Praise for Martin Malone

'Martin Malone writes stories of profound originality. He has a great sense of history and how it can be made special for a modern reader. His work searches out the spirit and language of many countries, and it is enticing from the first sentence ... a writer to watch.'

— *Stand* UK

'A brutal story, brilliantly told'

— *Alan Sillitoe*

'Powerful, disturbing, and profoundly moving'

— *The Good Book Guide*

'Extraordinarily accomplished and beautifully realised'

— *Irish Examiner*

'A human story told with real emotion and sensitivity ... Malone brings this story to life with an insight and understanding as only one who has been there can ... an excellent read'

— *Morning Star*, UK

'A traditional Irish story with occasional stunning images'

— *The Irish Times*

DEADLY CONFEDERACIES

MARTIN MALONE

DEADLY CONFEDERACIES

and other stories

NEW ISLAND

DEADLY CONFEDERACIES
First published in 2014
by New Island Books
16 Priory Hall Office Park
Stillorgan
County Dublin
Republic of Ireland.

www.newisland.ie

PRINT ISBN: 978-1-84840-345-1
EPUB ISBN: 978-1-84840-346-8
MOBI ISBN: 978-1-84840-347-5

British Library Cataloguing Data.
A CIP catalogue record for this book is available from the British Library.

Typeset by JVR Creative India
Cover design by New Island Books
Printed by Clondalkin Digital Print

New Island received financial assistance from The Arts Council (*An Chomhairle Ealaíon*), 70 Merrion Square, Dublin 2, Ireland.

10 9 8 7 6 5 4 3 2 1

This book is dedicated to the memory of Sean Judge;
actor, director and a friend to the Arts.

The breeze at dawn has secrets to tell you.
Don't go back to sleep. ~*Rumi*

Also by Martin Malone

Novels
Valley of the Peacock Angel
The Only Glow of the Day
The Silence of the Glasshouse
The Broken Cedar
After Kafra
Us

Short Stories
The Mango War & Other Short Stories

Memoir
The Lebanon Diaries

Radio Plays
Song of the Small Bird
The Devil's Garden
Rosanna Nightwalker

Stage
Rosanna Nightwalker

TV
After Kafra

Versions of some of these short stories appeared in/on, *The Sunday Times*, **the** *Sunday Tribune*, *Stand UK*, *Literary Orphans Journal USA*, RTÉ Radio 1 and *Commotions*.

Martin Malone's short stories have been broadcast by BBC Radio 4, the BBC World Service and RTÉ Radio 1, and published in *The Dublin Review*, *The Stinging Fly*, *Bridport Anthology UK*, *The Fiddlehead Can*, *The Malahat Review Can* and *Phoenix Best Irish Short Stories*.

Twice shortlisted for a Hennessy Award (*Mingi Street*), he is a winner of RTÉ's Francis MacManus Short Story Award (*Love in a Cold Shadow*) and the Killarney International Short Story Prize. *Halabja* was longlisted for the 2012 EGF *Sunday Times* Short Story Prize, the world's largest prize for a single short story. *The Stand House* won the 2013 Cecil D. Lewis Literature Bursary Award. *A day unlike any other* was shortlisted for the 2013 RTÉ/Penguin Short Story Award.

Contents

The Caulbearer's Awakening   1

Love in a Cold Shadow   25

Big Sis's Little Trouble   34

The Archbishop's Daughter   43

Taming the Wolves   55

A day unlike any other   70

A Lasting Impression   79

Thursday Market   91

Café Phoenicia   99

Wicked Games   112

The woman who wanted to do nothing   123
for ever and ever

Halabja   132

Deadly Confederacies   151

A Sort of Jesus Disappearance   179

Doll Woman   195

Netanya   208

Prairies   219

Ritual   227

If Something Doesn't Get better   239

That Time in Kurdistan   251

House of Dara   265

The Red Caboose Motel   273

Mingi Street   285

The Stand House   297

The Caulbearer's Awakening

There is an outdoor toilet in a yard, concreted over except for the verges where Nana grows pansies and other sorts of flowers. My favourite is an orange flower that gives off a strong scent of wet peaches. She tells me their names, but I always forget. A garage faces an empty street of boarded-up houses. A takeaway on the corner of the next street is owned by Peter, and he wraps his fish and chips in reams of white paper. He'd asked Glen and me what part of Ireland we lived in, and we said the south, and he said it was good that we weren't anywhere near the trouble.

The people who work in the shops are different to the ones at home. Here, they smile a lot and call you 'Love' or 'Darling', but mainly it's 'Love'. Back home, they scowl as though we owe them something, and we do. I know this because Mam sends me to the shops to get stuff on tick. I don't have a problem with this, for everyone in our street is aboard the same Titanic. But we don't get called 'love', and I suspect that even if our slate were clean, 'love' would never leave the mouths of those shopkeepers.

His travel bag is packed, and on the double bed we shared. The sun is pouring in through the sash window, and it carries a scent of window polish. Nana had taken down the net curtains to wash. She said they had gone dirty-looking. She'd said this in a self-wondering manner, as though her eyes had been letting her down, if the sun hadn't come full on the window she would never have known. The window itself was grimy and dusty, with bird dirt on the sill. Nana's a short woman with grey hair that she buns under a net. There's a slightly wounded and worried look to her features – wounded by things that had happened in the past, and anxious about the future. She has peculiar friends, like Mrs Hickory, who keeps black poodles and who is always giving out about Pakistanis, and Mrs Dickory, who lives in Canton and makes home-made lemonade, and had been married and divorced three times. I wonder if she calls her exes 'love'? Maybe the Welsh don't in such cases.

Aunt Paula never comes into our bedroom. She more or less keeps to herself, her bedroom, the good sitting room and the kitchen. She watches TV with Nana in the not-so-good sitting room, mostly *Coronation Street*. She is always talking about Sandy in *Crossroads*; he is in a wheelchair and has long, fair hair. Uncle John had said the wheelchair was a better actor than Sandy, and she gave him a cutting glance. He pretended not to notice, like it was a normal thing for people to be giving him such a look. His feet smell, and he leaves his shoes outside the bedroom at night to stink up the long and broad landing.

Nana doesn't like him. They don't like each other. I often wonder what keeps married couples together.

I say to Glen, 'Are you okay?'

He nods. He is better looking than me. People find it easier to get along with him. They don't say so outright; they say that I'm like Grandad, which is the same thing as saying it. I hand him my comics, the glossy ones, DC thirty-two-pagers, of Batman, Jet, Superman, for keeps.

'For keeps, Moss,' he says.

He is surprised, because I don't part with anything unless I'm getting something in return. The look of surprise is phased out by one of concern, and I can see that he is thinking about his knee, and whether or not the lump there is more serious than people are saying.

I say, 'I said so, yeah. Of course.'

'I can swap them … for sure?'

'Why would you want to swap them?'

'Just saying, if I wanted to …'. He is establishing true ownership.

'You can swap them.'

'I won't unless it's for the Thor comics, Moss, and that's a holy promise.'

'That could be a fair one, if they're in good condition.'

It is what we do at home, swap comics. Weekly, we get the *Victor*, *Tiger*, *Topper*, *Hotspur*, and when we're finished reading these we exchange them with our friends for the likes of the *Wizard*, *Beano*, *Dandy* or *Valiant*. Mam gets in the *Bunty* and the *Mandy* to read, but we don't bring those along on our swap outings. Lately, though, our thoughts have turned from swapping to collecting. Glen has this idea fixed in his head that our comics will become very valuable in time, if they're kept in good condition. According to him, it makes perfect sense. Old automobiles, he cites as examples, and antique furniture. Antique comics.

'I'm sorry you're going home,' I say.

'No more two-a-sides,' he says.

We used to kick a ball about in the park, and sometimes we matched up against two other boys. The other day, we beat two Iranians thirty-one to fourteen. We played in the hot sun, with Glen sticking too near the goal area because of his knee, till one of the Iranians threw up near a fresh dog turd he had skidded on.

Grandad looks in. He is wearing a grey suit. He has a narrow face, with hollow cheeks and the same blue eyes as Nana. Nana comes from a farming background in Rush. Her people used to collect seaweed from the beach and use it for fertiliser on their crops. We have loads of photographs of Nana's people, but we don't know who they are. She is going to write their names on the back of them, she says, one day. Sifting through photographs of people you don't know is like looking at blank headstones.

'Are you ready, Glen?' Grandad says.

'Yeah … okay.'

I like having a bedroom to myself. I like the way the morning sun shines in through the window and wakens me, caressing my face. I like listening to birdsong, and the noise of passing traffic, and the small talk of Nana and Maureen, the next-door neighbour who talks. The neighbours to the other side are alive and well, but they don't talk to Nana. The next-door neighbour who talks to us has ginger hair, and is very pale and freckled. Gwyneth, her mother, lives in the house with her, but she never comes out. She is ninety-six. She has lived in Albany Road all her life. Maureen says her mother is fretting about a newspaper article she had read about the houses in Bangor Street being set for demolishment in twenty years' time. I'm looking down at them. I check that my willy is inside my pyjamas in case they look up … it slipped out once before without my knowing.

'Can you imagine,' Maureen says over the top of the wooden fence, which is much lower than the fence the other neighbour had had put up, 'I said to Mum that it'll never happen. Our street is safe as … as … houses. "You're not to worry, Mum" I said … but she worries, she's such a worrier, love her.'

Nana says, 'The poor thing.'

Maureen sighs and then continues. 'I mean, she'll be 116 if she's around when it happens. She'll be long gone … *I* could be gone.'

I think they miss the point. Maybe people like to bank on having a nice place to haunt.

Mam rings from the Vatican Pub in the evening. She asks how I'm getting on, and reminds me to be good for Nana and Paula, and not to be left alone with Uncle John.

'I'm fourteen, Mam,' I say.

'Not yet,' she says. 'Don't be in a hurry to grow up.' '
About Uncle John … what's …?'

'Who's there with you?'

'No one. They've gone back into to watch *Coronation Street*.'

'Just don't be … right. And …'.

'And?'

She is scaring me a little.

'Has he ever … now, you can tell me … touched you, you know?'

'What?'

'Has …'.

'No.'

'If he ever tries to, you go straight to Nana.'

'Mam …'.

'So, how is your pocket money lasting? I'll send you over a couple of pounds with your grandad.'

I'm in the bedroom, reading. The door is locked, and the window is open a bit because the night air is clammy. Maureen's cat is up to something, or up on something, because the mewling is loud and the hissing louder. I used to own a black cat. My friends hung Maggie just to see the look on my face. They're not friends any more. I'd spoken with Glen on the phone too. He said that some of the lads weren't talking to him because he'd been on holidays to Wales and they hadn't been anywhere.

'Don't let those lads bully you, Glen.'

'I won't.'

Silence.

'When are you going into hospital for the operation?'

'Operation?'

'I thought …'.

He hadn't been told. Shit. Then, neither had I; I just know. I'd wanted to ask him about Uncle John and if he had said anything to Mam about stuff, but he just kept pressing me about his knee and the hospital until I told him that it had to be looked at by a specialist, and there would be a small operation. Telling him this felt like a lie. I said it because he was going to find out anyway, and he was never going to let up asking me until he got the answer his ears wanted. His ears, because his heart already knew.

'They're going to chop it off,' he said, his voice breaking.

'No …'.

'You know Mam is fucking always saying that you were born with the caal.'

'Caul.'

'I'll have a false leg.'

According to Mam, I was born with a piece of membrane – a caul – covering my face. She said that happened to one baby in a million, but she could have been exaggerating. I don't know if there are other mothers who boast about having a so-called mystic in the family; God only knows what the neighbours say about her in private. Sailors used to pay good money for cauls because it was a seafaring tradition for the owner of one to never drown. Mam insists it's a birth sign indicating a healing touch and an extra eye. Just like Great-Grandmother Jennifer, who, eh, drowned in the River Foyle, a fact that Mam described as an aberration, meaning that Aunt Jennifer hadn't used her gift properly.

On and on he went about losing his leg, until I heard Mam calling him to hang up; there were others waiting to make a call. I thought she might have rung back to give out to me for upsetting Glen, but she didn't.

The next morning, Nana asks me to come down to the shops with her. It's Saturday. This evening we'll walk to St Mary's Church for confession. It's over a mile, but I don't mind walking. So, in the shop, Nana buys bread and milk and packets of digestive biscuits. Then we stop at a fruit stall. The man calls her 'Mrs'. Nana calls him 'Nick'. She buys potatoes, bananas, pears and peaches, and as he's bagging these for her she runs her eye on the postcard pinned to a canopy upright.

She can't make it out and squints hard, pushes her face closer. Then she draws away. Nick is smiling at me. He doesn't look at Nana, and he's trying hard to stop himself from smiling, but he can't kill the weed of a smirk. I simply must read it, and the postcard is of a man and woman passing by a bathroom window. The man says, 'There's old Fred, washing his balls with a toothbrush.' A funny card, but it's not funny. What is, is Nana squinting hard to read it. I don't think she'll be reading too many more of Nick's postcards.

Shopping with Nana is usually a drop into town once a week. We take a bus, and eat lunch at Wimpy, or in Mackintosh's department store, where she has an account. She always buys me a book or comics, and sometimes we go into the pictures. She has seen *The Sound of Music* eight times. *Paint your Wagon* she had sat through once. She said it was an ordeal. *Zulu* she loved. Mrs Hickory thoroughly enjoyed watching all the Zulus getting shot. She cheered madly, and the usher asked her to leave. 'Ejected' is what Mrs Dickory said. She had sat between Nana and Mrs Hickory.

'Did you ever hear the likes of …' she had said, shaking her head as she told Grandad. Grandad drew on his cigarette and exhaled, ran his hand over his hair, which he always kept oiled, as though it were an engine that would seize without it.

He said, 'She just got carried away.'

'Oh it was awful. I was so glad that Michael Caine wasn't killed … she would have gone crazy altogether.'

It's a film about Welsh soldiers in Victorian times in Africa. Mrs Hickory said that one of her ancestors had fought at the battle. That's probably the real reason why she cheered so loudly. Nana just tried to act as though Mrs Hickory were 1,000 miles away.

'I was ever so embarrassed,' Mrs Dickory went on, 'really … you should have been there. And she got ever so cross with me when I told her to shush.'

Aunt Paula smiled. She had been meant to go, but my aunt has a problem with leaving the house. She doesn't go walking or shopping. It takes a lot for her to bring herself outside. 'Collapsed nerves' is what Grandad calls her condition.

The phone rings in the dead of night. Its tone is loud and constant, boring deep into the silence of the black hours, drawing me from deep to light to half-sleepiness. A door opens, then another. Feet on the landing on the stairs. Aunt Paula says, 'Hurry …'.

'It's Pat,' my uncle says in a loud whisper.

Nana says in a loud whisper, 'What is it, John?'

He says 'Shush' to her.

I climb out of the bed, thinking that Glen had lost his leg or had gotten one of his mad ideas and run away. Opening the door a little, I see Aunt Paula looking over the banisters, one hand in the pocket of her white robe, the other clutching a tissue.

'John, what is it?' she says in a shrill voice.

'Pat's young fella is after being killed.'

'Oh,' she says.

'Bill,' he says, 'a hit and run ... this bleddy phone brings nothing only bad news ... first about young Glen and now ...'.

Nana says softly, 'Bill. William.'

After the call, they move into the kitchen to make tea. I go back to bed and think about Bill. I'd only met him a couple of times. He didn't really get talking until Glen mentioned toys and showed him an Action Man he had in his bag. Then his eyes lit up, and he started on about a war film he had seen, and how he had no money to buy soldiers but used beer-caps instead.

'Beer-caps?' Glen said.

He nodded, and brought us outside to the shed and showed us his collection.

'I don't play with them all that much, not any more,' he had said. 'I want to get a job and buy a camera and start making my own movies.'

'What sort of job?' I'd said.

'Dunno. I used to work with Uncle Kev and me cousin Michael on their fruit farm, but there's only work during the summer, and this summer he had no work for me he said. Dad had a few words with him about it.' He dropped his voice low. 'Cos there was work ... we found out.' Dead.

Grandad has been away for a week. He went to Bill's funeral; he'd been home when the accident happened.

'Convenient', Uncle John had said. 'I think Bill's death is a sign for Grandad to think on things.' I'm not sure what those things might be. The bounce in his step has gone. His mind is always distant. He brings me on excursions. We walk into town; even with his bad foot he can walk fairly quickly. It's about a mile farther on from St Mary's church. Along the way we pass the red toy shop with the glass cabinets of model soldiers. I collect lead cowboys and Indians. I have wigwams, a cavalry fort and 7th Cavalry soldiers. I'm always adding to the collection. You can't buy these at home, at least not in my town. Maybe in Dublin, but I've never been to Dublin, except to spend some time in a hospital there after I woke up at home with one of my eyes closed. Grandad thinks toys are a waste of money. He doesn't say so outright, but I know by the look of him that he disapproves: his face sort of draws back into itself. I think that's because he never had a childhood. How could he have? Even Mam and Dad hadn't. They're always talking about food being rationed during the war, and getting an orange as a Christmas present. Grandad and Nana are war parents and Mam and Dad are war babies. They say this is why they don't like to see waste. Waste didn't exist during the war. If it did, they would have eaten it.

We go right on by St Mary's Church, and pass the blind shop and its display of wickerwork crafts. Today we're doing a double tour. He's taking me to the museum, and then to Cardiff Castle. I like to look at the models of the Bronze Age villages and the Roman helmets and armour. I always think of the head covered by the helmet – what sort of person was he? Friendly? Kind? Cruel? The heart that had beat behind the armour ….

On the lawns in front of the castle is a bed of red and yellow flowers arranged in the word 'CYMRU', Wales, and next to it a flower bed in the shape of a red dragon. We cross the wooden drawbridge, its black chains slack as unburdened clothes lines. Grandad buys the tickets from a kiosk, and ice-creams from a van, because we have to wait for a tour guide to become available. A peacock flies from the branches of a tree and struts across the shaven grass. The keep is built on a high hill. I don't see how Grandad is going to be able to climb all those steps. The tour guide is a chirpy little man who leads us round the castle, shows the garden in the clock tower, the maze on the floor that the royal children used to play on, the gold mosaic pattern in a wall, the first bedroom with an en-suite bathroom in the United Kingdom, the banquet hall with its wall paintings, the Roman part of the curtain wall, the battlement walks, the archers' lancet slits, a door that King Richard III would have passed through, a spiral staircase – I don't like the atmosphere. It's as though we're haunting the dead, a reversal of how things should be.

Outside, the sun washes away that feeling. A peacock spreads it wings, a feather falls away. People are leaving the dungeon restaurant, a line of heads partially obscured by a grass embankment. A young woman is fixing a straw hat on her head. I think Grandad is looking at her, but I realise he isn't when she moves on – he is focused on the keep, probably wondering about the climb, or the points at which he could stop for a breather or a cigarette. Or both. The Welsh flag on the keep mast gives feeble flutters. He removes his trilby, mops his brow with a handkerchief, and looks at the patch of dampness there as though he can't believe it's his. I think to say he can stay here while I go ahead, but before I get to speak, he says, 'Are you ready?'

'I'm fine.'

'You don't like heights,' he says.

I walk alongside him, and I bet to myself that we'll be taking the bus home. If we do, I'll know he's in trouble, because he is the sort of man who prefers his legs to bring him places. We cross the small bridge over the moat. It is swampy, and flies hover above the scummy water. He looks up, and though I want to reach the top and go inside and see the interior of the keep, I know I don't have to really do that as there are photographs in the brochure of its grey walls, of the misty views. 'I think I could get a little dizzy going up there,' I say.

He looks at me like a man who has been thrown a lifebuoy.

'And it's very humid,' he says.

Then a young bearded man in motorcycle clothes and wearing two prosthetic legs passes us by, aided by two crutches, and takes to the first steps grunting and groaning. We have to climb … it's a pride thing now.

About two hours later, we are sitting on the bus. Grandad's face is crimson, tie knot no longer perfect, top shirt button undone; even his jacket has come off, and sits like a greyish dog across his lap. Rolled-up shirt sleeves. He wears braces, and a white vest with oval holes. I can see this because of the way he is sitting, slightly slouched, as though he has not a breath of wind to call his own between shirt buttons. He smiles when he notices me looking at him. It is his let's-make-the-best-of-things smile. Off the bus at the church on the bend of footpath he fixes himself, and we take it slowly on the short walk home. The sun has gone in.

In the hall, I notice the sitting room door is slightly open. Whispers. Paula emerges, and says stiffly, 'We have a visitor.'

Grandad hangs his hat on the wooden wall rack above the umbrella stand that holds more walking canes than umbrellas – canes that Nana buys for him to use, but he never does. All second-hand ones, well-worn. She should buy him a new one, something he can mark with his own wear.

Paula says to me, gently, 'We won't be long.'

I stroll on down the hall, passing the door to the study and the other to the basement, and turn on the TV before moving into the kitchen. Thirsty, I go to the fridge to see if it holds some of Mrs Dickory's lemonade. It does, so I pour a glass. Not until I have done this do I notice him sitting at the table with its new plain blue oilcloth.

'Hi,' he says, 'I'm Michael.'

'Hi,' I say, 'I didn't see you there …'.

'I know.'

He has long, fine red hair. Pale and freckly. Long fingers play with a red Zippo lighter that has a motif of a swastika. Half a cigarette is parked behind his ear. He has round brown eyes. The bottom half of one is shiny, which I think is a flashing beacon.

'They're having a pow-wow about me,' he says.

'Do you want lemonade?'

'Anything else going?'

'Coke. But I think it's flat. Glen always leaves the cap loose.'

'Glen?'

'My brother … he's gone home.'

'Oh, he's the lad with the cancer.'

'We're not sure about that.'

'How old are you?' he says.

'Almost fourteen,' I say, and then ask, 'You?'

'Nineteen … You're the clever one, who reads a lot, writes poetry and stuff? Listens to jammy old records?'

'Who said I was clever?'

'Me dad. He said his brother, what's his name, your grandad, is always blowing your trumpet.'

I begin to hope we don't have to share a bedroom.

He says, 'It's in the tap water.'

'What is?'

'The cancer.'

'I don't think so.'

'It makes sense. They pour all this shit into it … chemicals and that.'

'I mean I don't know if Glen has cancer.'

'He has a lump,' he says, 'a tumour then … same difference. Where did they get the clever bit about you? And what's with the girl's name? Ruby is it?'

'It's Reuben, Ruby, but people call me Moss after Nana's brother who's living in the madhouse.'

'Moss?'

'Yes.'

'Moss. That's almost as bad as Ruby.'

When they come in from the good sitting room, Grandad says a scarcely audible hello to his nephew. John asks if he had a good journey. Grandad has not shaken his nephew's hand. He is a man who shakes everyone's hand, and for him not to offer a hand to his brother's son tells me a lot.

Paula says, 'You don't mind sharing your room, Moss?'

Nana says, 'Oh no … we'll put Michael on the fold-up in the study.'

'That's fine by me,' Michael says.

Paula, glad of an excuse to leave, says 'I'll go get the linen.'

It is late at night after Michael has gone to his room that I learn he has done something awful back home, in Ireland. I should have been in bed. I normally would be at that time, but I'd decided to remain in the sitting room and be still. I caught most of the kitchen conversation, but not all. Uncle John had said, 'He can't stay here. I …'.

'He has to.'

'If the guards find out that we …'.

'We just say we knew nothing about it.'

'Paula …'.

'Will you just shut it?'

She'd said this so viciously that I hurried on to bed, climbing the stairs on the balls of my toes, skipping the creaking step ….

The things I notice. Grandad will not stay in the same room as Michael. He has taken to eating his dinner a little while after us. He looks at Michael at times when Michael isn't aware of this looking, and it's a look that I never thought Grandad capable of giving. He gives me pocket money, but says I'm not to mention this to Michael. Grandad has lost weight; his energy isn't as it used to be. He won't go into the study to listen to his music, and Aunt Paula turned a deaf ear when he said he was wondering if he could move his player and records into the good sitting room.

Michael stays in the study for long periods, emerging for meals and to watch the sports on TV. He gets no calls from home, and doesn't make any to his parents. The cacti in the conservatory have died.

He says, 'What?' to Nana's question.

We are in the kitchen.

'Would you like to come to confession with us?'

'Are you mad?' his eyebrows rise in surprise at her invitation.

'I think you should.'

'Why?'

'It might do you some good.'

'I don't believe in God, or in any of that stuff.'

'Well, can't you come along? It's a nice evening for a walk. There are a few garages along the way, you might find those interesting … compare prices to those at home.'

'You won't keep on at me to go to confession?'

'No.'

'Or to go to Mass tomorrow?'

'No.'

'And will you give me money to bring home a couple of bottles?' Michael says.

'I'll see how you behave.'

'I'm old enough.'

'You're not twenty-one, and that's the age limit for enjoying a drink … you were less trouble when you were a child.'

'What does that mean?'

'You know very well.'

'Me Ma was right about you.'

'Is that a fact?'

'She said you were a cranky and a nosey oul' bitch.'

'With a son in the guards … did she not tell you?'

'That's nothing to boast about.'

'You may say. Well, Alan is stationed in Dingle … and it's something for you to think on … the fact that he is a guard.'

'Is that a threat?'

'Yes.'

He shakes his head. Sunlight shines up the copper in his hair. Nana says, 'You'd have met him at the funeral if you'd have gone to it.'

'You weren't there either.'

'I had Moss to mind.'

'He could have gone with you … Oh, I see, I forgot, things are tight moneywise. Ma said ye were poorer than church mice, I forgot.'

'Get yourself ready; we're leaving in five minutes.'

'And you couldn't chance leaving him with himself.'

At this, the air fries. Nana seems to balance her thoughts on the balls of her feet, rocking herself, but she won't fuel this matter further.

'Be ready. Because if you're not … I'm ringing Alan. And let me tell you something for nothing, young man: you'll regret it if I do.'

'I'm sure you'll tell your Alan about your man too … that's why you and my uncle stay with them, isn't it, to keep an eye on him?'

'If you're not in the hall in five minutes I'm making that call. And about an hour later there'll be a knock on your father's front door.'

'You don't like me very much, do you?'

'I see nothing in front of me except a young man who thinks about no one but himself.'

'Give it a rest, will you?'

'I …'.

'Jesus, will you ever just stop talking? Your voice goes through my head.'

The sun is shining as we step out onto the pavement. Nana wears a light raincoat, and carries her bag strapped over her arm, always held at her midriff. The corner of a pixie sticks out from her coat pocket: she is always afraid of being caught out in the rain and getting her hair wet. She had considered getting a blue rinse like Mrs Dickory, but decided it wouldn't suit her. Michael says, just to nail her down, 'Now don't be bothering me to go to confession.'

'You can wait till we're finished, or light a candle and say a few prayers,' Nana says. Passing the red toy shop I mention what Bill used to use for toy soldiers, and how different brands represented different branches of the army.

'He brought us into his shed and showed them to us,' I say. 'He had almost a box full, and hey, did you ever play with him, Michael?'

His lips tighten, and something appears to give in his eyes. He turns pale, even his freckles seem to lose colour. By now we are on City Road, and walking by a string of used-car forecourts. The traffic is light, and the skies are half dark and half blue, and the dark half is coming our way.

The church is empty. A scent of incense and another of candles burned to their ends reaches my nostrils. Nana always times it so we can get in near the end of the queue. Michael hasn't said a word since I'd brought up the subject of Bill's beer-cap army. He doesn't stay with us in the confessional pew, instead moving up a few rows from the altar. I am thinking of his ashen colour, of how his lips seem to have clamped a tight cordon on his words, and the nervous fidgeting of his hands.

Nana steps into the cubicle, the door held open for her by an old man bent over in two. I am struggling to come up with something to confess, and can't get beyond a few swear words, but these seem to do for the priest. His name is Father Owen Jones, or so it says on the sign outside his door. In fact, he even helps me to remember a few of my sins, and gives me an example of another type.

'Did you say anything bad about someone?'

'Yes. About my cousin Michael.'

'I see. What did you say?'

'That I hated him.'

'Anything else?'

'I called him a you-know-what.'

'I don't. Tell me it out straight, good boy.'

'I said he was an out-and-out bollix.'

'Indeed. Anything else?'

'I said he was a flute.'

'Flute as in a pipe?'

'As in down below, Father.'

Silence.

'Hmm. Why did you call him such names?'

'He made me mad.'

'Why?'

'He's always saying that my brother has cancer, and he hasn't. He has a lump on his leg, that's all.'

'So you said the first thing that came into your head?'

'I did, Father.'

'You do know that you shouldn't hate anyone, isn't that right?'

'Yes, Father.'

'You're going to try not to hate anyone, isn't that so?'

'Father.'

Leaving the confessional booth, I see Nana standing over Michael, her arm draped across his shoulder. She is leaning over him, whispering. When I draw near I see tears rolling down his cheeks. He doesn't care who is watching.

All the way home, he is silent, and his silence is catching for we're silent as well, too afraid of saying anything in case it turns out to be the wrong thing. A word could be enough to start him crying or to spark his temper. As we turn the corner at City Road, and enter Albany Road, a thought comes to me. I sense that there are uncomfortable truths among us: I don't know what they are. But people don't break down in church without reason. And Nana is aware of Michael's reason, or at the very least is partially aware. And kitchen talk from John and Paula are other jigsaw tiles. And Bill ... why is it every time his name is mentioned the air freezes over? Michael's face seems to fill with strain: it's like his life is fine until our cousin's name is mentioned. And when the name is said, my aunt, uncle and grandparents stand like monolithic boulders in a stone circle staring at him.

In the depths of night, I toss and turn. With gentle street noises from Albany Road drifting to my ears, I put the pieces of the weeks together. I think Glen is in trouble, for sure, and the realisation sickens my stomach and brings an ache to my heart. As for Michael and Bill ... well, like the adults, I have no idea about what we should do about what we know.

Love in a Cold Shadow

Gone. Blue beret, blue cravat, Irish tricolour flashes, the lot. Burned, he said, in the range. The accomplice sat in at the table having breakfast, smiling.

'Tim, where are they, really?'

'Mammy burnt them. She said she burned them, I didn't see her burning them. I just smelt them. They made a very grey, smoky smell.'

Tim's seven. He's my only son from my first marriage. I'd a daughter, Nancy, but she caught meningitis and died. Nance was 5. She'd be 9 now. Tim has no memory of her. Sally's my first wife. She's 39, slim, and keeps her hair short and blonde. She wears earrings, and has a small birthmark on her earlobe. She used to be self-conscious about it.

Tim stays with me. It suits Sally; she's taken up the threads of her acting career. She got bit parts and walk-on parts in some TV soaps and short films last year. Since then, not much. She's honest about her lack of work. There's a play opening in the city next week that she hopes will run for a few weeks. Then there's talk of a TV commercial.

I arrived early to collect Tim. Kildare are playing Usher Celtic in the final in the afternoon, and I want to get dinner over and cleaned up before heading off to watch the match. Judy's my second wife. I met her through a dating agency. She's got a 16-year-old son called Ian. We don't get on. But he gets along with Tim, and that's important. Judy and he have gone to visit his father in London. He's dying of cancer; has it in the prostate.

Sally stayed on in the family home. She bought out my share of the house. I gave my share to Judy, who in turn handed it to Rob, her ex, to buy him out. That was four years ago. All done amicably, I have to say, considering. At the time I felt we were all trying to out-civilise each other.

'Hi Bob,' Sally says, pink towel wrapped around her hair.

She's off on a shoot today. A commercial, I think, promoting venison. She's got lumps of the stuff in the freezer. Christmas presents, she says, the ultimate alternative to turkey. Sally's a vegetarian, and hasn't eaten meat of any sort since she witnessed her uncle taking an axe to a dead turkey's head. She says she'll never forget that evil bastard, doing such a thing in front of a 5-year-old.

'Fine … I was just asking Tim about my UN stuff.'

'Oh, that … I burned all that rubbish.'

'Rubbish? I didn't think it was rubbish.'

'Well, you should have collected it like I told you to do ages ago.'

'Did you burn everything?'

Sally stands at the sink, looking out at her small garden, the climbers on the walls that have stopped climbing, the rose bushes growing wild, the sweet wrappers mingling with the weeds.

'Except the medals,' she says quietly. 'They're in the press in the sitting room.'

Sally doesn't ask what I want them for. She blames my overseas trips for breaking up our marriage. Eight times abroad, four tours of duty in Lebanon, two in Cyprus, and one apiece in Iraq and Bosnia. There is an overseas veterans' reunion being held in the Royal Hotel in Dublin. The gear I want is part of the function's dress code.

Sighing, I leave for the sitting room, where Sally has torn down the wallpaper and emulsioned the walls in primrose. The chandelier I'd always thought too large for the ceiling hangs, monolithic, the spectre of many arguments, oval light bulbs piping up from imitation candleholders, strings of glass beads … highly ornate, ridiculously expensive.

I find the medals. Six medals mounted on a strip of board, their ribbons stained with primrose paint, and the medals with white metallic paint. I hear the door closing.

'I'm sorry,' Sally says, leaning against the wall, her hands behind her back.

'You're a bad bitch.'

Turning about, I make to walk past her. Sally holds her hand up, her chin going in a little with determination.

'You need to hear what I've to say.'

I look at the medals on my palm, and then put them in my jeans' pocket.

'I'm going away,' Sally says.

'And?'

'I won't be coming back.'

Right now, I don't care where she goes. She is dating some Scot who talks through his teeth. I can't think of his name. A good-looking fellow with a hungry gleam in his brown eyes. He writes songs and poetry, strums the guitar.

Well, tell me, I think, before I grow a minute older in your presence, tell me. She owns the house, so it's not about signing papers. What then?

'We're moving to the States.'

'Yes. In what way can I help?'

If there is a smidgeon of sarcasm in my tone, I don't care.

'I want to bring Tim with me.'

Something cold hits me all over. I've minded Tim since he was 3 years old. She couldn't be serious.

'No way.'

'He wants to come with me.'

'Of course he'd bloody want to go with you … what else do you think a child would say to his mother, eh?'

I rub my neck. It aches. I am not going to become embroiled in an argument with Sally. She'd only make me lose my rag and say things I don't mean. Besides, arguing with Sally is a well-worn route I never want to travel again. I walk by her, into the hall.

'Tim! Come on, we're leaving.'

Tim calls back, 'Ah, Dad.'

'Now, son, come on.'

Waiting in the car, I watch Tim kiss his mum goodbye, take his pocket money from her and put it in his weekend bag. I ignore Sally's tight wave, and drive up the street a little more quickly than I'd come in. I couldn't bring myself to mention what Sally had said.

That evening, Judy rings and says that Rob has passed away. She is staying on for a while, longer than anticipated. She says that Rob left her everything: house, money, car, everything. He never stopped loving her. When she says that, I think I am going to get sick into the phone. This Rob she's gone soft on is the same one who'd beaten her to within an inch of her life. I say nothing, then think that my saying nothing is to blame for Judy's sudden coolness, and say that Rob was a fine man.

Judy kept pressing to find out what was on my mind, so I told her.

'I'll do gaol for her,' she says quietly, willing to serve a prison sentence for the pleasure of harming her. Judy says such things quietly when she is serious about it.

'He won't go.'

'You've asked him?'

'No … no, I haven't.'

'Well you should. That's the first thing you need to sort out.'

I haven't asked Tim because I fear what he might say. Tim loves Sally. He looks forward to spending his weekends with her. She goes out of her way for him on these days. Making tea, I study Tim. He is lying on the red-and-black rug in front of the TV, watching *Wrestlemania*. Nance … there're times I can't help looking at Tim and seeing his sister beside him. I've an ache in my heart; an ache I share with Sally, an everlasting bond of grief, if not a unifying bond.

'Tim?'

He looks up, eyebrows raised. Taking a deep breath, I ask. Tim's cheeks redden. 'I don't know what to think … I don't like the idea of Mammy leaving, and I don't like the idea of leaving you and Judy.'

'You have to decide, Tim …'.

Tim clashes his action figures off each other, then stops.

'I don't suppose you and Mum will ever be friends again?'

'No, no. Not close friends, son.'

Tim's blue eyes moisten. He bites his lip.

'How do I tell Mum I don't want to go?'

I am saddened that he's been nudged into making a major decision at such a tender age. It bites at my heart, souring my stomach.

Sally doesn't believe me when I ring to tell her. She says I've influenced Tim, have turned him off the idea of going to the States. No matter what I say, she won't be convinced. I tell her to come around and find out for herself.

'I wouldn't darken that cow's door,' she says.

It hurts.

'If you thought anything of Tim, you'd darken any cow's door.'

'Not hers.'

'Rob's dead. Judy's gone over to take care of the funeral arrangements. Be brave and say what you've been saying when she comes back, right to her face, right. Fuck you, Sally, fuck you for all of this hassle.'

She'd got me going. I think she'd set out to do just that. She always knew how. You live with someone long enough, and you get to know the easiest routes to rile them. A certain cough, a shoe left lying about, a suspicion of unwashed hands coming from the bathroom, forgetting to tuck something important in the grocery trolley, telling her you can't afford to pay for something when she knows that you can. A marriage full of skirmishes, in which I usually held my own.

The next day, I bring Tim right over to Sally's house. We see the Scot on the way out, walking toward his car. He issues smiles, a wave, but doesn't delay any.

We follow Sally down the hall into the kitchen. The air smells of burned toast, and a drop of marmalade sits like a fat, yellowy tear on the breadboard.

'Tell your Mum what you told me, Tim,' I say gently.

Tim looks at Sally. His chin dimples. I know he is about to cry, and would if he spoke.

'He thinks America is too far away to go just yet. What he'd like to do is visit in the summer and see if he likes it there … then he can stay if he wants.'

Sally puts on a smile. Tim hasn't yet lifted his head.

'And he's loads of projects to finish in school; he can't leave them behind unfinished.'

'I understand, Tim … that's okay. And you will visit next year, won't you? I'll come over and bring you back with me, is that okay?'

Tim's nod is almost imperceptible.

After he went out back to play, Sally put on the percolator. An aroma of fresh coffee fills the air. She'd been quiet in herself for the last few minutes, talking with Tim, trying to stem his quietly falling tears. No, she wasn't mad at him, and his idea was the best. It'd give her time to buy a house, and set things up for him. He'd be coming out to a lovely room, and by that time she'd know all the best places to bring him. It had taken a few minutes for Tim's tears to subside.

'I see Nance in him,' I said, over black sugarless coffee.

'Yes … he has her eyes.'

'I meant what I said … I'll encourage him to visit you … not that he'll need encouraging.'

Sally sips at her tea.

'I'll be doing my own encouraging.'

'Right …'.

We make to leave when Sally says she has work to find.
Kisses and hugs for Tim, and a reservedness towards
me, like someone taking in a cold food she doesn't like.
I bring Tim to the cemetery. We aren't long there when
Sally arrives. She parks behind my car in front of the
grave. She puts her carnations in vases. My own flowers
are in side-urns, flanking the granite headstone. There
are moments when we are a complete family again.

Big Sis's Little Trouble

For weeks, leaflets and brochures had been deposited everywhere a body might sit or lie or shite in our house. Information concerning Pro-life, and some other crowd called Anti-life. It was all to do with having a baby or not. I didn't read into the stuff too deeply, and some of the words made no sense to me. I think tossing a coin is probably the best way to solve a problem that people can't agree upon. But maybe life is too precious to decide on the toss of a coin; if it is life, I mean like before you're actually born – I don't know.

I had strong suspicions that Big Sis was planting these things – sowing seeds like. She probably got the idea from Mrs Doran down the road, who brought a coffin into her dying husband's bedroom. But Bollix Doran – everyone calls him Bollix because he is one – got better, and now he sleeps in the coffin in the spare room. We've got a few oul' ones like Mrs Doran in the estate – ones that go out and buy next year's Christmas presents on Saint Stephen's Day. Da calls them 'Oul' cunts'. He says this about anyone he thinks has gotten one up on him. I used to think the world was full of cunts.

Da said, as he settled his arse into the table, 'I don't know who's leaving all those leaflets in the jacks, but he'd want to quit.'

He'd? He was accusing me. I'm the only other one in the house with a mickey. But I kept my mouth shut, because I sensed big news was coming from Big Sis. Big Sis with the big arse and bigger tits and big fluffy black hair and big blue eyes Jesus Christ himself would have got down off the Cross for, if he wasn't already down for her other goodies.

Da has a thick face, like he is always in bad humour, but he laughs a lot. He watches that old shite, *Father Ted* and *Only Fools and Horses* and *M*A*S*H*, on the plassie, and he says *M*A*S*H* reminds him of his time in the army. Well, Ma told us he was never in the army. He was with the sandbags – the reserves – and gave it up after a week scrubbing dishes in Lahinch barracks. He's a painter decorator, and he hates the Poles because they undercut his prices. We all thought he was going to collapse with a heart attack when he answered a knock on the door and two Poles offered to paint the outside of the house for €150. They said Mister B. Lox Doran sent them down to ask. Bollix is sore at those who didn't visit him when he was dying. Da said he wouldn't go see the hoor off, not even for two free tickets to watch Ireland play Brazil in the final of the World Cup.

Ma handed us our dinners, and gave out to Little Sis for not setting the table properly.

'I did, Ma,' she said.

Da said, 'You did in your hole ... where's the salt? Have I to use my finger as a knife?'

'Red, language,' Ma warned.

Little Sis went to get the salt cellar and a knife, asking herself what his two legs had died of.

'Did you say something?' Da asked.

'No,' Little Sis said. 'Jesus no, I never said *something*.'

Ma sat into the table, and frowned at the burnt pork chop on her plate.

'We need to start going to Mass,' she said.

I couldn't figure out how a burnt chop made her think of that. Da shook his head. He isn't into God and shite like. She started slagging Da then, teasing him. She said she used to love rubbing his carroty hair. He's little on top of his head now, except a couple of wisps making a last stand. Freckly head. She calls him 'Red', the name a headstone to lost thatch.

I also had half a suspicion that Little Sis was aware of Big Sis's dilemma. Little Sis is skinny with hardly any diddies. Her hair is skinny too, and so are her lips. Both of my sisters think that I'm a prick and a ladyboy wannabe. They've said so to my face, which they also insisted was an exaggeration, meaning I had less than a face. Up until I was 10, last year, I used to go into their bedroom, then they banned me when I started noticing and saying stuff about their figures. They said

I was ogling their bodies. I suppose I was. But I was just being curious; not being a pervert. I understood where the girls were coming from though, because we have a pervert in the family, on Ma's side. Uncle Johnny is someone we never talk about, or the things that he did when he was a priest. He's in gaol somewhere in England. Da said if he ever laid eyes on him he'd ram a broken beer bottle up his hole. Which hurt Ma, because Uncle Johnny's her brother, and she knew him before he grew fond of feeling up children. She says a collar does wicked things to a man's thinking process.

It could be that Big Sis is a pervert too. She used to walk around the house wearing only a bra and knickers until Arnie Duncan, our 80-year-old across-the-road neighbour keeled over by his netted curtains with his hand on his mickey and the other on a pair of steamed-up binoculars. Horny Arnie, we called him. He's in an old folk's home for a year now, waiting to die. He has the same horn he had when the doctor found him. We found this out from Mrs Doran, who knows everything about everybody in the estate, and who is fond of saying that she's never wrong about this or that. Da shut her up when he said, 'Except for your Bollix dying that is.'

So then, we were in the middle of dinner like I'd mentioned, and out Big Sis comes with, 'I'm pregnant!' And the man who's always saying he never panics, that he would have been the calmest person on the *Titanic* … Well, Da nearly swallowed his fork whole. Ma put a hand to her mouth, either to keep her dentures in or to check that the words didn't come from her mouth.

Little Sis's sniggering fell away when Big Sis hung out the culprit's name to dry.

'Curtis Maguire! Curtis! You knew I fancied him, you bitch!'

Da's hands were by his plate, fingers curling up and uncurling, his cheeks red as cherries, lips white and shiny like the edge of a razor blade.

'Shut it!' he said, slapping the table with the flat of his hands. *The calmest man on the Titanic had spoken.* He snarled, 'I suppose the fucking rat wants to marry you?'

Ma said, 'He's only 17, Red. No young one gets married nowadays just because they're … they don't want to go making two mistakes.'

Big Sis said, 'He doesn't know.'

He glanced at us in turn and said, 'Is that why that litterture shite has been in the house?'

Mam said, 'Red …'.

'Well now, we'll have to deal with this little problem,' he said.

Mam said, 'Hold on there … what do you mean?'

Ma's a Catholic and Da is a Protestant. And that makes us Procats or Catprods, I suppose. They don't go to Mass, so the truth is they're pagans … but I think even pagans believe in something. So they're not even pagans.

Da shook his head and said, looking at Ma side-on with something like fear coming to his eyes, 'She's too young; she can't have it. Her life will be ruined.' He turned his eyes to Big Sis and said, 'You don't want it, do you?'

'I don't know.'

Then she did the sister thing: she turned on the waterworks.

'Did he … rape you?' Da said, with hope in his tone. Like his daughter's condition wasn't her fault.

'More like she raped him,' Little Sis said.

Ma reached across the table and clipped Little Sis's ear. 'Go to your room!'

Little Sis opened her little mouth, but Da cut her off. 'Now!'

She pushed back the chair, and ran from the kitchen, along the hall, pounded on the stairs and slammed her door shut. We all looked up at the ceiling, where, according to the pleading in Da's eyes, is where all his answers lounge.

There was absolute silence for a few seconds, broken then by Big Sis's snuffling and Da's constant sighing. The dagger glances that Ma was sending Da had a noise, too.

'No,' Ma said, 'it's no possibility. Not a hope. The child will be born … even if it's over my dead body.'

I said, 'Nice image, Ma. Thanks for planting that in my head, you're a pal.'

Da seemed to notice me then, and he hiked a thumb to the hall and said, 'Go to your room.' He said it quietly, like he was doing me a favour.

I went. No problem. My wardrobe is above the kitchen, and I often hear great bits of news whenever I put my ear in there. Like the neighbour Ma told Da couldn't keep her legs together. I thought that a terrible disease and imagined myself walking splay-legged to school, drawing sympathy from my pals. But the next day I saw your woman coming toward me on the footpath, and her knees were close together. There isn't much point, I thought, in having a disease that you can be easily cured of. Another bit of news I could have told the sisters was the fact that Ma and Da were thinking of having another baby. Funny how your plans can come alive through a third person.

I put my ear in my listening post.

'Who-do-you-think-is-going-to-feed-and-look-after-this-baby?' Da said, pausing between each word, 'not-moi!'

'Curtis Maguire,' Ma said, distantly.

Curtis is creepy. Goes all weird in the eyes sometimes, like he was seeing stuff in you that a mirror wouldn't tell.

Da said with measured patience, 'F this.' then he flared up thick, 'I'm going to ring that … that … that FUCKER …'.

'Da!' Big Sis said.

'Shush you!'

'Ma!' Big Sis said.

'Shut it!'

Within a breath he was on to Curtis's dad and told him all and then he was listening. After he was finished speaking with Bill he said, 'Jesus!'

'What?' Ma said.

Da said, 'He told me that was the fourth this week.'

'Fourth!' Big Sis shrieked.

'Red?' Ma said.

'Four, aye … fucking four. Wan is expecting twins.'

'Oh Jesus!' Ma said.

Silence.

Big Sis said, 'Does twins hurt more than one, Ma?'

'I fucking hope so,' Da said.

'Red,' Ma said.

He softened then, 'And some long-time childless married woman has a bit of explaining to do to her husband.'

That's typical Da: making himself feel better by thinking how others were worse off.

'Twins,' Ma whispered in alarm.

Well, Big Sis didn't have twins. She'd a bouncing baby boy. She called him Red-Mond, which is the height of arse licking. Little Sis is cute, she says, by taking her smarties. There's one for every day – Tuesday and Thursday tasted horrible. She was raging because she had to gobble Friday's ahead of itself. I can't figure out how the smarties stop a woman from getting pregnant, but I know how condoms are supposed to. Ma showed me using a parsnip. She said she didn't want me getting young wans in trouble, even if they wanted to get themselves into that trouble. That's progress, I suppose.

Da is always playing with Red Mond, which sickens my hole because he doesn't bring me to the park to play soccer any more. But then he's a lot on his plate, especially after Ma told him to prepare himself for more little trouble.

The Archbishop's Daughter

Everything has a shadow of some kind. Maybe even a shadow has a shadow.

– Amos Oz

Dear Monsignor,

If I've strayed from protocol and addressed you incorrectly, forgive me; I meant no disrespect. Don't you think that the words 'Archbishop' and 'Daughter' make for an interesting and somewhat arresting banner? It brings us straight to the heart of the matter.

What I have to tell you is of genuine significance. This isn't yet another sad and lamentable tale of child sexual abuse that continues to drag the roots of the church screaming towards daylight. My secret, soon to be yours (though I suspect you already know some detail) is at once amazing, heartbreaking, romantic, and yet conversely it is none of these.

What I have to tell you concerns another type of abuse, of a nature that I haven't quite managed to define. The secret I want to relate to you is a recently discovered

one, and the pain and shock of it has not fully taken its
leave of me. Nor is this a case of a man putting a foot
forward in the hope that he will be given money to go
away quietly, with the secret locked tightly in his heart, its
trail to turn cold on his tongue. Money does not interest
me; I mean this, though I am by no means a wealthy man.
I can hear my own death knells in the offing. I am too
busy with the process of dying to worry about money.

Why do I write to you, Monsignor, and not an Irish
Archbishop? Rome is where the power is – Rome is the
Authority, the Dragon, the Ivory Tower of the Infallible
One: Il Papa. And so I write to the sinless soul. I want
him to know that I did not reach the end of my days
in total ignorance. Il Papa has, through his silence, his
covering up of truths and sins, sinned against me. May
God forgive him, and your church.

Let's begin.

My wife, Monsignor, is the daughter of Ireland's
most famous or infamous Archbishop, and her mother
is a nun. His name is Laurence John Roche, and his
friend and long-time lover is Sister Emma Pearse – their
daughter's real name is Eleanor.

I'll let you digest that for some moments before
bringing you further.

It is of course the reason why he never made
Cardinal.

Irrespective of what I can see and now know (I feel
none the wiser because of it), it's important too that I
tell someone of religious pedigree this story.

To refresh your memory.

Laurence John Roche was born in 1895. His father was a doctor, and his mother died when he was a year old – a fact that Laurence did not discover until he was 16 and at boarding school. He had always thought his stepmother, Deirdre, to be his real mother. The effect of this revelation on the boy, according to his biographer, was devastating. I've read the book, and isn't it sad that, for all of its 675 pages, there is not a single clue to be found of what had been really going on in the late Archbishop's life? The writer must have been bound by awe and respect for the Archbishop, and/or by the country's libel laws. Fear, too. Then again, Monsignor, you are acquainted with how we Irish like to bury things. We are the Ostrich Nation.

In all his regal glory, the Archbishop is there between the covers in black-and-white photographs of his ordination, his meetings with Pope Pius and later with Pope Paul, with President de Valera, with whom he was great friends. All that information is contained within those 675 pages, and while the details and facts of it I presume are true and accurate, it is with what's not written about him that we must concern ourselves. Let the public and academics pick over the bones of the man they think he was, the things he did and didn't do – he is part of the long road that has led the Church to possible ruination and moral bankruptcy.

In his defence, he came from a society where truth was harboured like the last few good potatoes of a famine cottager. A man leaves his community and dons a white collar and black garb and becomes what? A moral compass for the community? A teacher? Perhaps. But he could never lose what was ingrained in him: to hide things, to move paedophile priests from parish to parish – and Archbishop Laurence John Roche did that sort of thing, because the importance of preserving secrets had been bred into him like good manners. To say that he should have known better is to try and escape from the fact that he did not. There was the secret of his dead mother – a secret kept from him by his stepmother and his father, his friends and neighbours in Cootehill. He had his own secrets about life in his first boarding school, saying only that terrible things had happened to him there. A didactic man, austere, saturnine. A great scholar and teacher, who by his very appointment to Archbishop had created enemies for himself within the religious community – he was the bog-man from the north of the country. What good ever came out of Nazareth and Cavan county?

His friendship with the poet Patrick Kavanagh? There are documented accounts of their meetings, and the song that evolved from Kavanagh's poem, 'On Raglan Road' held perfect resonance for the Archbishop. He 'tripped lightly along the way', yes? 'Her dark hair would weave a snare that he would one day rue'? 'He loved too much and by such by such is happiness thrown away?' 'When the angel woos the clay …'.

Ah yes, for I believe that Eleanor's mother had beautiful, long, dark hair, as does Eleanor, even now, still, though she is – I was about to write 50 years old – 46. I am finding it difficult to come to terms with her age in all of this. She was 14, and not 18, when I made love to her. What does that make me? A friend of the Church? An ally? A stealer of innocence? Yet, I was ignorant, kept in the dark – this is some mitigation, I expect.

A photocopy of a black-and-white photograph is attached by a Baloo the bear magnet to the fridge in Eleanor's (our) kitchen. It shows a baby dressed in a cardigan with the cuffs rolled up. Behind her is a pristine pram, its flank shiny. She lies on a blanket spread on newspapers – one of the banner lines reads 'TAKEN', which, Monsignor, when you think on it, is both ironic and appropriate. For much was taken from Eleanor, and had to be, I suppose, when you consider that she is a princess of the Church, which is far removed from being a princess of royalty. It is a graceless thing, which is ironic when you consider grace to be a big word in the Church. Amazing Grace, the grace to enter the Kingdom of Heaven ....

On her wrist, circling the sleeve, is a silver bracelet with a capping that contains a fragment of bone from the remains of Saint Therese. This did not come back with her from Wales (where she had been fostered by an aunt too ill to make the fostering a permanent arrangement), but she has it now; after forty-three years. A long wait, isn't it? A long wait, too, for her to be handed back her real identity. It sometimes crosses my mind that it might have been wiser to let her go to her grave thinking that she was the person she had been all her life. But this would probably have been the greatest betrayal of all.

In the end, a relative of the Archbishop stepped in to resolve the issue of the infant's 'no fixed abode'. Her relationship to the Archbishop is not clear to me. It appears that she was a doughty old woman with an iron will. She insisted that the child be given to her married daughter and son-in-law, a childhood friend/foster-brother of the Archbishop.

When Eleanor arrived at her new home, she was malnourished and underweight, and it took the O'Learys three weeks to settle her from constant crying. She was given the name Patricia, and her age changed to slot in with the other children in the family. Neighbours who inquired about the new addition to the family were told that the child belonged to a sister of Michael's who had got herself into trouble with a married man. Not an uncommon occurrence back then.

Eleanor can recall being brought in from playing in the back garden to meet with a man in the sitting room. The Archbishop had called on four occasions to see his daughter, but she only remembers two of his visits, and only some of the things he'd said to her.

Eleanor told me of the excitement in the house prior to these visits – the polishing and cleaning that went on, the Wedgewood delft that was rarely used was taken from the locked kitchen cabinet. The sitting room was reserved for special guests and as an occasional treat for members of the family at Christmas time and on birthdays. There was a charge in the air – a humming and electrifying energy. These days she has items belonging to him in her possession: a prayer book, and between its pages old memorial cards and novenas to the saints he must have prayed to, a letter. As she entered the room, she remembered the fall into silence, the slow departure of others – leaving her alone with this man the others had called 'Your Grace'. In that room, with its smell of new floral-patterned carpet, and photographs of dead people, and a bookcase rich with brown-covered *Encyclopaedia Britannica*, she felt a tiny bit afraid, a tiny bit special. She wondered why none of her brothers and sisters had been brought into see him. Why her? Had she done something bad? Had someone told him what she'd shouted at Dougie Molloy for putting a frog down her back? The names she'd called him? And his mother too, for that was the only way she could get him to stop laughing at her.

She stood a few feet away from him in her new blue dress, her hair in a ponytail, new black shoes mirror shiny after Dad had that morning spat on and polished them.

'Come over here, child; don't be staying over there.'

He sat to the edge of the new sofa and looked her over, his hands on her upper arms, gently squeezing. Then he put his palms flat to her cheeks. He stared at her until he saw a mist come to her eyes; he feared she might begin to cry. Gently, he rubbed the top of her head and said, sighing, that she was a lovely looking girl. Eleanor is sure that she is able to remember this particular visit because of his sigh, for it was long and loud and filled with a pining sadness.

He asked her about school, and she said that she liked Mrs Doyle but not Mrs Kenny. She talked about the frog that was put down her back, but not about the things she had said afterwards. All the while she was talking, he was smiling, but it wasn't a happy smile – she sensed that. Now she recognises it as the smile of the forlorn, of someone who for a split second sees how things could have been, and yet could never have been.

'Are you happy, child?'

She nodded.

He said it again, after a timid knock on the door to remind him that he had an appointment to keep. 'Are you happy?'

'Yes, Father.'

He made the sign of the cross over her, and spoke in a strange language. At the door, he stopped and smiled at her. 'Be a good girl for Michael …'.

She was 10 years old when he died. Imagine not knowing your own father was dead? Imagine her foster parents looking at the news on TV, and the front pages of the newspapers screaming at them in bold – listening and hearing and digesting all the good and bad said of the dead man, while under their roof lived the Archbishop's daughter, and they could never tell a soul because they'd been sworn to secrecy. Very often it is the ordinary man and woman who are true to their promises, unlike others, who lean weight on an oath and then find they can't keep it. There were many times when Michael and his wife hadn't got a loaf to put on the table, and here was a story they could have sold for a holy/unholy sum. It's a barb, Monsignor, and I apologise for it – occasionally I give way to anger over all that's happened to Eleanor, and by association with her, me.

So, her father was dead, and she was given a day off school, like all the other children. An Archbishop's death, especially one of his standing and influence, was a notable event.

It is neither here nor there how the shell containing the secret was cracked open. There is proof at the end of my words to you – a facsimile of a letter. The original is kept in a safe place. There is no anger in me toward the Archbishop and the nun whom he loved. If they had not come together I would not have met Eleanor, had two beautiful sons, and a granddaughter, and the child's mother in my life. I have no anger, just a profound sorrow that runs deep to the heart and beyond. I want the Church to open itself to the world about Eleanor, to hand back my wife's real identity to her openly. In other words, to create a miracle for me: for the Church to come clean.

I have no more to say. But this does not mean that I should have the last word.

The Letter from the Archbishop to his daughter.

My dearest Eleanor,

By the time you read this you will be, God willing, in the prime of your life. It was my express wish that you were not to be told of the circumstances surrounding your birth and of your parentage until at least thirty years after my death. My primary concern was to protect you, your mother and your foster parents from unnecessary and stressful intrusions into your lives. You are by now aware of the position I held in life, and that there are very many who will not give you a moment's peace when this secret breaks. I ask you not to divulge it until your children have grown.

Emma, your mother, is a very good person and a very spiritual woman. I loved her from the moment I laid eyes on her. Our friendship spanned for over forty years, and during all this time I was head-over-heels in love with her. Every breath of mine wanted to be with her, to be in her company. I wore your mother down over that period, Eleanor, and I would have given everything up for her and to be with you both. Your mother is a special woman, and I don't have to explain this to you; members of your real family will tell you. You too have her gift, and often, throughout your life, I am sure it has caused you much strife.

I feel that this was God's curse on me for my sins: to fall in love, to create a beautiful human being, and to have it all taken away from me. I am not a young man, and I'm going to my grave with a heavy and broken heart – broken by an immeasurable sense of loss, and at my hardness of stance and lack of forgiveness concerning certain matters. If a priest had fallen as I had done I would have had him severely chastised and banished. I see now that I failed in things where there was no need to fail. There are matters I know of, Eleanor, beyond the scope of the ordinary human, and yet I served a lengthy period in ministry not comprehending the power that is love.

I love your mother and I love you. Every wakeful moment, both of you are in my mind and in my heart.

Above all else good that I would wish for you, it is my hope that you find stability and peace in your life. Sometimes people don't find stability until they reach old age; some people have it all their lives and then lose it in old age.

I would like you to remember this when you pray, and I hope you can find it in your heart to do that, for me. It was written by Yaakov Yitzchak, the Seer of Lublin who passed away in 1815 (you know by now of the Brahan Seer, your ancestor – such things the spirits have to tell us).

'I love more the wicked man who knows he is wicked than the righteous man who knows that he is righteous. The first one is truthful, and the Lord loves truth. The second one falsifies, since no human being is exempt from sin, and the Lord hates untruth.'

Each time we forget this, Satan wins a battle and finds a home.

I will watch over you, my dearest darling Eleanor.

Laurence

xxx

Taming the Wolves

Every morning at the small café, he sits under the wine-coloured awning, from nine to midday, and watches the tourists, pilgrims, local people and pigeons. The skies too, the patterns of cloud, the contrails of jets. Feels the breeze and hears the songs from buskers and radio. Listens to the barrage of voices. Sometimes he feigns interest in a newspaper article, but he does so to lose the focus of someone watching him. Watchers are watched too, he understands.

He is a man with little else to do with his life. So, he sits and drinks espresso and picks at a Danish pastry, perhaps two. And looks, listens …. Why he likes to do this is beyond him. Natural curiosity? Distraction? It is, he supposes, something that brings him from the centre of his own being, not entirely a distraction, but close. His name is Garcia Leary, a 39-year-old son of an Irish turf-cutter and a runaway Irish nun. Bob was his childhood name. Garcia was his since he was 19, a nickname. It was one of two. The other, Spanner, was because of his olive skin colouring, perhaps caused by some errant Spanish chromosome.

At about noon, he always leaves for home, to an apartment down a cobbled laneway, not far from the Roman Arena, where once he had listened to Pavarotti. He has lived in Verona for three years, and shares an apartment with a woman eight years his senior, although he thinks that she might be a little older. Not that age matters, and she has weathered the years rather well. She is slim, brunette, with short hair and green eyes he no longer knows how to read, for all his skill at looking.

He used to busk, playing his guitar in nightclubs and cafés, singing popular songs, along with some ballads he had written himself, though he no longer sings, plays his guitar or writes songs. It is as though he has changed persona, become an altogether different man to the one who had walked out on his wife and son seven years ago, because he felt that, if he hadn't, the wires in his head would have melted. He had come close to harming himself and others.

He buys the day's groceries in a small corner shop two doors from the apartment. He walks with a lopsided gait, a result of a traffic accident eighteen months earlier. His skeletal frame badly shaken in the collision, he is sure that the full consequences upon his health have yet to mature. Maria had been driving. She'd entered an inner-city roundabout with her eyes on a handsome Latino pedestrian, and pulled out in front of a white Berlingo van. His side took the full whack.

He sustained two broken ribs and a broken ankle. Whenever he is stressed his head pounds, and there are days when an inexplicable tiredness falls upon him – it is not a tiredness cured by sleep. In fact, he does not know how best to describe these bouts of tiredness, other than to say that it feels as though something has abruptly vacuumed away his energy. Maria apologises now and then, especially after he catches her looking at the wreck he has become; her sculptured ruin. Worry and concern written are all over her elfin face, sown deeply in there alongside the guilt. He has no head for much, except watching. Apart from the headaches and bouts of tiredness, there is the neck pain. Constant, but tolerable – when it is not, he takes painkillers. But he does not tally his aches and pains to her, nor does he ever complain of the discomfort. The van driver died, leaving behind a wife and two sons. Maria's mind has much with which to contend, and he would not swap places. Besides, if he were to badger her, she would up and leave him. He ignores the fact that people can badger with silence, too.

She works part-time as an English teacher, and is usually at home before him. He knows she is not in, because the mail is lying on the blue doormat. He ascends the stairs, grocery bag in one hand, the other gripping the wooden handrail. Two of the screws in brackets holding the rail to the lime-coloured wall have worked loose, and they lie on the bare stair amid a film of plaster dust and brown plastic plugs. He leans too heavily on the railing – he keeps forgetting. Although he knows she is not at home, he calls her name. Momentarily, it seems to fill the silence and the emptiness. The landing is narrow. The attic trap-door is of glass to allow natural light to grace the hall and the stairway, which had previously always needed a shining light bulb to chase away their gloom.

'Maria,' he calls, entering the apartment.

He looks around to the fridge to see if there is a note pinned behind a magnet. He leaves the bag of groceries in the kitchen and the mail on the coffee table in front of the TV, for her to read while the soaps are on. He turns on the radio, and then goes to the window that looks down onto the street. Quiet. He'd hoped to catch sight of Maria. He loves the way she walks, her head tilted ever so slightly forward, the frowning expression she always wears. Every day she brings him news from the school about what she'd heard concerning the antics of mutual friends and acquaintances. She has a way of making serious things appear so funny, and he adores her smile – but she only smiles when she forgets ….

The clock with the gilded roman numerals on its red face tells him she is way past home time. He wonders if he should call her. She doesn't like him to ring her at work. He checks his phone. A message. Ah … she has to see someone, so will be late. *Won't be long.* Why hadn't he heard her message beep on his phone? *Do I go so deep into myself that I'm deaf to the world?*

He makes a sandwich, sprinkles oregano over slices of beef tomato, and takes a beer from the fridge. Sits in front of the TV, but does not turn it on. Rarely does he bother with watching television, and he becomes restless during DVDs that Maria plays. Usually romantic slush or sci-fi. He lets himself fall asleep during them. Prefers listening to the radio, as music soothes the beasts that sometimes come to roam the corridors of his mind.

When she arrives home, she barely acknowledges his presence – it occasionally happens, and he knows not to try to coax her thoughts into words. She remotes the TV to life, and helps herself to a sandwich he had left for her. Checks the mail. He smells her jasmine scent, runs his forefinger along the back of her leg, squeezes her buttock.

'Change out of that blue shirt, Garcia – it's rank,' she says, moving away. He showers every other day, because it has become a habit. He is too hairy-chested, too hairy in general, she often says, for him not to shower every day.

'I have some bad news for you,' she says, sitting into the armchair.

'Let me guess … the landlord is increasing the rent?'

'No. I …'.

'He's dead?'

'No … this *is serious* … and you're not going to like it … but I think you need to consider this … just don't say a word, right, Garcia … listen and then decide.'

'I'm not able to make decisions any more. It hurts.'

'This is something you were talking about doing before the accident.'

'I see,' he says, understanding where the conversation is leading.

'I …'.

'No.'

'Why not?'

'It would be too stressful, that is the why. And I am quite certain that Rosemary and Anthony would want nothing to do with me.'

'You didn't think like that …'.

'I think like that now.'

'What's changed?'

He shrugs. *What hasn't changed?* he thinks.

'I don't know … but it has, Maria. I walked out on them, and I kept walking for years, and they're in the past, and I'm in theirs … and that's what I think now.'

'Okay,' she says, nodding.

She will not take the matter further, or argue her viewpoint … she does not pressure him, for the stress comes as a red cloud across his forehead, and the lightning bolts flash inside his skull. He sees his thoughts as voracious wolves, the rest of him as a tired traveller nursing dying embers in a forest white with snow.

The conversation, he senses, has led them around a corner. She is in deep silence, churning thoughts in her head, as though searching for the best approach to tell him something. She is by the window, smoking one of the five cigarettes a day that she allows herself. Homework copies are stacked on the table. Framed in the window, in the afternoon light, she fleetingly reminds him of some film star. The name won't come to him.

She says, looking out the window, 'Do you remember what else we discussed … had agreed upon … before the accident?'

'Yes.'

'About breaking up?'

'I remember,' he says very quietly.

'It is back on the agenda,' she says, facing him.

She'd resolved that there wasn't an easy way of delivering her news. The words, he feels, are sharp instruments, piercing. They inject a lump in his throat, waves of sickness in his stomach, and bring tears. The inner turmoil reveals itself in the slight tremor of his cheeks. He wipes his lips.

He looks at her. She can't meet his gaze. She shakes her head as though to free herself of his stare. Her features seem set in stone, and would not, he thinks, be out of place among those of the nearby Roman sculptures.

'I can't do this any more,' she says, jamming her cigarette in an ashtray and lighting up another with the Zippo lighter he had bought her for a birthday present.

'Do what, Maria?'

'This,' she gestures with her hand, 'living in a dump, looking at you moping about the place, dealing with your moods … living with the accident every day for the rest of my life.'

'I see,' he says.

'I have to put distance between it and me … I need to move on.'

She does not mention his lack of spring in the bedroom, his disinclination to discuss their future. There were times she had tried to raise the matter, but he had had an idea where she'd wanted to bring him, and constantly deferred the issue for another day or changed the subject.

'So your idea was to abandon ship,' he says, 'when I was back in Ireland?'

'What man wouldn't want to see his son?'

He calls her a bitch. But she has spoken the truth, if for a devious reason. Deviousness he would never have, until now, believed was in her character. What man wouldn't be curious to see how his son is doing, if not his ex-wife? What sort of man is he?

'You don't care about them, Maria … you just wanted to use it as an excuse to get shot of me … would you have come with me to Ireland?'

Her silence answers. She is leaning against the window, her cigarette not going far from her lips. There is a series of rushed draws, and then a long inhalation and exhalation. She waves the smoke out the window.

'Who is he?' he asks, feeling a pain in his neck, a heat coming inside his head.

'It doesn't matter, Garcia,' she says.

So, there is someone else.

'How long has it been going on?' he asks.

'Does it matter?'

He massages his neck, stands and goes into the bedroom for his painkillers. Takes a bottle of water from the fridge and washes them down. Slams the fridge door shut – jars of this and that shudder in the quake.

She sighs.

He says, 'I can't go back to Ireland.'

'Really'.

'So,' he says, 'why push me in that direction? What else is going on with you?'

She shrugs, and because she feels that he has come too close to her, she leaves the window, sitting into the table.

'I just don't believe that you can't go back, Garcia … I don't know what you did there that keeps you away. You never said.'

He nods. He put his hands in his jeans' pockets, because he talks with his hands and it annoys her. His mouth, she likes to say, doesn't need his hand as a conductor's baton.

She says, 'It's perhaps fortunate for me that I have no idea.'

'What do you mean?'

'I've no idea what I mean by that.'

He is certain that she fears that owning the knowledge would place her in danger. What does she think? That he is an IRA man on the run? A drug dealer? A murderer? Some other class of criminal? He throws each of these at her, but they bounce off her rigid expression.

'Are you leaving or am I?' she says.

'The apartment lease is in my name, isn't it?'

She doesn't answer. Her new lover has no place, or else none good enough for her. Perhaps he shares accommodation? The idea comes to him that this new man is young, perhaps younger than him, definitely younger than her.

'I'll go,' she says.

'I like it here,' he says, 'and I can't walk out on anyone any more … I can't do that.'

She stares at him briefly, then leaves the room to make the call, to pack. Meanwhile, he brews a fresh pot of coffee. Wise perhaps, he tells himself, to go out for a while, to lessen the pain of watching her leave. He could say hurtful things that he would later regret saying. He is not violent. Obviously, she considers him a risk, although he had never lifted a finger to her in anger. He must have said something to her at some stage in their relationship about why he had quit on his wife and son. He can't remember. Yes, he had come close to choking the life out of Rosemary, because she had pushed him to breaking point – she had done what Maria is doing. But he had changed, and perhaps the accident had wrought that change; now, he lets things go – the things he cannot change.

Emerging from their bedroom with two rucksacks, one plump and the other much less so, she flits around the living room and kitchen, bagging ornaments, small, framed lithographs of the Roman amphitheatre, and other touches she had bought to make their apartment a home, keeping an eye on him as she proceeds.

Minutes later, a car horn beeps. And then she is gone. Without a word of goodbye – just a look commingling *goodbye* and *sorry*. He hears the plop of a rucksack descending each step, the *oh God* as the handrail loses more screws, the opening and closing of the front door. He looks out the window in time to see a yellow Renault turn a corner.

Bereft, feeling as though a part of him has been lost, he opens a bottle of whiskey. The apartment feels strangely naked without her touches. She forgot the painting of the galleon caught in high winds and raging sea – or perhaps she hadn't forgotten, had instead made a decision not to take it, because she knew he liked it a lot, and she would think of that whenever she laid eyes upon it.

Over the next couple of days, he sits for longer than usual at the café – middays run into late afternoons. There is no reason for him to hurry home. On Tuesday, he espies the new couple walking under an archway. He watches them. They are a distance away, across the esplanade, between him and a mill of people and pigeons on the wet flagstones. The skies had cried this morning, briefly. Maria and whoever. Holding hands, her leaning in against his shoulder, smiling. He is young, this new man, and walks properly. Should he go and warn him of her wandering eyes, her poor driving skills, how she cannot tolerate the company of human wrecks – how her carelessness had put one man in a grave, and another within sight of one? Or has she already told him? It's possible, he supposes, but unlikely. She probably gave him a sanitised version of events. In her mind, the van driver had been driving too fast – *he* had not seen *her*. His statement to the Italian police, asserting this as a truth, had most likely kept her out of gaol. It also helped her case that the driver had previously been banned for drunk driving. Still, the truth is there – buried – but it never alters, or loses its sting.

Infrequently, he had thought of his son and former wife, and had asked himself how they were getting along without him. A couple of times he'd stared at his mobile phone and wanted to dance his fingers on the digits. One time, he had done it … the call rang into an answering machine. Anthony would be 15 now, Rosemary 36. They probably think he is dead. Rosemary would have received his life insurance – *that's after seven years of being missing, yeah? Then you can be declared dead for legal purposes.* He isn't sure, but maybe for that reason alone she wouldn't be thrilled to hear his voice. What happens to paid out insurance on a man who turns out not to be dead?

He's never before experienced the swell of loneliness that now pervades his whole being – wreaking devastation with his nerves. In a fit of temper last night, he'd wrenched the handrail free and let it fall onto the stairs. He drank several shots of whiskey in quick succession, as though this might quell the fire raging within his bones. Thinking, thinking – his thought-blades that cut and tore at his soul in a bout of prolonged mental anguish; a torture that seems to happen to him mostly at night, when the power of the past is strongest. It is the wolves circling, beginning to close in. He'd rang Maria, but she wouldn't answer. Clicked him off after telling him to 'Fuck off and leave me alone' in response to a dawn phone call.

There they are – the new couple. Sadness bites. He looks at his phone on the table, lying on the top of the newspaper, beside his notebook … the number not Maria's. He rings, mindful of someone watching him – a someone asking himself about the sad-looking man at the corner table, apprehension replacing the sadness as he waits, phone to ear.

'Hello?' a man's voice answers.

'I'm looking to speak with Rosemary … Leary.'

'Who's this?'

'She used to be friends with my wife.'

Silence.

'My mother died last year … I can put you on to Herb, my stepfather?'

Silence.

'Hello,' the young man's voice says quietly.

Garcia says, 'No, it's okay. Who are you?'

'Spanner.'

So he has my nickname.

He is forcing himself beyond the shock of learning of Rosemary's death.

'How's your father?'

'He's dead.'

'Oh … and what happened to him?'

'He was lost at sea.'

This is what she had told him.

He hears a voice, a man asking who's on the phone.

Garcia says, 'I'm terribly sorry to learn about your mam and dad.'

'That's life,' his son says, 'but thanks.'

If someone is watching him, what he sees is a man with tears streaming down his face. His son's voice … Rosemary …. If he had stayed, could he have prevented her death? Had his leaving her wounded her deeply and set in train an illness? No. She'd wanted to be rid of him. He should not have left; not when it was she who'd wanted to leave.

She'd hurt him in the way of women who know their men. She said he hadn't got the spark to make it as a singer/songwriter – would never amount to anything much more than a caterwauler in a pub. Their interminable rows pushed and pushed him. He had to leave so he could tame the wolves that were sniffing around the shreds of his sanity. He hears now their howling from the woods of his mind.

With some considerable mental and emotional effort, he stands. Looks around. He will walk for a while, that helps. He might catch sight of something beautiful that adds a reason for a living – flowers, a magical pattern of birds in flight, young lovers holding hands. Perhaps he will sit in the coolness of a church and light a votive candle for Rosemary. Do small *living in the now* things to disperse the pack of wolves.

She'd found happiness with someone else – good. His son thinks his father is dead. Good, too. Clouds have silver linings. The world moves on. He has given too much of himself to the people-watchers here. It is time to find another café. Perhaps another city.

A day unlike any other

He notices, because she is ignoring him, grey skies overhead and black clouds to the west. Two magpies; one follows the other across his eyeline. A sudden lift of wind touches rain-kissed daffodils into a frenzied dance on a margin of estate greenery. He is also aware of a fleeting metallic scent of rain, the slow and heavy trawl of traffic in both directions. Thick bad breath of diesel fumes. Up ahead, a speed van. A black cat with two white paws waiting outside the closed doors of an Indian restaurant. Driving a Nissan Almera, a man for whom he had once worked. A car the same make and model and navy colouring as one he used to own. Beside him, her strong silence.

They had been walking for a mile, from the bridge over the river, along the main street, towards the rented house they call home, but know that it is not. For something to say, he says, 'It's going to rain.'

The young woman grunts.

He says, 'You'll be grand.' After his remark fails to elicit a response, he adds, 'We should get a hurry on.'

But she does not quicken her pace.

They are passing the Pakistani's house; it has slates halfway down its gable ends, resembling, to the young man's mind, a German soldier's World War II helmet. He remembers saying this to her before, and so refrains from mentioning it, and the fact that his mother used to work for Mr Sood, for she also knows this. He thinks that perhaps the problem with them is that each has run out of new things to tell the other.

She says, 'Don't …'.

'I wasn't about to,' he says.

'You say it every time we pass that fucking house.'

'Sometimes you mention it before I do,' he says.

'Only to stop you telling me.'

Once, they had both worked at a banking call centre. It was where they'd first met, in the staff canteen. Their salaries were poor, but combined it made for fair. In the downturn they lost their jobs, his going shortly before hers. Swamped in debt, their home was repossessed, so too his car. Even the baby she had been expecting turned out to be a mirage. It was as though their coming to live together had cursed them. The crash, he corrects himself, it wasn't a curse – it had to do with the crash. Cunt of a year, 2008. Blame the government – smug Ahern and his 'go commit suicide' to his detractors. Bluff 'Diddy Man' Cowen and his picture in the art gallery – fair play to the guy who did the stunt. All members of the LLLS – Living Like Lords Society – on their fat fucking pensions while the rest of us are shit in the loo. No flush.

*

In the sitting room, he turns on the TV and lounges on the sofa, his shoes and coat on.

'It's your turn,' she calls to him from the kitchen.

To make dinner, he remembers. He doesn't want to cook. She will pick at whatever he cooks. Critique with small sighs.

'Use the nailbrush – your nails are filthy,' she says, as she passes through the sitting room to the bathroom.

He watches her, shakes his head, then rubs at the dark stubble on his face.

She's getting so fucking fat, he thinks, while I'm losing weight.

The doc had told her she needed to have that lump in her left breast checked out. Another entry in a long list of shitty happenings. What is he supposed to say? They don't tell you that. Oh yeah: listen, hug, comfort, console. How do you manage that with someone who carves you with her eyes? Fill her with optimism, he supposes. Paint her a pretty picture, say she'll be grand. Think positively. It might be what she needs to hear, even if she knows they are all out of pretty pictures.

'For …' she says, emerging from the bathroom. She is biting her tongue, he knows – he should be cooking something.

She is using that antiseptic wash on her hands instead of washing them. And she never washes her hands if she only peed.

'Did you use all of the toilet paper?' he says, remembering that she had a couple of days ago. Using the last leaf of bog roll is like taking the last Oreo biscuit on the plate: out-and-out selfish.

'Have you got the dinner on?' she says.

'No.'

'Well, I'm not cooking … end of story,' she says, slouching into the armchair, crossing her legs and folding her arms.

'What's left out there?' he says, then sighs.

Payday is tomorrow. Visiting the doctor had taken up their last fifty euros – money they'd put by over two weeks to get her to the doctor. They'd applied for a medical card, but hadn't got any word back. She had called the department and been told there was a delay in processing applications.

'I dunno,' she says, 'a can of tuna maybe, pasta.'

She'd been crying too. Fresh tears had fallen a few minutes ago.

'Oven chips?' he says.

'I think so.'

'Crinkly ones?' he says.

He only ate those, while she prefers thin cut like you get in Mickey D's.

'Thin,' she says.

'Beans?' he says.

Her silence brings his eyes from the TV.

'Get up off your fucking arse and look,' she snaps.

'Why don't you fuck off with yourself!' he says irritably, but with an added something that is close to bitterness, and worse, outright dismissiveness.

Then she goes bawling her eyes out.

'It might be … what did the doctor say? "be-nine", right?' he says, 'it could be … you don't … we don't know yet. The doctor said it was best to be on the safe side.'

She dabs a tissue to her eyes. He'd never seen her eyes so red from crying. Not even after she'd miscarried.

'It might be nothing,' he says.

'It is something,' she says in a knowing way.

He stands, considers hugging her, squeezing her shoulder to show that he is there for her. It would be a lie. Of course he would stand by her, but the hugging and touching and kissing is stuff of the past between them. He hadn't realised that until this very moment.

'I'll do us egg and chips,' he says, squeezing her hand.

'We've no eggs.'

'Beans it is.'

'Peas.'

'Peas, so,' he says.

He hates peas, especially mushy. He wants to say this, but she is sick. If not with cancer, then from the worry of possibly having it, and so she doesn't need to hear him bitching about little stuff.

He is glad to be in the kitchen and away from the sight of her misery, and would murder to have money for a couple of pints. He wonders if she told her parents. Not over the phone – it would have to be a sit-down job. Probably at their place – he wouldn't be present. She wouldn't tell him that she had broken the news until she had it done. They owe both sets of parents a lot of money; handouts for this and that to pay bills, and had long exhausted those sources of revenue. Still, desperate, he'd asked his dad the other day for a loan, and was met with a sigh and a quiet refusal. He hadn't got it to lend, he said. Her parents had said that she should move back in with them – her bedroom was there. For her. So, without saying a bad word about him, they had managed to cut his feet off at the ankles. Her mother never liked him – her father likes no one.

No chips. Croquettes. Bought cheap from Tesco. After they've eaten, she says she is going out for an hour.

'Where?' he says.

'Mam's,' she says.

She has no money for a bus, and her parents' house is a long walk.

'Do you want me to go with you?' he says quietly, half hoping that she doesn't.

'No, Mam is collecting me,' she says.

'You …?'

'What?'

'Nothing.'

Later, she sends him a text to say that she is staying over. He retires to bed shortly after midnight. He misses her. Even if there is a divide in the bed, and they had taken to sleeping back to back, it had always made him feel good to know that she was within touching distance.

He feels empty without her. Unable to sleep, he returns to the sofa and watches a DVD she had said they'd watched before – he'd insisted he had not. Minutes into the movie he remembers its middle and ending. She is so often so right about things, while he misses the mark.

He texts her goodnight with an x, and waits for her response. But there's no reply.

In the morning, the cold awakens him. He checks his phone to see if she'd messaged him, and shakes his head on his way to the bathroom. Jen never fails to answer his texts. If she didn't text she would ring, or send a 'call me' message.

The toilet paper holder is empty. If she were here he would be angry with her; now that she is not, he finds her inconsideration somewhat endearing. He knows himself well enough to understand that his mood is tempered by the notion of his money waiting for him at the post office. Usually they stroll there together, and afterwards treat themselves to lunch in 'Cake K' before doing the weekly shopping. Rent and electricity and gas bills are all overdue, but he tries not to think about them. Messages her to say he will meet her at the PO at the usual time. Other things he does not dwell too long upon: his mother's birthday; a score he owes to a friend for a spot of hash; his car; toilet paper. Her sickness.

His father had called him last week to remind him of his mother's birthday. A couple of scratch cards, son, a birthday card, son, eh – so I won't have to listen to her whinging. He can stall his hash friend for another week. His mother will get over the disappointment. She will not show her hurt so as not to cause him any. As always. *Fuck the recession and the whole shower of bollocks that led us there – we need to go fucking mental like the Arabs. The only fuckers here that you hear whinging up a mighty fuss are those about to lose their slice of fucking cake, farmers and ….*

He waits for her outside the post office in the mall. There is no sign of her. He joins the queue, hands over his welfare card, signs the docket and collects his money. There's a dance of coins in the slip tray. Several times he had looked back at the queue to see if she had joined, hoping to see her smile, a tiny wave, hand busy then in the handbag for her card. A plastic card she hates.

He buys credit for his phone, feeds it, then calls her. No reply. Next he dials her parents' landline. Her father answers like he'd been expecting his call.

Her father says, 'She's staying with us for a while, yeah, until she gets these tests done.'

'I'll be round,' he says.

'No. Leave it for today, don't call … until tomorrow, how's that?'

'I did nothing on her, Mister Dunne … it's not my fault. Why is she running out on me now?'

'She's terrified. Let her be with her mother for a day or so. It's a woman thing, yeah?'

Her old man had been pleasant to him. He hadn't expected that. But she hadn't wanted to speak with him, and that hurt. He considers ringing back to ask her dad to remind her what day it is, but she wouldn't forget. Money isn't something you forget when you have none. He lunches in a café they had not eaten in as a couple so as to lessen his pining for her.

Afterwards, he buys toilet paper – the good-quality sort, not the thin stuff; you might as well use your naked fingers – a six pack of beer, and crisps, and tells himself to hold off spending more until she is with him. They had made shopping a social occasion.

Walking home, he thinks of yesterday, how the wind had disturbed the daffodils into a dance, how she'd refused to talk, and when she did she'd been short with him. How quiet she had been, quiet among the thorns of her tears, making today for him unlike any other.

A Lasting Impression

Sometime in spring, Josh Frayne turned about on the steps of the Railway Arms Hotel with his wife at his elbow in her wedding dress and threw handful after handful of coins into the air. Silver threepenny pieces and sixpences pirouetted on road and footpath, tinkled to silence on a manhole cover, dancing hares, Irish wolfhounds and harps. We kids hurried about on our hunkers picking up the bits of silver rain. And then the guards came, and they put an end to it. I didn't see Josh for twelve years, and then I walked into the factory to start a new job, and there he stood at the clocking machine, issuing timecards, regulations and glossy employee handbooks to the new employees. A forklift went by spouting out noise and diesel fumes, and he repeated himself because our response had been muted; he wanted to be certain that we were sure about his rules. In the intervening years he had put on a lot of weight, and grown his fair hair long. There were pockets of sorrow under his eyes. He wore a green overcoat with two biros in his breast pocket, and black shoes with an intricate scroll around the toecaps.

After depositing the other new guys at their respective workstations – the various shops: Press, Welding, Paint, Assembly, Foundry – he led me to the Maintenance Section, where he himself worked, in a Portakabin wrapped round with a Plexiglas window that wore an arc of soot like a dark grin.

'So, right, you're the new cleaner. We're getting in a floor-sweeping machine at the end of the week, and you'll be minding that. I have a roster for the places I want you to keep clean, okay?'

'Okay.'

'My name is Josh … you're Tommy?'

'Mick. Tommy was one of the guys that you dropped off at Final Assembly.'

'Mick, so. How old are you?'

'Nineteen.'

'You don't look nineteen. Jesus, you could get away with being sixteen.'

'My birthday was last week.'

'You've a birth cert to back it up?'

'Will I bring it in?'

'No, not yet … just make sure you have it. You don't know the problems I get in here. You have no idea. People … Give me a dog any day.'

I didn't know what to make of him. He was my boss, and that came across for sure, but he was something else too: he was a boss who believed he didn't have to ram the fact home. He looked at a calendar, crossed a date with a pen, turned and said, 'My ex-wife wouldn't let me have a dog because she said she'd hate to see its shit on the lawn and hair on the carpet, but in my experience cleaning up dog shit is easier than the shit I sometimes see coming across that door. I've got a couple of Grade A schemers, and a few who would stand on their mother's back to get ahead, even if only by a little. So be careful who you talk to.'

'Okay.'

'Everything gets back to me.'

'All right, Boss.'

'You can call me Josh. Now, you tip along to the stores and draw what you need from Bergin; he'll give you a personal locker, and another to store your cleaning equipment. If you've any problems, tell him to give me a ring. Then later you can clean the dirty smile off that fucking window.'

Silence.

'I think I know you from somewhere. Are you one of Billy Stone's kids?'

'Yes.'

'I can see the likeness. Is he still alive?'

'Yeah.'

'Working?'

'He's foreman out in Tiny Lawrence's yard.'

'Tell old Billy, he must be old now, that I was asking for him. He was a soapy arse jockey – he fell off a horse at Cheltenham and lost me a pile.'

He said this on a chuckle to let me know that his grudge had burned out a long time ago.

At lunch, he joined me at the table. There were a couple of fitters beside us, and they knew Josh well enough to get away with ribbing him about things.

'Sally's giving you the eye,' one said.

'Stop that now,' Josh said.

'Definitely is,' said the other man, Mossy Flynn.

He lost his finger in an accident a week later. I remember because the hard brushes on my sweeping machine scooped it up.

'Aren't you married, Josh?' I said, on noticing his wedding ring; I knew that I shouldn't have gone there the very instant I'd spoken.

The atmosphere turned cold enough to chill our well-subsidised roast chicken dinners.

'Was. I told you that this morning when I was talking about dogs – what do you think ex means?' Josh said, carving through a breast.

'I'm sorry,' I said.

Mossy said, 'There's nothing to be sorry over. Not when you have a woman like Sally after your tail.'

'Still, the marriage …' I said, wishing I had kept my mouth zipped.

'What happened there anyway, Josh?' Mossy said in a low voice, glancing at his friend beside him.

I took a dislike to the man. He knew well what had happened to break up the couple, and was seizing the moment to try and prise it from Josh, just out of meanness. And I had given him an opening.

'What caused us to break up?' Josh said, looking at the peas and chicken he had speared with his fork.

'It's none of my business, I know, I know,' Mossy said.

'It was the only way I could get away from her mother.'

I decided to keep myself to myself after that, and to think twice before opening my mouth. I didn't have much to do with anyone really as we cleaners were lone wolves, and there were only a few of us. Josh said I'd got the job on the strength of a phone reference from my previous employer, who'd said I was good for nothing only cleaning up. Luckily for me, Josh didn't take what people said at face value.

No one had to make sure I was doing my job; if a place isn't being cleaned it's noticeable. I swept the areas Josh had designated for me: the long and wide corridors, between the storage aisles where the firm's portable workbenches were stored. When I got the red-and-beige machine, it made life easier. A salesman called Dunne showed me the ropes, and handed me a few quid to tell Josh that it did the business, and this was easy to say because it did. It was like pushing a pram that had a dead man's clutch. It wasn't hard work – the only bad part was emptying its bin. It never ceased to amaze me the amount of dust that gathered, because

I couldn't see the dust on the concrete floors; a very fine dirt brown. It made me think that just because I didn't see dirt it didn't follow that none was present: that's a philosophy I've always believed in since then, carrying it with me when I left the factory a year later to become a cop in Cardiff. I'd always wanted to become a policeman, but because I couldn't get a hold of the Irish language I couldn't join the Irish police.

About a month after I'd started in the factory, I was in the main toilet area talking to Carty, a nice old man who kept his domain spotless. He said a lot of people had bad toilet manners: they parked snot on the walls, wrote sexually explicit graffiti, and left shit streaks along the bowl. Monkeys wouldn't be as inconsiderate, so he maintained. He had slicked grey hair, deep blue eyes, and he smoked like his life depended on it. Cigarette smoke, he insisted, killed the smell of shit and its germs. He said that one of the foremen had been on his back a while ago, looking for a way to sack him, reporting him for loitering and not doing his job. 'What he didn't know was,' Carty said, 'I knew he was scheming to get his brother into the factory. His brother wanted a cleaning job. It was what he had done for all of his working life. Blood is thicker than water. Jobs for the boys. Mind yourself and your job,' Carty warned.

The following afternoon, I went and told Josh, and he rubbed his lips and fiddled with his wedding ring. I wasn't too sure why he wore it, but I was to find out before too long.

'He's an out-and-out fucker that lad.'

'Carty?'

'Not him. No … Dunne, Tommy Dunne. He'd have his fucking granny working in here if he thought he could get her in. He'd dig her up and bring her in, I swear to God.'

'Tommy Dunne?'

'Yeah … his wife is in the pay office, his two sons are working in Welding, his brother's on the forklift, and last week his sister got a start. And she'll – mark my words – ride her way up the ladder and into the Managing Director's arms. No flute will be safe.'

'Tommy Dunne,' I said, 'that's the man who showed me the ropes on the cleaner. I thought he was a salesman, and he …'.

'What?'

He stared at me. I had to tell him about the bribe.

'You thought he was a salesman, Mick? How in the name of …?'

I nodded. 'But I never saw him before.'

'Yeah, okay, he's back after three weeks' holidays, so you couldn't be expected to know who he was. He's one of the top guys, God saves us, and he has the MD's ear, right? And like I said his sister will have a hold of more than the MD's ear. You have the picture?'

'I do, sure.'

'Mick, lad, you've got to wake up to what's going on. If you want to be a cop, you have to learn how to see … really *see*.'

Silence.

'How much did he give you?'

'Fifteen quid.'

'Hmm, he offered me twenty-five. I told him to shove it up his hole. Unless it's from a win on the horses or the sweeps, an inheritance, you should know that there's no such thing as easy money.'

'You're right, Josh.'

'A day's pay. What did you do with it?'

'Nothing.'

'Well, he hasn't come near me yet to make a report. Maybe he won't. I don't see how he can, because in my book it's as bad to offer a bribe as it is to take one. Still, because there's no underestimating the sneakiness of some people, we better make up a story.'

If Dunne ever had a plan to come at me over accepting money from him, it never came to fruition. Looking back, I doubt if that was his intention – I think he simply wanted to ensure that the deal to buy the machine went through without a hitch, and I suspect he was a little put out over Josh leaving the final decision up to me, as he'd said I'd be the one using it the most. And people like Dunne sometimes forget how many pies their fingers, and accomplice fingers, are in. But they came at me in other ways.

About a week later, I was helping to shift some filing cabinets in an office when Dunne's sister, after some idle chit-chat, said that I looked very young. In the afternoon, a ginger-haired man from Personnel came on to the floor and asked me to produce proof of my age, to bring it in the next day. Josh said they were hoping that I'd have lied about my age on the job application form, and would use this as an excuse to dismiss me. They had done something like that to a guy on Final Assembly who'd refused to work night shift. He had said on his job application that he would be willing to work nights – I guess he was hoping it would never come about. The fact that he had a wife whose mind wasn't there didn't elicit much sympathy from Management. Granted, the union kicked up a little, but Tommy's brother was the Rep, and all his shouting the odds and threatening strike action to Management was purely for effect. People were fooled by his phoniness, and thought he was a great man for going in hard against the top guys. Very few stopped to consider the fact that there was no overwhelming necessity for the guy to be sacked, because there were plenty of men willing to switch from days to nights because of the generous shift premium. When someone said this at a union meeting, Tommy's brother shrugged and said, 'At the end of the day, he broke his contract and that's why we're all here. It's what they keep throwing back into our faces.'

When I showed my birth certificate to the Personnel man, he brought it into the Administration offices and had it photocopied. Some time later, no doubt after they'd scrutinised the original for signs of tampering, he handed it back and said, 'How would you like a transfer to the Welding Section?'

I remained silent, and he continued, saying that there'd be extra money and a shift premium. Suspicious of his proposal, I said I needed a few days to think about the offer. He had made me feel as though he were doing me a favour, offering me a promotion, which he was in a real sense, but it wasn't one for which I'd applied. When I went looking to tell Josh, he wasn't around: he'd called in sick, and then we learned his wife had died in hospital. He brought her home to their house to be waked. After hearing the news, I hung out in a shower room that wasn't used as such, and which was located in a part of the factory that hardly anyone had reason to visit, except for the likes of me and Carty and a giant from Foundry who sometimes went there to cry, and who some months later killed his mother on Christmas Day.

Carty had a bad cold, and the end of his nose was so red you could find your way in the dark with it. He had a tawny shirt with the sleeve rolled up higher on one arm. After he listened to the offer I'd been made, he took a long pull on his cigarette and told me that they wanted to shift one of Tommy's brothers from Welding because he had difficulty in meeting the daily quota and he also didn't want to work nights. He was a skinny man, not in the best of health. Carty knew him. 'A smile never dawned on his ugly puss,' he said. The man had been dying for as long as Carty could remember, thirty years at least.

When we met there in late afternoon, close to finishing time, we must have been chatting for about ten minutes when the door opened, and in walked Tommy Dunne with his face aglow, like he was a saint after a long prayer session who had made a God connection. Carty's lips drew in. He said nothing, just looked at Tommy, waiting for him to say something. But he just went off and set things in motion.

A coffin was the appropriate resting place for Josh's wife. That's how bad she looked. He was broken. Apparently, they'd got back together six months before she died. He'd taken her in because she was dying. I didn't tell him about the day's events, and nor did Carty; we thought it would have been inappropriate.

When he returned to work, I noticed how the pockets of sorrow under his eyes seemed to have grown bigger. He was distant, always seemed to be half-listening, like one of his ears was elsewhere. Carty got fed up with the hassle, and tore all the clocking cards into confetti after he got his final pay cheque. They moved me into Welding on 'promotion'. And Josh had nothing to say to us about our comings and goings – I don't think he was really aware of our going until long after we were gone. By the time his thoughts were back in focus, there was nothing that he could do to reverse matters. He brought Carty out for a meal and a few pints, and once he stopped at my welding machine to chat, and said that I shouldn't be hanging around; I should go chase my heart's desire. Then he asked me to open my hand, and into my palm he pressed a sixpence piece, 'For luck.'

A hangover morning, still and drying out after a wet and windy few days. Bitterly cold, too. I haven't been back in town for many years; I returned to bury my father. Yesterday, Josh had shaken my hand at the cemetery, but I hadn't realised it was him until I had time to reflect in the evening – there was a woman with him. She looked a little like Sally, but I couldn't be sure.

And now it is my turn to behave as Josh had done all those years ago: to repair, if only temporarily, a bridge of love.

The hotel steps on which he and his wife had stood as a newly married couple are gone, burned to ash, and the site built up as a shop and apartments. The factory lies derelict, holding nothing except empty spaces and the ghosts of old schemes and schemers. Today is similar to the day when I had first laid eyes on him. He was merry, his wife beside him, spreading his good fortune by creating arcs and bursts of silver rain. And I do that now, in memory, in gratitude for the things I learned from him: the coinage is euro, the wish a secret, and I walk on and away from their dance and fall.

Thursday Market

Before Thursday's first wash of light around the market square building, there's the jingling of tubular bars, the flapping of canvas like a flock of wounded birds searching for impossible flight, the clanging of trestle tables being set in place, a maze of stalls spreading from the old building that houses a display of sarcophagi lids, bearing long-dead names of men who'd amounted to something in another age.

The old market square building is now a heritage centre, this you should know, one of the few changes since your last visit. Its modern treasure hoard is a wealth of Bord Fáilte brochures, guide books, glossy leaflets, encouraging tourists to spend time here, money there. Coloured beads and knick-knacks, almost weightless in consideration for your flight home, you see, easy packing, a little something for you to show someone where you'd holidayed. Forgettable experiences kept unforgettable through memento. These days, fresh fish is sold from a refrigerated van parked near the entrance to the cathedral. At the railed cenotaph to the fallen of 1922 you can buy clothes from a Pakistani and sofas and carpets from an old traveller man who did business with your mother. A new man called Cheap Jack sells gardening implements and toys. A young guy with hunched shoulders and a perpetual cigarette, unquenchable like the Olympic torch, sells pirated DVDs. Here, in the Thursday Market, you can still buy items at a cost a little below that in the shops.

But you're not listening so intently now. I can see the drop off in interest. So I don't remind you that back in the fifteenth century a name inscribed on a sarcophagus lid decreed us our Thursday Market.

Into the silence I say that a deed good or bad can carry a long way into the future.

Yes, that is so true, you say. Bitter? you add.

Perhaps a little, I say.

Not over us, you say. Not after all this time.

I say quietly: No, not over us. You.

You look away, the tips of your fingers touching the cellophane packaging of the plain biscuit on the saucer, resting there like a headstone against your cup.

To bring you back from the faraway place you had brought yourself, I say there is the well too, long sealed over, now grated but visible, a curio. But I think sometimes it's not possible to unravel the knot in a harm.

I used to love touring the stalls, you say.

I tell you some old memories to loosen the knot I was tying, and you shake your head in this small café down the road from where you used to live. This café is new – on its ground stood a bicycle shop that was dark and dusty and oily, like a forge, smelling of new and old rubber and saddle soap. On a crooked shelf, a dozen or so rear lights glinted the red eye at a turn of the sun or the fall of a car's headlights. Silence then as our fresh cappuccinos arrive. My heart gives a little flutter when I remember the last time we sat in a café and you complained about the crack inside my mug. Well, the manager didn't know where to look as you listed off the names of germs that lived in the tiniest of fissures in delft.

That was the day before you left town, when you sat my ring in the palm of my hand and folded my fingers over it. You had been edgy since we'd met, and I knew something bad was coming, but I didn't believe it involved the returning of a promise, a dream.

Market day, fifteen years ago. Almost.

I think how you are slim as ever, your hair is now auburn, your eyes the same colour and shape as my ex-wife's. I think how it is you are dressed so stylishly – it is easy to notice that you have done well for yourself. I am sure my dress down of blue T-shirt and faded jeans tells you as much about my status. And yes, I also caught the glance of your eyes on my paunch, the rinse of your eyes over my thinning and greying fair hair.

I wonder why you've come back. There is no one and nothing here for you, except a cemetery that holds your parents, and perhaps that is why you're here, an anniversary? It isn't just me – is it?

I don't like to ask. You were never one to explain yourself. At least not fully.

You ask if I'm married, and I nod, but don't tell you it's been over for a while and that I have no idea why the ring is still on my finger. Why is it you asked, I think, for you had seen the band of gold?

Children, you venture.

One, I say, and no more, because when I think on him even for an instant a lump races from my heart and blocks my throat and my eyes fill. You've a daughter, I say. This throws you. I say I heard from a cousin of yours who had been home on holiday. She saw me in Tesco and remembered that you and I had been, as she put it, an item.

Yeah … yeah, you say, I'm divorced and have a daughter. Beautiful. She's staying with her father in Tucson for a while. She didn't want to come to Ireland.

A shrug tells me her decision had nothing to do with the destination. There is a fleeting expression of regret in your features, like you have mislaid something of importance and cannot for the life of you remember what it is.

What do you work at, Terry? you say.

When I tell you that I'm working in a bank, it doesn't surprise you. I'd like to refrain from asking you what you do, because I know it's something much better and exciting, because it's part of the reason why you folded my fingers over my ring. You wanted more than was in me to give.

When I ask, you tilt your head to one side as though deciding which success of yours is the best to push forward. In the end you can't decide, and you say you're a microbiologist and have written a stage play, which is, as we speak, being decided upon. You live in Manhattan. Something surrenders in your eyes when you see that your achievements fail to impress me.

You sip at your cappuccino and ask me for my son's name. I tell you and you sound interested, and so I give you a little about him. You seem reluctant to speak about your daughter, and the lines fall deep about the corners of your eyes when you say that she's a daddy's girl – your ex-husband. You say he's a businessman, and owns a string of hotels and a couple of racehorses, and you say this like these achievements are small. You say it because you realise your roots and whose company you're in, and you know such talk in a small town makes us speak ill of high-achievers who lose sight of their origins. Such talk is reserved for your class of society, where each can relate to the other about the things they have or intend to have. You say it because, in your eyes, he has greatly diminished.

You smile.

I ask if you're happy, and you sigh and look at your hands and stretch your lips and shake your head and say you haven't been for a long time. You made wrong choices in your life, you say.

And this *throws* me. The words, but also the meaning in your eyes, their grip on mine.

Are you happy, you ask. No, I say. I thought as much, you say. My marriage broke up, I say. This does not elicit sympathy from you but a shrug, as though to suggest this is no great surprise.

What went wrong, you ask.

As if this can be discussed at length in a café full of people in town for the Thursday Market.

A summary, you ask, firing high an immaculately groomed eyebrow.

I'm not ready to talk about it, I say.

So the break-up wasn't amicable, Terry.

We're friends.

Yeah, you say disbelievingly, I can relate to all that.

Well, I say … failing to think of anything to add.

Well, you smile.

You look at me then, and in that look I see the years melt away. You are you when all you ever wanted in life was me. Your eyes – the last time I saw them up close was at your mother's funeral some years ago, and I shook your hand, and you were busy with grief and didn't know it was me through your tears. I called up to see you two days later, but you weren't at home. It was a flying visit by you. We had no time to catch up on what was fast passing us by. I wonder if we could, you say, stopping dead.

If we could? I prompt.

You sweep in a breath of air and exhale.

What? I say.

Begin slowly at first, of course? you say … pick up the threads.

You go on to say, Terry, you were never far from my thoughts.

This is so brave of you, I think.

I lean back in my chair and say this.

You shake your head and force a smile and apologise for being so naïve. And I've often thought of you, I say, I spent a lot of time getting over you. And I don't think I ever quite succeeded in doing that.

So, we? you ask, a flutter of something like hope and excitement in your voice.

I shake my head, and this response doesn't annoy or upset you. Because what you see in me is a man who will not give himself a choice.

Your son? you say.

Yeah.

You sip at your cappuccino though you don't want it.

Kids, you say, don't stay kids forever. What then, Terry?

This one, he's special. We have coffee every Thursday morning. Right now he's up rooting around in the market. He lives for it. You should see the stuff he buys.

Rubbish, you smile.

Sometimes, I say.

You'd have loved America, you say, quietly.

I've no doubt, I say.

When he arrives at our table, he lowers his head and looks sidelong at you and then at me. In his thick fingers there's a bag of market delights that he is anxious to talk about, but not to disclose to a stranger.

You are gracious, if condescending, when you speak to him. He talks to you as he does to most people, without agenda, and with a naïvety that gives me joy and often concern.

It's time I was going, you say.

We shake hands and you leave, adjusting the strap of your handbag on your shoulder. You don't even offer to pay the bill, and this is not you, for you were never mean with money. In a hurry, you see – because you had walked away from someone like my son. I'd heard about your special needs daughter and how you had small patience with her.

Yesterday I learned of your death, and in this café of returned dreams on market day I speak to you in my head, the things I would have said if life had presented the opportunity.

I would have especially liked to say this to you: what is yours you'll always run full circle toward. That day with your ring burning my palm I went after you, to ask you to keep in touch – to tell you that it didn't have to be all or nothing. Though you were within hailing distance, I remained silent.

The last I saw of you was at the edge of the market, disappearing into the maze, past a woman selling imitation Victorian jewellery.

Café Phoenicia

We're only passing through, he often liked to say, meaning life. He'd said it moments ago, into a silence that Chibli thought had not wanted to be broken. But for some people silence is a torture. Chibli Mahmoud told the old man not to be going on so, it was irritating. He knew too, though, that Salih was leading up to breaking some news. Taking to a bad bend in the road leaving the village, north-east and downhill to the coastal road, he went through the gears on his German imported Mercedes.

The stars had yet to drift from the sky, the June air cool, still. Along the route lay two French UN checkpoints, and perhaps another set up by the Amal militia (sometimes the militia had none), before they could breathe easily and be assured of reaching their destination. The Amal, Hope, controlled the city, and had checkpoints operated by children masquerading as soldiers, standing beside red-and-white painted oil barrels and rudimentary sentinel huts. Always begging, Chibli thought, if not with their mouths then with their eyes. Their superiors were men not much older. They trained the boy soldiers in the old Roman Hippodrome and the adjoining Byzantine City of the Dead, quartered under the spectator rostrums. Orphans all, Chibli had heard, parents lost to Israeli shells, indiscriminate roadside bombs, internecine feuds. War and anarchy, his mother used to say, afforded an opportunity for people to settle old scores with neighbours, to seize and redistribute wealth as disproportionately as it had been before, as always.

Traffic was light in both directions; there was no Amal checkpoint, and the French soldiers did not delay them beyond a cursory look at the back seats and the boot. Chibli always carried a few pastries from the café in a cardboard box in the boot – a sweetener of a bribe, accompanied by his business card and an invitation to join him for coffee whenever they were on leave. These, it appeared, would grow another day old.

There was more meat to be seen on a used toothpick than on Salih, his old companion, his assistant baker. Chibli did not know any other skinny bakers. They, like him, were all at least overweight, but in most cases obese. Salih no longer wanted to travel the eighteen kilometres to and from work, or to worry about the likely hazards they might encounter – people had been attacked by so-called bandits, dragged from their cars and shot dead, remains left on the side of the road or kicked into a wadi. Or, if the carjacked were lucky, merely beaten and robbed. Who was to protect them? The country was in tatters – the gendarmerie powerless to prevent the outrages, the army fragmented, with many of its soldiers 'twinning' their military role with the Amal.

'We are only passing through,' Salih said, over the song playing on the radio.

'Stop saying that.'

'Chibli, I need to retire. I must. I want to live out my remaining time in the village with one of my women, to lie in on the mornings … I am so very tired of it all.'

'You always say that and then you change your mind. You are worse than a woman for changing your plans.'

'I'm not well.'

'You have been dying since I first met you thirty years ago. There was nothing wrong with you back then, except fear of old age, and now that you're old you …'.

'Ah, Chibli, you can be so cruel. Not a bit like your father, Allah smile on him.'

Chibli glanced at the old man and then put his eyes back to the road. Daylight was beginning to wash away the night. He could smell the sea, still hidden in darkness, a sea that almost encircled the city. A ruin of a place: Israeli gunboats had only a week ago fired a barrage of shells at the houses on the north port in the Maronite district. Their warplanes had dropped leaflets telling people to evacuate their homes or go to the beaches or the archaeological sites, for they were going to shell the city unless the militia stopped their rocket attacks on Israel. The Amal had commandeered the historical sites and converted them into military bases. In addition to the hippodrome, no citizen was allowed enter the south side of the port with its Greek and Roman ruins, a beautiful colonnaded walk to the sea, the amphitheatre, the mosaic-patterned pedestrian way … it was the business to be in, too: stealing artefacts and selling them on the international black market, or to local UN personnel. A more lucrative business than trying to keep a café solvent, and now the night-time curfews were further undermining his efforts. Perhaps it was high time, he asked himself. Tempting as it was, he could not imagine himself pilfering his country's heritage … though the idea was one that revisited him every so often.

'I have six months to live,' Salih said as they turned right, passing a camera shop, a few garages, the army barracks with corner towers.

'Ah, Salih, the doctors gave you that long ten years ago.'

'It's true this time.'

'If you stay at home, those wives of yours will slice off your penis. They all get in such a mood. They get broody at the same time, too. Why did you marry such moody women?'

'It's a risk I'll have to take. They will mother me to the grave.'

'Hmm.'

'And you, Chibli, it's time for you to look at your life, yes? Our country … the mess is getting worse. It's 1985. Do you remember your Papa saying that everything would be fine by now? Look at us. Things are getting worse. Even my bones smell trouble.'

Chibli had been married, and was now divorced. He could not give her a child: she wore the blame for it willingly so as to allow him keep face in the village. She remarried, and last year had her first baby, and was now pregnant again. While her tongue had remained silent, the rest of her had not, and although she'd moved with her new husband to the next village, fifteen kilometres away, everyone knew his seed was useless. He had heard whispers and loud laughter behind his back, and women who had showed him a flicker of interest now showed him none.

They slowed at a roundabout entering the city; already there were men gathered in the hope of finding employment for the day from one of the outlying farmers who often had a temporary need to hire labour.

'When do you want to begin your retirement?' Chibli asked, bringing a hand to his shaven head. He was 32, and had lived in Cyprus for some years, returning three years ago to take over the business bequeathed to him by his father. His two younger brothers had no interest in helping him, preferring to live in Paris. He lived alone in the family home in Tayr Zibna, a spacious and comfortable apartment, the biting loneliness as much a part of its features as the antique furniture. There were too many memories; tastes not his, but that he had not the heart to change.

He lost the cakes at the final checkpoint 200 yards from the café to a boy who'd asked him cheekily but not menacingly if he had anything to eat. He was starving, he said. Café Phoenicia was situated at the corner of Rue Abu Dib, facing the Roman Hippodrome, its gate guarded by the militia. Some years ago, his father had moved premises to this location as he saw potential in being within spitting distance of the ruins where Charlton Heston had raced his chariot to glory in *Ben Hur*. Photographs of the star, signed by Heston himself, featured on a wall, along with the signatures of some of the film's lesser-known stars. Sepia photographs of Tyre were arrayed opposite, against a backdrop of a yellow-and-peach mural of ancient jugs and traditional coffee pots. But few tourists visited. Everyone had banked on the civil war petering out, but it had turned into a festering sore.

Chibli opened the front door, and switched on the lights then the radio to see off the silence. Salih said he needed to piss before putting the chairs, tables and sun umbrellas under the awning. To leave these in place overnight was to invite the militia to sit on or to steal them. Chibli set to making coffee and putting fresh pastries on the shelves, and called in next door for fresh pitta bread. Rarely these days did he make his own, whereas Salih liked to keep his hand in.

Early morning customers included old men who smoked and nursed the same Lebanese coffee for an hour, played backgammon, discussed politics (depending on who else was present), perhaps a couple of UN soldiers stationed in the Lebanese army barracks, a couple of the senior men in the hippodrome, hefty and bearded officers who strolled from the rostrums to the café, pistols on their hips, smoking, always in deep conversation with each other, likely discussing how their young charges were or weren't shaping up. Nothing, Chibli had overheard them say, makes for a better war dog than an orphan. New Zealand nurses, too, Rachel and Ann, from the Palestinian refugee camp, six kilometres south of the city, called in on Thursdays about 9.00 a.m., or late afternoon when the heat had gone off the sun. He liked Rachel, and had once picked up the courage to ask if she would like him to show her around the city. She smiled and said she'd already seen all there was to see, but thanks. Salih had seen him blush and try to pass off his invitation as not being a romantic proposal by bringing the women fresh chi and borma; they licked their fingers free of the shredded pastry and pine nuts, and laughed like some women do after receiving an unexpected and not entirely welcome invitation. Chibli did not know which was worse: the polite rejection, or Salih's noticing it, and his overzealousness to show that no offence had been taken. Indeed, he had felt none, just a pinch of hurt and shame at having mistaken her natural friendliness for interest.

This morning was different than others. The old men who usually came to talk and drink coffee did not arrive. Salih called in to him in the kitchen to say he had seen them coming this way, but they had walked on by, and he felt sure it might have had something to do with the two men who were waiting outside to be served.

'And also, they want to speak with you,' Salih said. 'Maybe the tax is going up again.'

'Who are they?'

'They came from the direction of the hippodrome, but they are not our regular patrons.'

'I see.'

'I will make the coffee.'

Chibli dried his hands in a towel.

'Chibli … ' Salih said quietly, after peeping out, '… they have locked the door and turned the sign to CLOSED.'

He had never seen these men before. They were slightly built, had light brown moustaches, and were dressed in mufti. Armed? He saw no weapons, but suspected they carried pistols, perhaps tucked in at the small of their backs. They stood. He wiped his hands in his blue slacks before shaking their hands. The younger of two gestured for him to sit. It was clear to Chibli that for the present the café was no longer his. The older man said his name was Khadum and his colleague's Darwish. The men picked up their cigarettes from the ashtray. Chibli patted his shirt pocket and removed his own pack, putting it on the table. He felt too ill at ease to smoke.

Darwish said, 'You know why we are here?'

'No,' Chibli shrugged, 'I have no idea.'

Khadum said, 'Don't lie.'

'I'm not lying.'

Darwish pursed his lips. Khadum gave a tilt of his head, and his stare brought tears to Chibli's soft brown eyes. Khadum averted his gaze and poured water from a jug into a glass. Then he mentioned a woman's name and Doctor Hammed.

'I know him, for sure … he is my doctor,' Chibli said quietly over the hump of a small cough.

Salih arrived with the coffee, a blue bowl of sugar, and the small red-rimmed glasses reserved for special guests, and therefore hitherto unused. Chibli watched the old man walk away. Yes. He had lost weight. Why hadn't I noticed this before? Poor Salih, he cannot afford to lose any more: he could slip between the bars of a storm drain.

'Have you paid him, yes?' Darwish said.

Chibli frowned. Was this it? He had forgotten to pay his doctor, and these two men were a reminder? Is this what things had come to?

'I owe him some money for my last physical … and he is to run some more tests on me. But I've had to cancel several appointments because of the war situation, you understand?'

Khadum said, 'Let me be clear. You paid him to carry out the abortion.'

'What?!' Chibli said, looking from one to the other.

Silence.

'No, no, no … you are mistaken, my friends. Very much so. You have no idea how wrong you are.'

'Chibli Mahmoud,' Darwish said, 'that's you?'

'Yes.'

In an instant, the two men had their pistols on the table, hands gripped tightly on the handles, their knuckles white.

'How much do you think your life is worth?' Darwish said.

Chibli was unable to speak. His lips flagged several times.

'This is how much,' Khadum said, 'ten thousand dollars.'

'As Allah is my judge, I …'.

'We'll be here in the afternoon for the money, four,' Darwish said, pointing at his watch.

Chibli noticed the leather strap, brown and frayed, cheap. Dark forearm hair like wild grass grew across it, like weeds overrunning.

They let themselves out. Chibli saw them flag down a military jeep, get in, and disappear around the corner.

Salih came alongside his shoulder, 'I heard.'

'I …'.

'Yes?'

'So?'

'It's not true. I …'.

'Salih, I know you know; my whole village knows.'

'Truth doesn't matter to them. They believe in the money, that you have it. Because your father had it.'

'I am being very much wronged here.'

'Go to the Imam, or their leaders in the city … you must. Now, before they return.'

'Who is in charge? These men change so often.'

At the Amal headquarters close to the sea, opposite the UN Custom Post, he met with people who half-listened and did not care a whit for his problem. Those who could sort the matter were unavailable. Even the Imam was absent from the mosque and his home behind it – he wondered if he should call round to the doctor. No, he thought, it would not be wise. If he had carried out an abortion he was in serious trouble. The men would not talk to him: they would kill Doctor Hammed on sight. The doctor was not stupid: he knew the risk he was taking by conducting such a procedure. He may well be as innocent of the allegation as I am of the one they've levelled against me. Perhaps he has refused to pay? Yes … it is in his nature not to; the doctor is a man of principles and very opinionated.

There wasn't an issue in getting the money, but not in the time frame they had given him. Impossible. And in the giving of it he would be bled of most of his savings; he had been left the apartment, the business, his brothers the bulk of his parents' money. A sizeable amount. Enough to live well, if sensible. His brothers were sensible people. More so than me, he thought, sitting in his car outside his café. I should have sold everything and joined them.

They had asked him for money very close to the amount he had on call in the Banque du Liban. Why not above that sum? How would they have found out his account detail? Easy: a clerk or the manager. They would know whom to bleed, and had passed on the information to people expert in how to draw blood. Paranoid! The whole country was infected with paranoia. Go to the bank? If he asked to withdraw his money and close his account, requested the sum in dollars – observe the response.

Afterwards, he told Salih it was as though they had been expecting him. He had hoped for surprise, a flurry of questions, reasons, but the transaction was as neat as a cut from a surgical knife. Completed in less than fifteen minutes, sheaves of forms signed. The teller smiled, he smiled.

In the end, he could not bring himself to close the account, for a reason he supposed came from his sub-unconscious: he simply did not want to leave; he knew he would not settle elsewhere; and also, now that they'd exacted their price, they would leave him alone. Like vultures, they would go to find fresh pickings. They had left him enough to keep his business afloat. These were far from stupid people.

The café had been empty all morning, and had seen only a trickle of customers throughout the day. The two waited outside for the men to return. In the hippodrome the boy soldiers jogged around the track, carrying their

AK rifles across their shoulders, chanting about Allah and glory. Clouds fringed the blue to the north.

They offered no greeting to the men when they called. Salih stood but Chibli did not, not even when Salih nudged his shoulder – he counted the money under their scrutinising eyes, put it back in the white envelope and handed it to Darwish, the younger of the men, knowing the other would feel but not wear the slight. Fear churned Chibli's stomach to ice, but there burned a flicker of fire in his heart. Snuffed by the siren of an ambulance, loud and diminishing, and then low and persistent when it reached its destination. He estimated its distance … the clinic? Eye talk from the men enlightened him. He sighed, and asked if it was okay by them for him to resume work, and did they want coffee.

'No coffee,' Darwish replied, fingers drumming on the table like he was bouncing thoughts he could not contain in his head. Relief and tension surged along Chibli's veins as the men stood and pushed back their chairs. Relief only as they turned and walked out. He prayed to be trading in Café Phoenicia when peace arrived on the wings of white doves, when the land had been sated with blood, when the tourists returned. That would be his revenge: to have survived.

Then, watching the men pull away in the jeep, he thought to ask Salih for the name of his physician.

Wicked Games

He slipped off the M50 onto a back road, and dipped his lights when he ran into patches of fog drifting from the pines like spasms of kettle steam. The road was one he had travelled many times over a five-year span a long time ago, when he was a kid, some years before his army days – like people, roads change, so a couple of miles on he slowed down. He was looking out for a petrol station.

The petrol station alive in his mind appeared on his left, and he swung in under the pumps' canopy, cut the engine and took in the ghostly aura – a garish blue neon garage sign, amber street lights, a rat easing past a wheelie bin. Something straight out of a Stephen King horror novel. He was tired. Last night he had gone to see Louise, hoping to chat about what had gone wrong between them. He found her as he cut across the Ha'penny Bridge, linking another fella's arm. She didn't see him. He glanced to his right, caught the reflections of lights on the dark Liffey waters, the breeze that curled off its back and shaved his features. Yeah, well, she hadn't sent him a Dear John so she could spend nights out with the girls – what did he expect?

He considered himself fortunate that the break had been clean – there were no kids involved. The whole bloody thing could have been so much messier. So he'd seen her someone else; tall, broad-shouldered and obviously loaded. There are people who smell of money in the same way people smell of poverty.

She didn't want a scene when he came home, didn't want him using his karate skills to mince her boyfriend's bones. As if he would; the choice was Louise's to make. She could have whom she liked on her arm; he didn't own her. The wedding ring wasn't a slave's collar. After all, he had been as faithless as her – a belly dancer in Tel Aviv. Intimate of intimacies without so much as birthing each other's name.

Red-brick shop and offices. Double doors to a garage, a car on the ramp inside. CCTV camera wore a red eye. Charlie Berry, the owner, was a rich man who lived two miles farther down this road, on an estate bounded by old walls leaning with age. A long gravel drive crawled to a country house once used by the Martin family as a hotel.

He rang the Berry place on his mobile, said he'd be a little late reaching there because of the fog. Mrs June Berry sighed.

'You have Paul's things?' she said.

'Yes, yes, I have.'

It's the reason I'm going to see you, he thought. Paul had been a close friend. Paul's things that his Tara refused to take in – all she wanted was his watch, his poxy UN medals, his wedding ring, stuff for his kids – nothing else. Pop them in the post. She didn't want army people stomping all over her house. One had been enough. Now that he was gone, she didn't have to tolerate lowlifes on her floor. When she had said that, Myles lost his rag and had called her a bitch, and more, but she cut him short like a person well practised at cutting people off.

'Good, well come along when you're ready,' Mrs Berry said.

He bought a coffee to go along with his cigarette, and got into his Suzuki jeep to enjoy it. He dropped the cover of the glove compartment and settled the paper mug into its recess. Sorted out in his head the questions they would ask, the answers he would give: he wanted his answers to be closed avenues – he would say nothing that would lead him to lie about something else. He was never good at lying, or at keeping a secret for that matter. Eye contact, too. Dislike and disapproval must be held back; he needed to keep his expression neutral, so as not to spark suspicion in Mrs Berry, or alert Paul's father that he knew him for being a terrible old fuck altogether.

He started the jeep to breathe some heat into his bones. Myles sipped at his coffee, tasteless, listened to the radio, and took long drags on a cigarette for which he had no genuine appetite.

It's a Heartache came over the radio. Bonnie Tyler? Maybe, he thought.

It surely is, he said, a right bloody heartache. He drove on, inching through the fog, determining not to drive back to Dublin in this weather. He would hole up in his jeep and wait until morning, when hopefully the fog would have cleared. There used to be a bed and breakfast around here, but the sign was down and the house demolished.

Passing the first set of stone pillars, the ones Charlie Berry had told him about a week ago, which were being fitted with automated gates, he slowed almost to a stop. Meeting the bend and the second set of pillars, he drove through, the gates lying open for him as an expected guest.

He pulled up in front of a series of broad semicircular steps. Paul's oul' fella had gone berserk when his son joined the army, ranted about loyalty to the family business (ironic for him to rant about loyalty), his temper worsening when Paul said, not without pleasure, that he had enlisted as an ordinary private and not as an officer cadet.

Looking at the mullion windows, the in-year cars parked on either side of his 06 jeep, he saw at first hand the lifestyle Paul had denied himself. Was it worth it? Hardly, in light of what had happened.

He rang the doorbell, heard the fall of feet on tiles, distinguished a woman's figure through the stained red glass. She opened the door. She was old but dressed young, smelled of perfume, hair dyed black, and the corners of her eyes were as badly cracked as stone-damaged glass. She sized him up without moving her head, then the suitcase and rucksack that sat at his feet like obedient hounds. Something in her eyes fell back a step.

'Come in, Mr ...?'

Annoyance rippled through him, but he tried not to show it – he'd told her his name by phone and email. Often enough for her to remember, if she wanted.

'Myles. Myles will do.'

'We're in the drawing room,' she said, leading the way.

Part of the 'we', he understood, included Charlie Berry. Paul's father sat in an armchair beside a flickering fire of artificial coals, the cast-iron fireplace adorned with embossments of flowers. Framed photographs of family and portraits of daughters were arrayed along the mantelpiece. The silver-haired man got to his feet, extended his hand, and said, 'Charlie.'

'Myles,' Myles said, the other's grip surprisingly strong. He had Paul's eyes, except his were bluer and colder.

'Sit, sit down, good man. A beer, what? wine?'

Mrs Berry moved to the drinks cabinet and lowered its drop-leaf.

'Beer'll be fine, thanks.'

'So, you served with Paul ... abroad?'

Nodded. Why was he saying this; he already knew?

'Yes.'

'I'll cut to the chase, then ... I've read the MP Final Investigation Report, and I don't accept its findings.'

Myles had nothing to say. He hadn't read the report.

'Our boy had no reason to shoot himself. Now, I ... I invited you here for you to tell us the truth. You won't get into bother for doing it. I'll take care of things for you ... so don't be worrying. Truth will always out.'

Such an arsehole. And what are they implying? That someone else shot him?

Charlie glanced across at his wife. Her face was blank, lips like tracings of red blood. An uneasy feeling came over Myles. He sensed that she had instigated this meeting just so she could examine her husband's demeanour. Her eyes seemed to be spitting shards of her heart at the man – and he understood not a thing.

Charlie Berry sighed, accepted his brandy without comment, and sat to the edge of his armchair. He had hooded eyes, like a hawk. Mrs Berry sat on the armrest beside her husband.

'Your statement ...' Charlie Berry said.

'I didn't come to discuss the findings of the investigation,' Myles said.

'You're toeing the official line?'

'No. My statement is a true account of what happened.'

Mrs Berry put her hand on Charlie's shoulder, as though applying a brake to his words.

'You see, Myles, we just don't believe it. It wasn't his ... style,' she said.

'Suicide isn't a "style", Mrs Berry.'

'He wasn't like that,' Charlie said.

'Have you spoken with Tara?' Myles said.

'She's a slut. I'll fix her,' Charlie Berry said in a low voice, the way people do when they mean things.

Mrs Berry said nothing, gesturing with a frown for Myles to do likewise – a woman confident that she could talk her husband into and out of doing anything. Especially doing stupid things. Myles understood that Charlie Berry wasn't thinking clearly. He was a hard soul – the sort who would insist on his shops remaining open on the day of his own funeral – a hard soul and a disturbed one.

He sipped at his beer, and drew the back of his hand across his lips. He wanted to say something, but didn't know where to start. Should he tell them about Paul, the excellent soldier? The guy who was always eager to help others out and who thought no problem too big? Or about the Paul who conned everyone into thinking he was one happy-go-lucky fella? Mention the single shot, and how shocked everyone was when the latrine's aluminium door was forced open and all saw Paul slumped, eyes open, jaw slack, the pistol lying at his feet?

No, say nothing about the incident – around it, leading up to it, but not the immediate aftermath. He didn't have to say anything, for Charlie Berry went over and started to surface his son's things from the rucksack, going from it to the suitcase. Mrs Berry put her hand to her mouth.

Shirts, army and civilian, underwear, letters bound with a rubber band, photographs in albums with motifs of cedar trees, one of the latrine he shot himself in. In the background, presents he had bought, a water pipe and cigars for Charlie, and a gold chain and cross he bought for Mrs Berry in Akko while on a sixty-hour pass.

'Charlie,' Mrs Berry said, quietly.

She wanted him to stop unpacking their son's gear, but wouldn't say so outright for fear of being ignored, and also derailing some catharsis Charlie might be going through. Myles considered the notion that perhaps she waited hopefully for the slip of tongue from her husband that would cut his throat, yield her a sentence – words he could not rationalise away.

He stood up from his son's things and stepped backwards to his armchair, his eyes on the clothes he had removed, a pile of memories for the wash.

'What happened? Tell us. We need to hear it,' Mrs Berry said.

Myles raised an eyebrow, fixed his eyes on a yellow flower in the rug and said, 'He received a letter from Tara. She said she was finished with him that evening. We had rain. August rain in Lebanon is rare, you know – the earth smelt its redness, a rusty smell – I was thinking that when I heard the shot. And I ran out and heard the boys saying that Paul had shot himself. I got a jemmy bar and prised the door ... he left a note. You got the note?'

'We read it,' Mrs Berry said, looking hard at Charlie.

'Youse didn't get along, Mr Berry?' Myles said, a gentle probe to remind the old fella that he didn't have to travel farther than his own shirt buttons to find one of the underlying causes for his son's death.

The old man remained silent.

'They didn't, no,' Mrs Berry confirmed.

'The letter said that,' Myles said.

'You didn't mean it ... isn't that so, Charlie? You were only teasing with Tara about the money, weren't you? He was only teasing, Myles.'

Silence.

Tara wrote and told Paul that his father was putting pressure on her for repayment of €20,000 they'd borrowed from him for their house deposit. They'd been hoping Charlie would turn it to gift money. He didn't. Wouldn't. Not unless he was given something in return ... leave the army and come back on board the family's *Starship Enterprise*. That was the surface reason ....

Myles had a friend in the military police who on the quiet told him Charlie baby was screwing Tara, and he didn't mean for the return of his money; he wanted his money's worth. Paul learned of the affair from Tara's sister, who thought he should know.

Myles didn't reveal that he was pissed off with his best friend for not confiding in him – especially after he had weeks earlier confided in him about his own marital problems.

'You'll stay the night, Mr ...' Mrs Berry said.

The offer was empty of sincerity.

'No, I won't, thanks. I've accommodation arranged. Thanks anyway.'

She let him out, not a word of goodbye from either of them, their son's best friend, lousy failure of a friend.

The fog hadn't thinned, so he pulled in to a picnic area at the mouth of a forest. In a while, he would let the seat back and try to fetch some sleep. He would probably spend most of the night wondering about Charlie and Paul, and when the bond linking them had first begun to weaken. About how the old man will point his finger in every direction and never at himself. Refusing to let the truth sink home, fending it off like an able politician – how he'll push the army for answers, doing so energetically so as to cast off any suspicion his wife might have concerning him and Tara. And of Tara's silence? For money, perhaps? Or threat? Myles did not bring himself there – that was a bridge for another day. She, he suspected, did not mind the affair at first, but grew tired of it. He could be wrong, though. Part of him took a comfort in putting her in a bad light – taking Paul's side. His buddy who couldn't share a burden, only with a bullet.

His mother, all the while, would observe Charlie's antics, derive satisfaction at the sight of him squirming. And then someone one day will whisper a fact in his ear, and he'll find out what he does not yet know – that his wife had known all along.

Myles stared into the fog-shrouded woods. He understood now why Paul had joined the army: to get away from his parents, to save himself – but he hadn't gone far enough. In the end, all he had done was give them another game to play.

The woman who wanted to do nothing for ever and ever

It is in 1878, when the days start to draw in and the nights stretch for too long, that Emma decides she has had enough of life. She is 49, and works as a maid in a house set well back from a lake that holds pike, which one catches only for show and not for cooking, for pike are full of bone and though it is twenty-five years since Miss Mildred choked to death from a fishbone, her death throes appear to have been indelibly lodged in the very memory of the old house.

This dark evening, Emma Dundon, daughter of Edward and Elizabeth, both long deceased, sits to the side of her bed in a small room, cosy from reddening coals in a fireplace that casts out smoke whenever the wind turns a certain way. A stout white candle burns in an oval glass holder, but a draught every so often attempts to gutter the flame. The light is weak, like a tired heart in an otherwise sound body. She had lost weight in the last few weeks, yet still feels well, or so she tells herself. Her mind seems to reflect the sickness of her body – she is snappy and broody and quiet, not at all herself. She displays still her seemingly tireless energy. Every morning, before the stars go out, she clears ashes from half a dozen fireplaces and replenishes fuel boxes with coal and logs before seeing to breakfast and the making of beds.

It was hard enough to do all these things when I was young, she thinks, but it's not getting any easier, and the Mister and Mistress won't take on help to replace Biddy, who died six months ago. They insist on standards being kept as they were … bugger me, I do say to myself, bugger me they do, will you sew that Emma and sweep the yard? Sew, knit, sweep, wash, scrub, cook, bake, fill fuel, run a bath, polish this, shine that, do the dishes? God almighty, I do say to myself, will you sprout another of me, please? A double, so this one, me, can rest a while. A pair of knees on me like red onions, joints creaking and groaning, and aches and pains all over my body – all clamouring to be the worst of them, and me unable to make that decision. Tired, so tired. Yet not sleeping, even with a sip of the Mister's whiskey in me. His whiskey these days is the only thing of his that comes in me. Mistress has no idea of where he used to put himself. Oh, stand in front of the fire there, warming his bits and bobs, his hairy behind looking at me, and he talking about the price of hay and what this gentleman said to this other gentleman, and then he'd turn about, full of himself again, and he'd slip into bed and tell me to bite the pillow and not his shoulder, and if I'd mind opening my legs a little wider and bring them up high. Wasn't I fortunate he was spent in that how do you do of some men, and never could rise a belly on me?

She stands up and begins to undress – exhausted. She wakens these dark mornings as though she'd been asleep for merely minutes. Another day of it comes far too soon. Drudgery. She pulls her sleeping gown over her short, lithe body. Good enough still to hold a man's attention, but she is rarely inclined these days to have a man in her, and makes do with the occasional hand to herself – she can bring herself to orgasm quickly by imagining herself with the gardener's son, Jed – quiet, muscular, tall, with rugged features – now there is a man who could have put a belly on her. He'd done so to his wife, pretty quickly as a matter of fact – two already and another on the way. She looks a beaten woman already, and she only 25.

Mind if I borrow him in my mind for a bit, love? Only for a minute or two, depending on the quickness and the lightness of my fingertips. Sure, who's to know or object? He'll do no harm only good, I think, but a body wouldn't know that for sure, would it? For they say that the mind can be the sickest place of all, and the body underneath is kept in the dark about the fact.

The Mister never comes near her these days, and speaks to her like he had never known her in that way. Three men all told in her life: one a man who was a butler in the house, and left shortly after Miss Mildred died – she was to go with him and in the end did not, for the Mister and Mistress needed her in those days, when their only child wasn't too long dead. And in truth, the child's death had stricken her too with a sort of melancholia that, once it grabs on to the tail end of a person's soul, never seems to let go. Gordon White, kind and lovely and sure to have made her a good husband – she did not love him of course. And he had yet to assert a liberty of her that their master had been enjoying for six months – it was from him she wanted away, and Gordon was her ticket. It was a certainty, she had reckoned, that someone would catch the Mister with her – she was surprised that the squeaking bed boards had not alerted anyone, and she had whined aloud with pleasure one night when he put his tongue to her. But no one ever found out, and their secret remained one – survived as a goodly few appear to do in this life.

The other man was Frank, and he was rough, and rode her as though she was one of the Mister's racehorses. She was not sorry to hear he was fired when the Mister caught him whipping a horse for no reason. He had bad teeth and breath and hands, with fingers that did not know how to touch things lightly. The marks he left on her occasionally come to her mind, and she winces at the memory.

She hears the fall of feet on the stairs. Once familiar to her ears – he used to tell Mistress he was going to read in the study. This was an old habit before she became a new one for him. A poker must have its fire, she used to say, and there was no fire of much note in the Mistress of the house. Life had left her like a patch of scorched gorse – you could see the blackness and smell the soot ….

She listens intently.

Surely he is not about to start up that racket again? She is surprised to discover there is a flicker of want in her. He knocks the door – it is timid, like the rap of old.

She goes to the door and opens it.

His stubby candle has burned down on one side, the tongue of flame high. Candle grease thick, like prominent veins in the back of a leg. His waistline had expanded since they had last been lovers. He is dressed as for the day in green waistcoat and tweed trousers, white shirt she had ironed that afternoon – remembering that it had not washed well, for there existed the faintest whiff of his perspiration. Oh, the sweat of him when he used to furrow inside her, sliding off his face and dripping like beads of rainwater into her eyes, the saltiness stinging her worse than the air in her room from down sweep of smoke.

'I have news for you, Emma,' he says softly.

His eyes do not hold hers – they move to the fire, and to the bed, and then to the window. He coughs into the fist he'd made of his hand. She steps back, and he walks by her. She catches the smell of his armpits – the faint whiff now loud. She closes the door ever so gently. He stands to the fire for moments before turning his back to it.

'News?' she says, folding her arms across her chest.

'Damn bad news I'm afraid.'

'Bad news?'

'Yes.'

He takes in a deep breath. She knows now that he has not come for her, and is more than a little disappointed – she is also somewhat surprised at herself.

'The Mistress and I are selling up … there's a bid made, and it's most likely that we will accept. We are going to live in Spain. It's for the mistress's health, you know how poorly she has been …'.

He waits for moments for her to acknowledge this, and when she does not he continues.

'The thing is … the Hudsons, the new owners, have their own staff, and have asked to pass on the news that there is to be a clean break. Do you understand?'

She nods.

'We'll pay and keep you to next May, and give you something in expenses and so forth thereafter, to help you on your …'.

'May?' she says.

'Yes … it's a while off, but we wanted to be fair to you and give you plenty of notice. You have given us much service.'

'Fair,' she says. Service, she thinks.

'You must have someone you can stay with?'

She remains silent, for he knows she has no living relative. Awkwardly, he says, 'The Stevens are looking to hire help … I could put a word in there for you if you like.'

The Stevens – they have six children, and provide a meagre wage that sometimes isn't even paid, and the accommodation is shared. What would she be at, sharing a room with a young one?

He says into the silence, 'I suppose not … but they will ask about you, you know. Your reference will be first class, rest assured, any house would be glad to take you in.'

'Any house.'

He waves a hand.

'And the books … help yourself to any of them that you fancy from the study. I know that you like reading. Are you still reading poetry?'

'A little.'

'Good, good-o, good for you.'

He nods several times and rubs his hands together.

'I best be off back to the mistress or she'll be wondering where I'm gone, eh?'

'She'll think that you're in your study.'

'No,' he says, 'I'm afraid, Emma, she knows that's where I wasn't a lot of the time.'

'I see.'

Hastily, he says, 'But she doesn't think it was you.'

'No.'

'I said it was Biddy.'

She sighs and says, 'Poor Biddy.'

'None of the pleasure and all of the blame,' he says.

She cuts at him with her eyes. He throws out his hands in a gesture of helplessness.

'If I said your name she'd have you on the street, and no money coming to you. No beneficial reference either.'

'Who told her of your affair?'

He pretends not to hear, and so she does not ask again. He walks to the door, hesitates with his hand on the round brass knob, and then he is gone, leaving behind the odour of his perspiration and the scent from a crooked candle.

She sits again at the edge of her bed, and sips at the last of the Mister's whiskey. Then she extinguishes the candle with a harsh breath and slips under the blankets. The house is awakening around her in creaking floorboards, and a door that needs jamming with paper to the frame in a room above her. The Mister can fix it.

Over the following days, she consumes more of the Mister's whiskey than is good for her. She has begun to write poetry. What she owns in this world fits into a single piece of luggage with space left over. She wants none of his books. She retires in the early hours, and is late in wakening and tending to her chores. Clothes are half washed, and the hair above her lips she let grow. When the Mister approaches to scold her for her laziness, she says she is feeling poorly, and when the Mistress comes to her she says she isn't at all well in herself, and that a fierce lethargy has come over her. She tells the Mistress a partial truth: that she can't get Miss Mildred out of her mind – isn't it the twenty-fifth year of the accident? A week it takes for her to succumb to the fever she'd acquired from walking naked in the freezing fog, shrilly calling out in a drunken stupor for a husband, anyone's … she giggled. Then arrives the day that she's dying, and when the Mister and his wife visit her with the doctor, she points to an envelope on the mantelpiece. Hesitantly, he takes it up and opens the flap. The Mistress is looking at him reading the letter and is awaiting her turn …. Emma's eyes close, and she feels herself slipping and slipping … pushing herself too, wanting to embrace death, to know the peace of nothingness.

The doctor says, 'She's gone.'

'The letter, Andrew …' the Mistress says, hand extended.

It is easy for him to hand it to her.

It reads: My epitaph, if you don't mind it being so ….

'Here lies a poor woman who was always tired, for she lived in a place where help wasn't hired. Her last words on earth were: Dear Friends, I'm going where washing ain't done nor sweeping nor sewing, and everything is exact to my wishes, for there they don't eat and there's no washing of dishes. Don't mourn for me, don't mourn for me never, for I'm going to do nothing for ever and ever.'

Ends

(Epitaph from an English graveyard, circa 1860.)

Halabja

Unwilling to face into the biting cold, he had delayed in bed until he could no longer tolerate his mother's shrill voice. There was a certain sharpness to it that he would not dare to bring her beyond, and now she was close to the summit of her temper. He dressed in a hurry, and called out to let her know that he was coming.

She said he was the laziest of boys, and his sister muttered that he was a lizard-face for disturbing the quiet in the home. His grandmother smiled. She was deaf, and he thought she enjoyed being that way so she could hear nothing of the shouts and threats, or any of his father's loud snoring. Mother said he liked to snore because he knew it upset her and kept her awake. He hadn't always snored: it started when he put on the belly and began to drink too much arrack.

The Stupid Man, she often said of him, but not in a bad way. Well, he thought, not when Grandmother's, his mother's eyes, were on her lips.

An imperceptible breeze slipped off the flanks of the snow-covered Zagros mountains, the foothills of which tapered to merge with the town's cemetery road. He rode the bay mule his brother would take back down the mountain. Wickerwork panniers carried kindling to light the evening fire, logs, lumps of charcoal, a sharpened machete, fresh pitta bread, beans, tea leaves, sugar, and some toffee sweets given to him by his grandmother. He was 15, Kurdish, dark-haired, green-eyed, thin, and short for his age. Cotkar Amedi, called after an uncle on his mother's side whom he had never seen, who lived only in photographs and the occasional spoken memory of him. He bore more of a likeness to his father's twin, Salar, who lived across the border in Iran, in Marivan village.

Other than to complain about his late arrival, his brother had little to say. After spending two nights with the herd in the mountains, Memu was usually gruff and silent, anxious to be on his way. But Cotkar had questions he needed to ask. Had he seen any wolves or wild dogs? Had any of the goats been taken? Had he come across any more corpses of deserters from the Iraqi army? Last month, Memu had stumbled upon the remains of three young men in a ravine. All of them had been shot in the back of the head. They'd been buried in shallow graves, and pulled from them by either wolves or wild dogs. Out of begrudging respect for their souls, and the bad luck it might bring if he had just left them there to rot, Memu swung a pickaxe to the ground.

'No ... no dead runaways. No wolves, I haven't seen a wolf in years,' Memu replied, 'just a pack of starving dogs. Don't let them get too near.' He fell silent, and then added, 'There are no werewolves, Cotkar.'

'I know that.'

'Why do you go on about werewolves?'

'I don't … I said wolves.'

Memu smiled and put his finger to his nose, tapped there, 'I remember the nightmares you had after you saw a wolf man movie.'

Cotkar felt himself bristle, but what could he say? He had nightmares, but that was a long time ago when he had been just a child.

'No wolves, but say your prayers … this place is alive with ghosts at night, Cotkar.'

'I'm not a child, Memu.'

'Say your prayers.'

Silence.

It would take Memu an hour to descend, longer if he delayed to speak with anyone along the way, but that was a rare happening. He watched his brother leave, tired and slightly hunched over, astride the mule. He was wearing a smile now that he was on his way home to be fussed over by their mother and their grandmother. He would drink tea by the wood stove, smoke cigarettes and eat a hot meal. They would tease him about his stubble. And just as he readied himself to get up, they would insist that he drink fresh tea and warm the cold from his bones. Having teased him enough, they would then start to praise him for how hard he had worked, the fine man he had turned into.

The shepherd's camp was a small clearing enclosed by grey boulders, a mud wall that had once been a gable end of the family's former home, and a copse of spindly pine; a flatbed truck stripped of its tyres served as a half-gate, the other half, made up of oxide sheets of corrugated iron framed in by and nailed to wooden beams, was dragged across before dark. It was there to illustrate that the property was owned more than as a security measure. A loop of blue rope served as a handle to pull it open then drag it behind. Its rut of passage ran four fingers deep in the soil. The tiled roof had long gone from the two-room home. Pitched on its concrete floor was a five-man canvas tent, army surplus, and draped over its leaky patches were strips of yellow tarpaulin. The cab of the flatbed was in good condition; its doors could be secured, and under the seats Memu liked to hide his secret things. He was unaware that Cotkar had a spare key. On some windy nights, the cab made for better shelter than the tent.

The snow had retreated back up the mountains a kilometre. Grass and purple flowers were beginning to show through the slush. Landmines hidden by the snow had moved in the melt onto the dirt road, a few anti-personnel, a smaller amount of anti-tank. Cotkar had seen them on the verges – Memu had shown him these some days ago – warning him to keep the goats and himself clear of there and other certain patches of ground.

On the trails beyond the camp, in the copse of the pine, his goats nibbled; to draw them to him he would tinkle a bell or rustle a bag of feed or spread hay in a line. Close to darkness, he would corral them in the crude wooden pen that had a natural cutaway in a boulder, and into this narrow space they would cram at night, or earlier if it rained or lightning forked and thunder clapped. Or if they caught the scent of danger.

This would be his fourth occasion to spend two days with the flock. Rafik, his grandfather, was now too sick to work, and was in hospital in Sulaymaniyah, near death. He did not mind the shepherding so much. He had the radio for company and also the dog, the shotgun for protection. He had food, and his mother's and grandmother's prayers. Like they had done with his brother, they would make a fuss of him when he returned home. They would tease him, but not about his beard, for he had hardly a fuzz – instead they'd tease him about the girl. They would not do that, of course, if his father was present. He was a very serious man, who wasn't happy unless he was talking about serious matters. He did not like the Iranian soldiers in town, nor had he liked the Iraqis who had been there before them. But lately he had come to hate the Iraqis because they had murdered Kurdish people and levelled Kurdish villages. They didn't want Kurds living within twenty-five kilometres of the Iranian border, and they believed that by doing this they would quash the Kurdish resistance, the

Peshmerga, allies of the Iranians. He tried not to display his hatred because he had always taught his sons not to hate any living being. A distance outside of town, battalions of the Iraqi army's northern division had dug into long, serpentine and deep trenches. On the other side, close to the border, the Iranians were holed up in similar conditions. They preferred to kill each other from a distance as it was easier, it meant fewer of them died, and they didn't have to think about the killing – they had only to worry about hitting the target and not of the consequences of success.

He watched his brother until he disappeared around a bend in the track. The way was empty. Suddenly, a stabbing pang of loneliness visited. A sigh escaped him. It was a sigh that seemed to come from the well of his soul. For minutes he stood rooted to the same spot, looking at the emptiness; he did not want to turn about or avert his gaze out of fear of losing something precious.

He wore the clothes his brother had worn until he had outgrown them; his grey woollen hat, brown jacket, baggy black trousers. He was in his father's brown leather ankle boots that had had two owners before his father. Tattered, the brown was scuffed away at the toes and heels. He had good black shoes for weddings and funerals and celebrations, a pair of trainers and another of rubber boots. He shared a bedroom with Memu, a small room with two beds, a single bedside locker carrying a brass ashtray and a lamp, and a wardrobe with no doors. On top of the steel wardrobe was a tan leather suitcase, which Cotkar believed had never gone anywhere. His father had bought it many years ago in the event of someone someday having to go somewhere. It held spare bedclothes, and there was thick dust on it. Cotkar used to wonder if that was what happened to people who stayed in the one spot for all of their lives.

He made tea, and ate a round of pitta bread before going to walk among the goats, to see if any were ailing and that none had wandered. He carried the shotgun barrel broken over his shoulder, a pair of binoculars, and sweets in his jacket pocket. Half an hour earlier he had found his brother's porno book rolled up in his sleeping mat, but had put it away for later, when it was dark and he could see the pictures under torchlight. He preferred it that way. It seemed natural. It was an old porno book, the words were in English, and he could not understand them except for 'Fuck' and 'Fuck me' and 'Vagina'. 'Pussy'. His friends had told him what these words meant. The girls in the pictures must be, he thought, as he climbed toward a rocky vantage point where he could look down on Halabja, very old women by now. Perhaps 40. What would their husbands think of them if they saw these pictures? Their children? He did not think it was right, and yet it was so nice to look at the ladies. The women lived very far away – it wasn't as though they lived in the town and were the mothers, daughters, sisters and wives of people he knew – so there was no harm in kissing these naked women, especially the blond woman, and in pushing her to his penis. He was at odds with himself though – he liked to say prayers last thing at night, before he pulled the zipper of his sleeping bag over his head, and he felt ill at ease switching from looking at dirty pictures to saying his prayers to the Yellow Serpent and the Peacock Angel, prayers for his family, his hopes, for good fortune. Prayers taught to him by mother, of the Yezidic religion, who believed that God made the world and then entrusted it to the care of seven holy angels. There was no resolving the dilemma. He had tried before to ignore the magazine and had failed, and so he decided to simply keep the two apart – distinct and separate actions.

He sat on the spur of rock, and sucked on a toffee sweet. His fur-rimmed hood covered his head like a religious cowl. He liked to smoke, but again he didn't like to until it was dark. Two sides to me, he thought, the daytime me and the night-time me. He looked at the town below: khaki-coloured houses, all level-roofed, made of mud and stone, some with TV aerials, the streets measured the same. The town was devoid of character, of dominating features. A population of 70,000 souls. Every house looked the same, the streets smelled of poverty and make-do. It resembled a place shaken out of God's boot. If you wanted colour, you needed to look to the sky or to the mountains. Especially the mountains after the sun had peeled away the snow.

The sun up and the sun down, he loved these. Night of the full moon, too.

He saw it then. Beautiful. In full flight. He picked up his binoculars, zoomed in. A golden eagle soared across the blue heavens high above the town. Casting its shadow on the rooftops, the school, market area, waterhole, cemetery, on its way to its eyrie in the mountains. The glide, the lazy flap of wing, a king of the sky. Alone, aloof. He had never seen one fly over the town – it was usual to espy one sweeping over the plains, throwing its shadow over the grasslands, the minefields, the burnt-out tanks and other military vehicles. But not over the town. A portent? As with his brother, he watched until it had flown out of sight. In its immediate absence, he experienced another fleeting sensation, not of loneliness, but something else entirely – panic. He bit hard on his sweet. A shard of it lanced his gum. He cursed, and pressed the tip of his tongue to the cut, panned the town with the binoculars, hoping to see the girl or her brother, the lazy shit.

Patterns of grey smoke weaved from stove pipes, rugs spread on rooftops to dry, a butcher sliced strips of meat from the carcass of a hanging cow, chickens in wire cages, plastic wares for sale by his cousin. An Iranian army truck brought in rations for the Peshmerga manning the checkpoints at some road junctions. He watched the town come alive, and liked and at the same time disliked his remove from the activity; tractors and trucks coming and going on the streets, the marketplace yet to be at its busiest. Memu would be home by now, or at least very near to it – he would stop at Jaf's stall and buy a newspaper and some cigarettes. It was old Jaf who had thrown the porno book in a barrel, and thought it had been burned to ash, but when the old man went inside to get more stuff to burn, all the while mumbling to himself about his useless son and his bad ways, bad books and bad video cassettes, Memu reached into the rusted barrel and said, 'What bad ways is the old man on about?' He hid the book in his jacket before the old man returned from his shop-cum-home home with a cardboard box.

Old Jaf often gave a story about his son doing well for himself in Germany, and Memu would nod and say that was good and ask Jaf to pass on his regards. No one was ever sure if Jaf liked to say these things out of pride, or to make people feel small, or to keep the memory of his son alive among people who would otherwise forget that he had a son.

He sighed, lowered the binoculars, and got to his feet. It had turned colder and he was hungry. His gum had stopped bleeding. He walked back along the trail, stopping once to scan the mountains, the woods, the rocks and trails. Looking out for wild dogs. Or wolves.

When he reached the camp, he put a tiny pot of water on the camper stove to make soup, and while waiting for the water to boil he fed the dog. The dog had no name. It was old and not able to walk very far, and he could not remember the last time he had heard it bark. Outside the tent, its flaps tied back to let in fresh air, he sat on a camping chair and ate his soup. The radio was on, playing a song his mother liked, which delayed him from searching for a station that played more modern music. The dog sat by his side, its paw on a bone she had long licked clean, the strips of cold chicken untouched.

'If you don't eat, you'll die,' he said. She was as deaf as his grandmother. 'Are you suffering?' he said. Her ears were turned down, and he had heard it said that this was a sign of an animal in pain. This time she looked up at him. 'Well, I don't know what I can do about that.'

Memu knew. He had said the day she was unable to walk he would shoot her. It's when the back legs give out on a dog that you know for sure it's cruel to keep her alive. Cotkar hoped he would not be around to see it happen – if he were present, Memu might insist on him pulling the trigger. The dog was deemed to be his because as a pup it had pissed on him, in this way claiming Cotkar as its master. It did not occur to them that his leg at that particular moment might just have been the handiest place for the dog to piss against.

After turning the key in the cab door, he slipped his hand under both seats and found the small tobacco tin in which Memu kept his hash. He took enough for one roll and left everything else as it had been, for Memu had a nose for things that were even slightly out of place.

Just before midday, the shelling began. First, there was the strangest of silences, and then into that silence fell the heavy thudding of artillery shells. The Iraqis were bombing the town. He hurried back to the spur, carrying only the binoculars, and stood staring at the bombardment. His heart beat wildly. They had bombed before, but not with such intensity – the barrage was relentless, and they were bombing the residential areas that hadn't been at the core of their strategy before, but not near to where his family lived. Families were fleeing. Already there was heavy traffic on the roads, people hurrying on foot, leaving with nothing. He recognised very many of the faces. He knew they were screaming and shouting, that there was a furious revving of engines, people crying, but he heard nothing. Then, as suddenly as it had commenced, the shelling stopped. The panic activity of the people continued – it was as though they understood that the silence was an interlude, and they were right. Sporadically, for the next hour, the shells tore at the earth, at buildings, homes, and at flesh and bone. Cotkar wondered if he should return home, but his father had said that no matter what happened in town the work had to be done … the goats had to be protected from the dogs and from thieves still. His feet shifted from the anxiety that danced in his heart.

He heard the helicopters before he saw them. The beating of their wings, the droning of their engines. He counted ten, then fourteen. He dropped behind the rock to its side, lying down, and trained the binoculars on the helicopters, his elbows serving as a bipod. The shelling had stopped. The helicopters were outside the perimeters of the town, hovering like dark green demons. Next he heard the jets and the impact of their loads – separate clouds rose about fifty metres into the air in a tricolour of yellow, black and white. He could not see through the dense cloud caused by the explosions. There followed a silence. Most silences actually say something, but this one said nothing. As the fog began to lift, the horror of what he was witnessing gradually increased.

'No!' he cried, on his feet, the helicopters withdrawing. The world in zoom. Graphic. People were lying dead on the ground. Not a few, hundreds. He saw dead babies with yellow powder about their lips, people spewing up green vomit. He saw people laughing and then falling down dead. He saw others walk their last step. He saw a family of children lying in the back of an open truck, people running, burning as they ran. The bombs had landed in his home street, but they would be safe, yes? He prayed. Father would have got them all out of harm's way, yes?

No.

He ran till his lungs ached from the scalding by the harsh air, and then he stopped and walked until he was able to run again. He got a stitch that turned to cramp; his stomach heaved up soup and bread. Close to the town he saw streams of vehicles making for the Iranian border, and others coming his way in trucks, pulling over onto grassy areas outside the town. The mountain road led them nowhere, just to pretty sights, gorges and ravines and coldness. He walked into the crowd, mingled, but he could very well have been a ghost, for they took no notice of him.

Many were badly burned through their clothing. They stripped – their clothing had appeared normal, but underneath their skin burned. There were those in the throes of agony, and those who stood by, not knowing what they could do to help, and very many cried for those back in the town who were now lost to them.

Old Jaf came up to him, his leonine eyes glazed, and said on a cough, 'Don't go into the town, Cotkar.'

'I must …'.

'The poison gas has killed very many … stay with me until it has gone, then we will go back in … I promise. Stay with me. I have my car.'

Cotkar's lips were dry and cracked. Now that he had stopped walking and running, his sweat was drying into him and he was beginning to feel shivery. The breeze was blowing a smell their way, one of horseradish, and another smell that was sweet but indefinable.

'No …' he said.

Old Jaf shrugged and said, 'Okay, okay …'.

All around them, people were coughing, spitting up yellow liquid.

'Is that what you want to be doing?' Jaf said. 'Your father would not forgive me.'

Cotkar was unable to speak.

Jaf threw out his arms and said, 'I don't know, Cotkar.'

He looked around, shook his head, and stroked his grey beard. Cotkar walked on towards town, pulling his scarf over his nostrils and mouth. Jaf hurried after him, touching his elbow. 'No, wait. Think of what your father would want. He would want you to act like a man. To be clever. We must cross the border. The Iraqis will be here soon … we will come back when they have gone. The Iranians and Peshmerga have all pulled back.'

Cotkar pushed down his scarf and faced the old man. 'I'm not crossing the border. I will stay with the goats in the hills.'

'Good, good, yes … just don't be here when those jackals come in.'

'I won't, Jaf.'

The old man pleaded with his eyes for Cotkar to come with him, but Cotkar was stubborn. Realising this, Jaf turned about and walked away, finding a path for himself in the bustle of all that was going on. People hurried to board the wounded and old onto tractor trailers, the backs of covered and uncovered trucks and into cars. Cotkar put his hands to his ears to block the urgent voices, the groaning, the screaming of those in agony from their injuries, and some wounded could not scream – their throats and mouths too blistered and still scalding as the gas burned its way through flesh. They tried to scream, but these were silent screams. Others' screams were guttural, as though from an animal in its dying throes. Cotkar found this as unbearable to listen to as the loud cries. He picked up the reins of a grey pony and mounted, ignoring its owner's calls.

Jaf said harshly, 'Leave him, let him have it.'

In town, he dismounted and walked past dozens of dead bodies, mainly women and children lying in all manners of distressed positions, as their convulsions had left them. A couple of Iranians took photographs, ashen-faced as they snapped. Survivors milled past him, all in some degree of pain – an old man screamed and flung his arms in the air as though to beg a question of God.

Now that he was within sight of the family home he had raced toward, he slowed. There was a smell of rotten vegetables that seemed to push through his scarf at his nostrils. A cluster of dead chickens, a dead black cat, a dead man holding a dead child on a door step. A woman who liked to talk, silenced at the foot of her garden. Her son, a boy he had last week cuffed across the ear for calling him a devil-worshipper lay with his eyes open, his tears yellow, his mouth smeared yellow. The girl – Cotkar's mother and his sister used to tease him about her, Memu once too, but then he stopped after their mother gave him a stern look – caught in an embarrassing pose, her knees drawn up, parted. Roza. He had often dreamed of marrying her, but had never spoken a word to her beyond a shy 'Hello'. Gone. A short distance from his home – what was she doing this close? Frozen in death. He had never seen her in the vicinity. She looked – what? – emptied of herself? Tentatively easing past those sights, his heart fracturing, he pushed in the front door, and said, 'Mother …'.

He stepped into the living room, the room where they ate, talked, watched TV, where his father slept, his mother and sister cooked. They were huddled together on the sofa in an embrace, like a sculpture. His mother, sister and brother ….

Unable to tolerate the sight of his family, he went outside and banged his forehead against the wall in a mix of rage and grief. Oblivious to Jaf ranging alongside him in his blue Lada that was spotted here and there with navy dye to smother the rust. Oblivious to the old man venturing into the house, blind to his covering the bodies with blankets and sheets. In the yard, there were the carcasses of chickens and a mule. Cotkar's father and his grandmother.

Rejoining the boy, Jaf said in a measure of breath that would not have misted glass, 'We should go. You've cut your head. Here …'.

Jaf tore a sleeve from a shirt, and wrapped it around the boy's head and tied a knot. A petal of blood showed through.

'I need to find my father. My grandmother.'

'Cotkar …'.

He patted the boy gently on the shoulder, rubbing his neck. He did not have to say what his eyes had seen. Cotkar nodded, dried his tears with the back of his hand, and then said, 'One minute. I need to get some things.'

Jaf nodded. They left the street behind, driving slowly, the pony trotting behind, roped to the trailer hitch. Outside the town, Jaf said, drawing to a stop, 'You are sure?'

'Sure, yes.'

'You must take off your clothes, wash all over, Cotkar … they call it decontaminate. I heard the doctors say this.'

From the boot, Jaf handed him the things he had taken from his home. There were also things he had not seen the young boy hurry into a leather suitcase. He had something for him: a plastic carrier bag.

'Here, these clothes belong to my boy, they should fit. Maybe you won't like them … they are very western.'

It was dark by the time he reached the camp. He had walked the pony because it was overburdened with weight. He let the reins fall to the ground, removed the hessian sack and suitcase plump with items he had taken from his home. Ornaments, family photo albums, a little money his mother had managed to squirrel away, a couple of rugs, his father's heirloom sword, and the shell that had crashed through the ceiling and sat across the broken TV, an unexploded shell with Iraqi Army markings. One of these was a motif of an eagle, the emblem of the Iraqi northern Nebuchadnezzar division.

In the darkness, under torchlight, he corralled the goats, pushed closed the oxide gate, smoked Memu's joint, cried. He planned to return to town at first light. Jaf had said that the collection of the fallen would begin as soon as possible, but no one knew when 'possible' would happen. He had taken his family possessions here for safe keeping, the former family home, because he knew that the Iraqi soldiers would loot and destroy. They had taken lives, and would take what was left of those lives.

He stayed in the tent. The dog was gone. He recognised that as a sign. His gum was very painful, and he felt a stinging sensation all over his skin, as though it had taken a reaction to the fabric. It was below freezing, and yet he felt hot. His fingertips – he had touched his grandmother's face, his mother's, his father's, brother's and sister's – began to itch and throb. He had breathed in a dilution of the poison gas they had inhaled. A weakness came over him shortly after 3.00 a.m., and the batteries gave out in the radio. There might be fresh ones in the cab, but the dogs were outside. He heard their growls, the scuffing of their paws, the anxious stirring of the goats, the ninnies of the pony. But it was him they wanted – lured by the smell of burning flesh. Though the shotgun lay within easy reach, he wasn't too sure if he could fetch it before the hounds came rushing in. Or if he even wanted to ….

Deadly Confederacies

We were skint, and Jack's oul' fella refused to lend him a tenner so we could go to the pictures. Mister Kelly was mean, and the sort of man it is easy to dislike. Money had been left to him from the sale of a family farm in Rush, County Dublin, and he'd paid cash for a terraced house in our u-shaped council estate. Cheap too. Off the relatives of a woman called Granny Flanagan, who'd fallen out her back and broken her neck. An accident, so it was said by the Legion of Gossips in the estate. She had taken to the drink, and there wasn't a day that she didn't fall. In light of what was to follow, Granny Flanagan's death might not have been so straightforward an affair. Jack and Mister Kelly, at the time of her death, were renting another terraced house up the way from the widow granny.

Jack couldn't remember his mother, and his father kept no photographs of her, or if he did he never showed them to Jack. He was an old fuck with grey whiskers like what grows on mould. He spoke in a low, gruff voice that matched his manner. He grunted at Jack. It was as though the old fuck believed that was as much of his voice that Jack deserved. If he were in a bad mood he shouted at his son. Standing there listening to him speak to Jack in that way used to make me so angry. Angry enough for me to often want to bring a poker to his skull – and I guess that would have happened if his heart hadn't given out on him a year later.

Jack and I had come in from Black and Decker, where both of us had recently got jobs working on the assembly line, assembling portable workbenches. It was two days to payday, and we wanted to see a picture that was showing for one night only: *Night of the Living Dead.*

Jack tried humour, telling his father about zombies and how they were like the gossips in the ring, women who ate the hole off you just for the sake of saying something. But the mean fucker's lips went hard and his face looked like a boulder had come to lodge there.

'Make your money last ye,' the old man said. 'Go 'way from me the hell.'

'I'll give it back,' Jack said quietly.

'You're getting nothing out of my pocket. Not even a dried snot. Off now with the pair of ye.'

Jack swayed a little. I thought he was hoping to see a melt, or that he was restraining himself.

Finally, I said, 'Let's go … my dad'll give it us.'

His oul' fella grunted a grunt that a pig wouldn't be capable of matching.

'What's your problem?' I said.

'Get out of here, you, whoever the fuck you are.' Then to Jack he said, 'Who the fuck is he? Is that the lad the oul' ones are always saying to me is like your brother? Is that the little bollix?'

He knew who I was – he was letting me know that if his son meant nothing to him, I meant less.

'Come on,' Jack said, taking a strong grip of my elbow.

He pushed me, like you would a friend to keep him away from involvement in a row that he had no chance of winning. I could have broken past that shove, but a part of me thought about the consequences.

'I think ye two are bent and twisted queers!' the old fuck shouted.

Jack had to push against me all the harder.

'Ignore him,' he said.

Jack was like that. Cool under pressure. He was bubbling like lava inside. He would not let his old man away with insulting us. Some weeks later, his father started to lock his bedroom door at night.

Suppose it was like that song about the Vietnam war, 'we ruled the day and they ruled the night.' Words close to those, anyway. But that's how it became in that house: his old man ruled the day and Jack the night.

So after he refused us the loan, we wandered around town, had a couple of pints each on the slate in The Castle Inn. On our way home, about elevenish, we saw the picture-house woman, Kitty Moore. She was on her high nelly bike, heading down Station Road. She lived about two miles outside town. Once she got over the railway bridge she'd be pedalling on a dark and unlit road, with few houses around. Jack, with the beer in him and the prospects of facing into his old guy, and wanting to delay that, said, 'Let's go and scare the living shite of her.'

'Yeah,' I agreed. I hadn't got much to go home to either.

Not many liked Kitty, for she was severe-looking and sharp spoken; she wouldn't let you away with being a small coin short for a ticket. One night, she and the usher asked me to leave, saying I'd stolen in, that her stub count didn't tally with the number of heads sitting in the balcony. How she knew it was me, I had no idea. The usher probably reeled off names. It wasn't as if the house was full – most were couples not there to watch the film. I was an easy pick, then. But they were mean: they could have let me stay. If she had, and let it be known that she were doing me a favour, maybe I would have said to Jack, 'Ah leave her, she's sound.'

Would it have shaped our lives any differently? I think not. Of course, she wouldn't have died that night – that would certainly have made a difference to her, and her disabled mother.

She pulled into Rourke's shop and garage forecourt, and parked her bike against the pebble-dash wall near the air hose. She walked briskly, with a peculiar gait like that of a duck, past the front door of the bungalow. She knocked on a sitting room window that glowed of pale blue TV light.

We stayed in a corner and watched her as she went indoors. It was Jack who knew she wouldn't stay there for too long. I wondered, as we hurried along Rathbride Road, how he could have known. When we reached the 'y' in the road, a mile and a bit from town, and a half from her corrugated-iron bungalow (that I didn't know was hers until I saw its photograph in the *Evening Press* some days later), I had it figured: he had watched her before.

A north-easterly breeze, carrying spits of rain, whipped against our faces. It began to raise a lament that spooked me a little. We stepped into the furze between the 'y', squatting behind dense gorse that had the first smell of spring on it. The road was empty. We smoked our last cigarettes and wished his father dead. I asked him about his mother, the question falling off my shivering lips. He heard and said, 'She won't be long, now … the crabby hoor.'

'She could have a heart attack,' I said, not in the least bit worried if she did, but I wanted to fill in the silence, the shift in mood that had come into being after I'd mentioned his mother.

'I'd say she has the takings on her … in her bag in the basket,' he said.

There was a basket strapped to the front of the handlebars. All the oul' wans had them in those days.

Oul' wans that liked their stuff under their eyes the whole time. Then, a miniature moon cast a weakish glow of light on to the road. She was pushing up a slight elevation now, the wind hard in her face, the light bobbing along ahead of her on the rain-slickened road. Sheep bleated, moving off road on to her path. As she approached the junction, Jack whispered, 'Get ready.'

'What have I to do?'

'Use your fucking imagination. Stay close to me …'.

She tinkled her bell against the presence of sheep. Harsh little pings that the drizzle seemed to rust in mid-air, for I never heard a tinkle as strange – maybe her exerted breathing affected the tone?

'Now!' Jack said, cool as you like.

Within a heartbeat, she and her bike were in the furze. I can recall the back wheel spinning to a stop, the slow dying of torchlight as the dynamo wound down, her cries loud then muffled, snuffed – and then what followed was a complete and utter stillness. The wind died, the night sky choked on rain for seconds. Or so it appeared.

I struck a match, then another. Twin miniature beacons flickered under the shelter of my free hand. Jack's hands remained tight on her throat. Her coat was open and bra raised. The matches went out, burning the tips of my fingers.

'She's gone,' he said, panting hard and struggling to control his breathing.

He was on a high. Me too.

'Do you want to see her?' he said.

'Fuck yeah!'

We cast a fresh and quivering glow of matches over her upper body, her lifeless eyes the colour green of marbles I used to roll. I went to touch her breasts, and he slapped my hand and said, 'No!'

'Why not?'

'Just do as I say.'

His breath smelt of Tayto cheese and onion crisps. Dead beer, sour on the tongue.

'Get the money and stuff and let's get the fuck out of here,' he said, calm now.

We took the long way home, across the plains, doing an arc of about three miles, her things in our pockets. We didn't talk, except for to recite the same alibi.

We left her there, like we'd leave a shit in the woods. No looking back.

Because murders were rare back then, a huge oul' fuss was made and the cops did their thing – but the heat goes off a murder after a while. That's what we learned – murder heat cools by degrees, and each degree of cooling means a step closer to getting away scot-free. But Jack, for a fella who liked to say he was smart, made a stupid mistake that almost had us licking prison bars.

The following summer, after he hadn't shown his face for a day and a half and hadn't answered to Jack calling him, we discussed breaking into his bedroom. The stink in his room came out and asked us to, more or less. He was stone cold in the middle of his bed. A Sunday. I remember the day because of the chicken Jack had roasting in the oven, and they only had chicken on Sundays.

Jack closed his father's eyes, opened the window to free the stench from the old man's work boots and stale fag ash and decaying flesh. Then he lifted the mattress, both sides in turn, and searched the bedroom for money, not too worried about making a mess, because the room already had a ransacked look. He found about 400 quid, a stash of porno books and a bank book that said the old man was down to his last 1,500 quid. Afterwards, maybe an hour later, he went next door and asked his neighbour to ring for a doctor, that his Dad was after dying. If Jack shed a tear over the old guy that was about the height of it – and the biting wind at the graveside might have been responsible for that extraction.

Weeks later, we started going out with the women we would eventually marry. Women who believed in love and having kids, being homemakers, who were very slow ever to think badly of us. A woman's intuition isn't bullshit – if you ask me, they only ever get into trouble when they ignore it.

*

Eleven years later

I picked her up outside a bus stop late at night. Deserted, apart from herself and a wizened up drunk in an army greatcoat, who staggered past the crooked bus stop sign. She said she was waiting on a cab. I said nothing about seeing her wag her thumb. She was broke, and relief at seeing a familiar face cleansed worry lines from her forehead. We knew each other – she'd often babysat for me and my wife. We got along fine. Always a joke going on, but no messing of the sort that I intended to try later. She was skinny, 19, had hardly any tits to speak of. Long flowing red hair and a beautiful fucking arse. Tight. Lovely word that, in the right context. I was, what, a couple of days from clocking up another birthday. The twenty-eighth. I wasn't getting any from the missus, so I had to make the most of whatever opportunities came my way.

'Get in,' I said, glancing at my watch to fool her into thinking that I was tied to time.

'You're sure?'

'Yeah.'

'How come you aren't working tonight?' Jo asked after she got in. She smelt of musk perfume.

'I am.'

I worked night shift in a warehouse that distributed to stores throughout the country. Small-scale centre. Two of us managed the night shift, loading aisles with pallets of grocery items for the artic' containers; the drivers loaded these: their doing this kept us a fair bit ahead of schedule. We were lifelong pals with bad stuff in common, so we covered for each other.

She said, 'What brings you by this direction?'

'Just taking a break,' I said.

Partly true. The full truth was that I'd been sniffing her out. I'd listened to her mother earlier that day, when she called into my house for her regular gossip coffee with Louise, my doll. She mentioned that Jo was giving her a hard time. She'd do nothing for her in the house. Smoked in front of poor Gerry, her asthmatic brother, who was also a bit retarded. Her father was a nice man, salt of the earth type. He passed the collection baskets around during Mass. Didn't drink either. A right holy fucking Joe. There's no one that good. No one.

'I might get myself a Chinese,' I said.

I raised the volume on the radio. Found a channel that played music, which I thought might strum her into a knickers slipping off mood.

She didn't clip her seatbelt; her legs were ever so slightly apart. Knees then started coming together and parting, like she needed to pee. White shoes with little heel – she was tall. I was thinking about her knees drawn high and wide, and my balls resting against the cheeks of her arse. I felt my cock begin to harden. I'd heard she was riding the bingo bus driver in his bingo bus when his passengers were in the hall checking their numbers. Sixty-nine, heh heh.

'Do you want a cigarette?' I said.

'Haven't you got anything stronger?'

'Such as?'

She canted her head in a cute way and looked at me, silently asking if I were serious.

'Yeah, I'll give you a joint. But you better not rat on me, Jo … right?'

She said nothing, so I told her again, and she said, 'I'm not a kid.'

'I'm well aware of that,' I said, giving her a smile.

It was a fine night, with a sky flush with stars.

We left the town behind. Something soppy played on CKR that she said I was to leave on when I went to switch channel. Marianne Faithful singing *Dreaming my Dreams*. I don't like it – the song is fine – but it *was* a favourite of my wife's. Bitch of bitches. The mood sort of slipped in the car. Plummeted, actually. She sighed long and hard. We were driving between stretches of the Curragh Plains. 5,000 acres of short grassland that's a crop of thistles, nettles, furze bushes, sheep and sheep shit. By day, racehorses thunder up the gallops and joggers take to a track around the woods, while others walk their dogs. Four-legged variety, mostly. By night, in certain parts, lovers park their cars. And that's where I was headed, swinging a left turn just before Chilling factory. I was telling her that this dirt road was called Colgan's Cut, after a highwayman who used it as his escape route after robbing the mail coaches. She wasn't interested. The young don't care about the past – they think the world started as soon as they developed memory.

She was sitting up, alert now, straight back. And her knees had come together.

'Where are we going?' she said, glancing out the passenger window.

'I thought you wanted to smoke a joint?'

'Eh, I meant for later, Tommy ... just take me home, will you?'

'Jo. Okay. But I'm having a smoke first. Okay?'

'I'm fucking bursting.'

'Number one or Number two?'

After the recent spell of scorching weather, the ground was hard and bumpy. I pulled off onto a grassy circular area surrounded by furze bushes. Monday night. I knew the spot was always empty early on in the week. I pulled in close to the bushes that were in full golden bloom.

'Well?' I said to her shocked face.

'Are you for real? What sort of question is that to ask anyone?'

'You in the rags or what?'

'Wait till I tell my Dad about this.'

'About you smoking weed?'

'Number 1,' she whispered.

'You can go in the furze. I've got a pack of wipes in the glove compartment if you need them.'

She wound down the window halfway. It wasn't an easy roll, as the dial on the lever was absent. She stared at distant lights then, but I couldn't be sure. People often look way beyond immediate and distant things. She stepped out of the car, shut the door, looked back in at me over the gap in the window and said, 'I think you're behaving a bit too fucking creepy for my liking.'

She took off at a mad gallop, heading for the dirt track. Her action caught me completely by surprise. She screamed as she ran. When I caught up with her, I spun her around. Pinched her nipple hard, and dared her to do something about it. She went to slap my face, but I caught her wrist and then the other. Dodged an attempted knee into the balls. She was coughing and sputtering, too winded to scream. Instead, she gasped on a spit, 'Please … no.'

She knew in that instant she was in serious trouble. Her eyes went incredibly large. She struggled to break free of my hold. But I was strong. I could have held her 24/7, no problem. She shrieked, and I told her to stop, and she wouldn't. So I clocked her one to the jaw. It silenced her. I went to touch her cheek, gently, to show that it didn't have to be a bad experience for her. But she bit me hard on the arm, near the elbow. I punched her in the face. And I felt and heard bone crack. She breathed a raspy sort of breath as I dragged her into the furze and stripped her of every stitch of clothing. I had an image of myself as a wolf and she … well … what she was: a defenceless young and pretty maiden. It was a big turn on, as turn ons go. She smelt of sheep shite and blood and vomit, but those reeking odours didn't fall on me until after I was done. That fuck's that,

I remember thinking. What now? I was in a cold and hot raging temper.

Dumped her body in the boot. Covered her with a blue picnic rug I'd bought in the V de Paul. I knew the bogs well. Still do. I eased from the Cut and crossed the road onto the plains, traversed the grasslands, her body going thumpity-thump in the boot. Crossed a minor road and kept going over the grassland, scattering sheep, easing under a railway tunnel put there to aid farmers to shepherd their sheep from one part of the plains to another. Didn't hit road again for three kilometres, all the while her body going thumpity-thump on the undulating terrain. Passed ancient ring-forts and a tinkers' camp near a fox covert. I heard their dogs barking and smelled the smoke from their wood fire. Not far from where we did in the picture-house woman. I was like Jack – cool as.

Drove the road past the Hill of Allen, and kept going to the heart of the bogland.

Back at the warehouse, Jack said, 'What the fuck kept you? There's covering for you and then there's covering for you.'

'Fucking car,' I said, 'it conked out more times.'

'Hmm,' he said, carrying on with wrapping polythene around a pallet towered with grocery products. Satisfied the tower wouldn't collapse under a wobble, he got in his forklift and began to raise the pallet. Then he eased down along aisle four. Aisles were marked out like track and field lanes. I looked at him. He hadn't noticed anything odd about me, nothing apart from the fact that I'd been away longer than usual.

A cold breeze drifted in through the warehouse, and the skies beyond the shutter spaces were navy coloured and still ripe with stars. I felt great in myself – I was bubbling, rich with energy.

After depositing the load, Jack went down the line and pressed the green buttons on the portable control boxes. The shutters began to grind and squeal their way toward home. While he was busy doing that, I crossed the floor to the loo and looked at myself in the soap-flecked mirror. I washed my face because it was bright red from exertion and excitement, then I slipped into a cubicle and checked my dick, eased the foreskin back into place. Less than an hour ago it had been pummelling away inside her, and a rush of pleasure at the memory trickled along my veins. I checked my arm, and there were deep teeth-marks visible, and blood too. I suppose it was the last physical mark she would leave on anyone. It didn't have to turn out in a bad way for her – it was her call. Back at the washbasin, I washed off the blood, but that bite mark impression, I could tell, wasn't going to fade for a few days. When I was a kid, a dog bit my leg, and the mark lingered for a long time. I applied a Band Aid and went out and joined Jack. I gave him a hand to sweep the floor and stack the empty pallets, making space for the day shift and the daily arrival of stock, which we would be shifting that night into orders for the artic' drivers. Fucking got so maddening that routine. Boredom used to have me climb the walls and chew on my fingernails.

Outside the factory doors, we lit up cigarettes and enjoyed the cool morning air on our faces. He was squinting into the morning haze, like he was trying to see future sorrows.

'You should sell that piece of scrap,' he said, on a sniffle.

'That might not be a bad idea,' I said.

He himself drove a red Ford Cortina with black trim. It'd belonged to a colleague's father, who bought it new with his redundancy money from Irish Rail. A shrine-mobile, it had scapulars, wooden crosses, novena cards and bottles of holy water – touches that Jack said he couldn't bring himself to throw out. We had that in common with each other, too: a total disbelief in some almighty figure that was going to reward or chastise us according to what we deserved. If God is almighty, then there shouldn't be wars and famines … simple fucking logic. No one I know ever came back from the dead to say 'Hello, how are ya doing, Tommy?'

On the way home, I drove past the spot where I had done in Jo. Didn't give in to the urge to drive up there to see if I'd left anything behind. Wandering sheep would bead the patch with droppings. Horses would pick out divots with their hooves, especially if it rained. Nature was already beginning to disturb and conceal.

I carried on by. I hoped Louise was out of the sack. I didn't want to listen to the moans she liked to drip-feed into my ears. She entered the bedroom about three p.m., drew back the curtains, and whispered, 'Jo's missing.'

'What?' I said sleepily, the bite stinging. Like Jo was haunting.

'She didn't come home last night,' Louise said, raising her voice a little.

She went to tug the blind cord, but I said for her to leave it. My mouth was parched, and the bite mark was throbbing harder under the plaster.

Louise waited by the window and looked at me, saying things with her looking.

'What's there to eat?' I said.

'I'll do you a fry,' she said.

She wore jeans, and a red turtleneck that had a coffee stain down the front. No matter how often she washed it, the stain remained.

'Are you getting up?' she said.

'Yeah, but I'm still knackered … so don't go fucking nagging at me to mow the lawn and shite.'

'They've rang the guards.'

'The guards?'

'About Jo … I told you … she's missing.'

'I wouldn't say it's anything to be going ringing the cops over. I think she's off shagging some lad.'

'She's not like that! You know that she's not. How can you say that?'

'I don't know what else to think … how would I? Jesus.'

'I'd be out of my mind if either of our daughters didn't come home when they were supposed to.'

'So would I,' I said.

Amy and Heather, 11-year-old twins.

'Make us that fry,' I said.

It seemed like everyone in town joined in with the guards to search for the missing Jo. Two days and the weather broiling and people were out in skirmish lines, searching the plains. The furze were thick golden islands, impenetrable, and hid countless small clearings. A little black purse with some coins in it was found by a sheep farmer at the Cut, and later identified as belonging to Jo. It contained the bus ticket she had bought earlier on the day she'd disappeared. Evening papers and the TV news devoted space and time to her. My stomach was beginning to grow ulcers, but I knew all I had to do was not to panic – news gets old quickly. New murders bury old ones … and new ones were always happening.

'Jesus Christ,' Louise said as we watched the TV.

Jo's old holy Joe, Bob, was beseeching anyone with information to come forward. He looked broken. But then he always had that broken look. It was like his face always knew that this day was coming.

'Do you think she's dead, Tommy?'

'It's not looking good for her.'

'What sort of sick bastards are out there? It must be someone who knows her … Bob thinks so, doesn't he? He said as much, didn't he?'

'Shush,' I said.

I went on three searches, spoke with and agreed with fellow searchers who whispered to each other in confidence that we were looking for a body. Into the mix came news of some fucking turf-cutters unearthing a medieval Bible that had been preserved for centuries in the Bog, not far from where I'd hidden the 'disappeared' Jo. I began to feel like I was running out of fucking space. It felt like my veins were being squeezed. Freaked me out some – then everything seemed to slacken off. I don't know why, but it did. I figured that the lull was just a respite.

Almost a year on, and her name again started to appear in the newspapers. Grainy images of her in a straw hat with a wide brim and a polka-dot band. None did her any real justice: she was far prettier.

I expected appeals on TV from Bob and members of her family to happen. She was gone. I would love to have said to them, get over the fucking fact and move forward. It's what the rest of us have to do. It's her own fault that she's not here.

I suspected that this would be the way of things: every year, for months, her name wouldn't register on people's tongues, or even in their minds. Flurries of activity then in the weeks before the anniversary, and after it had passed by. Time once more would wrap its foggy shroud around her.

It helped my/our position too, deflecting cop heat, that meantime other women had been attacked, that another had also vanished. Though they did bring the heat on me a little, because I was a suspect, like it or not, and not just because of Jo, but for the picture-house woman. Jack had done that stupid thing, which almost sold the pair of us down the fucking Liffey and out to sea.

Fitz was the guy who infrequently sought me out to invite me to help the police with their enquiries. I easily imagined his crestfallen look after he'd gone and checked out my statements – nothing hits a cop harder than him thinking his hunch system is fucked.

I don't think of her that often. Even now. Jo was a Sally and a Liz back in time. Neither of those women went missing or was harmed in any way by my good self, so I know for a fact that Jo is the odd bitch out.

Twice during the winter and inclement months I'd gone to move her body from the bog-hole, and on each occasion I'd heard this strong voice in my head saying not to go next nor near her.

Louise was happy that I'd moved on from the warehouse to work at the buildings. The money was much better in construction, and the work mostly open-air, which suited me. I'd served two years as a brickie before, and I'd worked it so I could finish serving my time. Fully qualified, my wages soared and I was in huge demand, even if times were hard in the industry. Travelling from site to site gave me an opportunity to suss out the lovely fillies on the pavements. Yummy mummies, fine young things, and sometimes it wasn't the mummies or the fine things that kept my eyes turned but something else about a woman that seemed to do it for me.

I'd flown to England with a woman I fell in with in a bar. She was called Liz. Though she was a little on the old side and running to fat, she was fit for purpose in that she had a dirty tongue, and sex-wise there were no holds barred. The only complaint I had was when she took out her dentures and placed them on my belly before she put her mouth to me. Shrivelled my cock it did, looking at her falsies staring up at me. It shook me a little when she said, 'I think you've hurt women, haven't you?' She claimed to be psychic. I replied, 'No. Jesus, no.'

Uncomfortable moments like that sprang up out of nowhere. For instance, one afternoon, Amy stood beside me in the mall. We were standing outside a shoe shop waiting on Louise to come out of Marks & Spencer with a roast for the dinner.

'Daddy, there she is,' she said.

'Who?'

'Jo who went missing, you remember?'

A poster of Jo on the shop window, smiling. Tanned face, smiling eyes.

'Please help … information to … Jo,' she read aloud. 'I used to like her babysitting us, she was very funny, Daddy.'

'She was … yeah … finish your smoothie.'

She sucked loudly through the red straw.

'Daddy, do you think she ran away?'

'Maybe.'

'Do you think she's dead?'

'Amy. They're not nice questions.'

'She didn't take her money out of her bank account or credit union … Mammy said that.'

'Really?'

'Yeah, really. So I think … I think … Daddy, pay attention.'

'I'm listening. What?'

'Aliens took her.'

'Maybe so.'

She finished her smoothie, and then told me she was bursting and couldn't hold it. Fuck, I thought. Fucking kids. We moved to the nearest loo, and on the way I saw Bob and one of his daughters handing out fliers. I couldn't think of her name. She was the spitting image of Jo. And she stood right in our way, like some fucking ghost – she smiled at people while Bob kept a serious face that showed his mood and his sickness.

'Bob,' I said, simply.

His daughter was talking to a tall, skinny woman in a red trouser-suit.

Bob shrugged and said, 'We can't sit around and do nothing. Can we?'

He didn't know he was talking to a member of a small group of suspects. Up close he had the appearance of a man whose heart had lost its chime.

'Is that your daughter running on?' he said.

'She is.'

'Mind her.'

'I will.'

'Make her street-smart. That's what happened to my Jo … she was too naïve, too trusting … she thought, you know, that no bad thing would ever happen to her. She was like her mother, God rest her … she prayed for the angels to keep her safe. Huh, goes to show you, doesn't it? Prayer is a waste of fucking time.'

'Dad!' his daughter said.

'It's true.'

I wished Amy would hurry up. I picked up a bunch of fliers and said, 'While I'm waiting …'. I handed them to people passing by in both directions. No one refused to take them, but I saw that a few, after taking a glance at Jo, pitched them into a bin before going through the double doors. People don't give a fuck. They might for a while, but the passage of time washes meaning away.

I was never as delighted to see her. Bob patted her head, said she was beautiful, and asked if she liked school.

'No,' Amy said, adding, 'are you Jo's daddy?'

'I am.'

Amy seemed to ponder this. Louise figured on my radar, weighed down with bags.

'We have to be going, Amy … Bob … the best of luck,' I said.

'I hope your Jo comes home to you,' Amy said to Bob.

My back was to them, so they couldn't have seen my expression. The expression of a man fully realising that his daughter had cursed him in a most peculiar way.

Eight suspects. A routine call in by the cops to see if there were chinks beginning to grow in my story, my conscience. Things that they could scrutinise; at which they could pick and poke. I'd made the shortlist. They'd told me this months ago, after I'd supplied them with a blood sample; back then they'd asked me if I'd volunteer to do that for elimination purposes. Clever. If I'd declined …. But I knew the sample wasn't worth a flying fuck to them unless they had a body to match it against. And they hadn't, wouldn't, so giving them my blood was no problem.

'Is that it?' I said.

'We'll let you know when it's time for you to go,' Detective Roche said.

He was clean-cut, young. A guy on the up, with not much for a chin.

'Am I under arrest?' I said.

'No,' Roche said.

Fitz, his older companion, was sitting across the desk, toying with a grey Biro he kept his eyes fixed upon. A ginger-haired man with deep lines across his forehead, like cracks in a ceiling.

'So I'm free to leave any time I like?' I said.

For the first time during this interview, Fitz spoke. He looked at me with clear blue eyes, and said, 'I'll break your fucking leg if you move … I'll say you assaulted me and that you slipped in the ensuing struggle …'.

I said, 'Maybe I should call my solicitor.'

He said, 'Sure, give us his name and phone number and I'll have Frank here give him a call.'

'I did nothing to deserve this shite,' I said, then I gave him a contact name and number for Denis Wallace, the solicitor who'd pushed through the purchase of my house.

'You sold a car in the immediate aftermath of Jo's disappearance,' Roche said.

'It was falling apart.'

He continued, 'You bought yourself an identical model. A different colour.'

'So?' I shrugged, pretending to be lost as to the relevance. 'We've been here before, guys.'

Roche said, 'The car you flogged … it matches the colour that a witness gave us. He saw a young woman get into a car like yours.'

Greatcoat man, I thought, but he was too pissed to take notice of anything.

'Like mine,' I said, 'but not. So …'.

'So,' Roche said, 'we found hair fibres from Jo on the front seat.'

'So,' Fitz said, with sarcasm and contempt, 'can you explain how come we found those in your vehicle?'

'Jo was in my car, that's easy to explain.'

They looked at each other. I formed the impression that Fitz had something else on me, that he had been told things. He had the look of someone who had a trump card that he wasn't going to play just yet.

I went on. 'I gave her a lift home after babysitting two or three times. She used to babysit for us ... do you not read those questionnaires you have people fill out? Because I said about taking her home in the one I filled out, and my missus said so in hers too. We both said that I gave Jo a lift home a couple of times.'

Fitz kept staring, trying to dig at the truth lurking behind the walls of my skull.

'Louise ... that's my missus's name, if you want to cross-reference. We share the same surname.'

Silence.

'Does an innocent man still need his solicitor?'

I couldn't hide the truth of my visit to the cop station from Louise. They'd called to the house twice to see me, knowing I wouldn't be there. Sussing her out was all, looking for anything she might say that could be used against me. Which set me to thinking.

'What's up with you?' I said, stabbing into the silence. She didn't answer.

'I'm talking to you,' I said. 'I said, what's up with you?'

She'd the worried and haggard appearance of a deeply troubled woman.

'I heard you,' she said. 'They obviously think that you have something to do with her disappearance. Why, Tommy?'

'No idea.'

'I do,' she said.

'You do …?'

She nodded, reaching for her pack of cigarettes on the table. She was trying to quit, but she hadn't got the willpower. She was afraid, and spoke with a tremor on her lips, but at the same time she was flashing steel. I wanted a fag too, but not one of her brand.

'Be honest with me, Tommy, for Christ's sake. You owe me that much at least.'

'I …'.

'How come you're a suspect?' she said in a knowing way.

I sensed that she was digging for a deeper answer. Teasing for a truth, a smidgen of it, trawling for a confession. Whatever. Worse than the fucking cops.

'Because of the car sale,' I said, 'of what happened to Jack's oul' lad and the picture-house woman. We found something belonging to her on the plains … a locket of hers … so really, tell me: why are you fucking asking me this? You already know it.'

An item of jewellery Jack had stupidly given to his then girlfriend, now wife, who'd worn it to a charity dance, where the picture-house woman's mother recognised it and demanded a closer inspection. There were no giveaway initials, just a scratch mark that the old woman insisted was graven on her memory. Jack and I sung the same hymn to the coppers, so we smoothed over the ripples of suspicion – but suspicion never dies. Our names, for sure, were logged in the picture-woman's case file.

And I looked across at Louise and thought that she was a noose beginning to tighten around my neck. Under my glare, her shoulders climbed. Nervously, she scratched at her thigh. We were both thinking of differing and the best means to end things.

A Sort of Jesus Disappearance

Barney, who had been on desk duty the night before, was intent on sleeping through the journey from the Lebanese border to Jerusalem. Carty was getting increasingly annoyed at Barney's lacklustre responses to the landmarks he'd been occasionally and excitedly pointing out.

'Akko!'

'Yeah …'.

'The Holocaust museum.'

Yawn.

'Look at that, Barney, a Roman aqueduct.'

In a jaded voice, Barney said, 'I couldn't give a bollix … I just want an hour's kip, okay?'

'You're in the Holy Land, you should …'.

'If the place you're talking about isn't a disco or a pub, fuck off … please.'

Eventually, Carty gave up and Barney fell asleep on the back seat of the UN minibus Louis had pre-booked for a week. A straw hat with a back-band covered his face, bony legs drawn up.

There were five of us. Tommy drove. He hardly ever smiled, and took himself seriously. He had a brown fleck in the white of his eye. Barney had called it a shit spot. Tommy didn't think it funny, and reminded Barney of his corporal status. Tommy was the best looking one among us, film-star handsome, and we intended to use him to lure women into our company. Alongside him sat Louis, who was the senior rank among us, but he would keep that fact quiet while we were on leave, hoping we wouldn't mention the times he'd shafted us on the duty roster for slights we had done to him, real or imagined. According to rumour, the Norwegians had him in their pocket. They supplied him with snus and Gammel Dansk – Norwegian snuff, and a concoction made from a variety of fruits – and insisted he had to have Viking blood in his veins. 'Viking genes,' Louis had said, unsteady on his feet in Thor Mess, feeling his chin, not amused when I pointed out that they'd said, 'Wiking, not Viking.'

'They can't pronounce the V,' he'd snapped.

We all wore new clothes bought in Ali's on the shack street outside headquarters, except for Carty, who had on his issue green T-shirt and khaki shorts. He had a red scapular around his neck and his dog tags. Now and then he took out the scapular and kissed its image. We thought it might be of Jesus, but it could well have been of himself. After three months in Lebanon, we were sort of mad for skirt, but we had to temper that with a visit to the holy places too, to take photographs of where we had been to show our families back home, to say we'd lit candles and said prayers for the people we'd been asked to pray for. A backdrop for our planned and hoped-for acts of depravity. So it wasn't a holiday, we'd lied to families, but a pilgrimage, making it sound like it would be an ordeal.

Soon, as we veered a left off the road to Tel Aviv, Barney threw his legs to the floor and said he was bursting for a piss. At 30 he was the youngest, Louis, at 38 the oldest, the rest of us fitted age wise somewhere in-between. We were all victims of something or other. Veterans of trips to Lebanon and Cyprus. A couple, Carty and Louis, had been to Iraq.

Tommy said, 'I can't over pull over here. The traffic's … and besides, I'm sure there's a law against urinating in public.'

Carty said, 'Hold it, can't you … you're not a child.'

'I said I was bursting,' Barney said, 'how can you fucking hold anything that's bursting? You stupid fucking Kerryman, you.'

Louis said, 'Use a bottle.'

'He's not pissing in the bus,' I said, thinking of the smell.

'Look at the tits on your one!' Barney said, tapping hard on the window to take her attention. She gave a small wave. Broad smile.

Louis slugged the last from a cola bottle and passed it back.

Carty said, 'You shouldn't be looking at women in that way … it's not healthy.'

'And she's carrying a pair of balls, too … but you missed that,' I said.

Pissing into the bottle to Tommy's, 'Don't get any on the floor,' Barney said, 'This is Israel, huh? Full of the fuckers who throw the shells into the Leb at us, bastards … ahhhhhhh, great to have the tank emptied.'

Carty said, 'The cap, Louis.'

Louis handed Carty the blue top, and he told Barney to catch. Because of cry-offs we had ample space on the minibus: a double seat each with Barney's a triple.

Barney capped his piss, sighed long and hard, lit up a cigarette, then thought to ask if anyone minded. He was heading for premature baldness. He looked like a slimmer version of Bob Hope, and things that fell into place for him usually happened through accident, not by careful planning on his part.

A song came over the radio that Tommy liked, and he raised the volume. Sinatra's 'Let me try again.'

Barney said, 'Is that what you said to your Missus, Tommy?'

Louis glanced sidelong at Tommy, not smiling until he saw it was okay to by Tommy's expression.

Carty was the only single man present. He was tall, built, as Barney put it, 'as though he'd been reared on a dinosaur's tit.' He had short, wavy black hair, Slavic high cheekbones and green eyes that were close-set and deep under his brow. He was Born Again; the list of things he had got up to until about four years ago was the stuff of legend.

Carty said, 'That song is a hymn ... it's what we should all do every time we slip ... look to try again.'

Under the weight of this platitude, I think even the minibus groaned. Tommy looked in the rear-view mirror and asked if anyone had a cassette. Barney reached in his tracksuit top lying across the back of the seat and said, 'Here ... Boney M ... for the holy soul there.'

'Rivers of Babylon,' Carty said.

Boney M and Belfast played as we climbed the hills leading in to Jerusalem (as though two troubled cities were acknowledging each other), passing red-oxide-painted war vehicles parked as ornaments on grassy strips, and new apartment blocks on disputed territory.

As the honey-coloured curtain walls of the old city came into view, Carty blessed himself three times in exaggerated sweeps, three fingers joined to indicate Father, Son and Holy Spirit. His eyes swallowed every new sight, his mouth open too, to help out.

None of us had been to Jerusalem before. But it was an old name among us. Book and spoken word from childhood became a reality: something we could touch and smell and taste.

Carty said in his lilting Kerry accent, 'He was here. Imagine that, lads ... we're in the place where Jesus actually walked ... this is his city. He breathed the air, he ...'.

'Sure, Jesus is Jesus … he's been all over the fucking world, like,' Barney said.

'But here … here, he came and lived among us, became human.'

'Us? Sure you weren't even fucking born then,' Barney said.

'Among the human race, you clown.'

Barney said, 'And youse Kerrymen haven't evolved to the level of humans yet … yere always getting above yereselves.'

'Are you looking for a slap?' Carty said.

We couldn't determine if he was serious.

Tommy bypassed several parking places for some nit-picking reason he didn't share with us; we circled the hotel maybe six times before he settled for a space Louis had indicated to him the first time around. Louis wore spectacles, and he kept pushing the bridge with the tip of his forefinger, as if pushing back thoughts he wanted to scream out to Tommy about his passing yet another perfect fucking spot. Mild-mannered Louis never called a spade for what it was to a person's face; he preferred to serve up his opinion behind a person's back; not solely out of badness; he simply disliked confrontation and engaging with the risk of having his words pushed down his throat.

Octagonal black-and-white tiles covered the reception floor of the Palace Pilgrim Hotel. Rubber plants stared at us from the corners, and crystal chandeliers looked down on an arrangement in squares of green couches and opaque glass-topped coffee tables. After leaving our bags in rooms on the third storey, we took up residence in the green area, and discussed what to do for the evening over Macabbi beers, or in Carty's case, a tomato juice with ice.

Carty said, 'We should go into the old city, before it gets too dark.'

Barney said, slouched, feet crossed, arms folded, unlit cigarette between his fingers, 'Tomorrow would be better ... we'd have more time, yeah?'

Louis said, 'It's been a long day.'

Tommy said, 'How about something to eat? I don't know about ye, but I'm famished.'

I said, 'I'm easy.'

The Tavern Inn – we volunteered non-drinker Carty to drive our minibus – was dressed seedier than a shebeen in bogland at home. Dimly lit, low-ceilinged, dark crossbeams, photographs of Jerusalem on the walls and paintings of nineteenth-century Palestine. Also, a few national flags: even the Irish tricolour had a space, something Carty told us, because it was something we'd missed. Disinfectant wafted from the loos, and creaking ceiling fans rotated with maddening sluggishness. We sat outside, watching a beautiful red sun begin its descent while Carty was inside asking the barman whose idea had it been to put the British flag above the

Irish tricolour, over the mock ochre brick fireplace. I'd gone in to say his eggs and chips had been brought to our table.

'I don't know, mate,' the young man said in a cockney twang, towelling a beer glass, 'I never noticed it to be honest. You can put them level if you want. Maybe it slipped, yeah?'

'Where's the owner?'

'In the States. Why? Do you want the manager. He's here.'

'Carty,' I said.

His hand spread like a map across my chest. I stepped back from it.

'Have you a lighter?' he said to Barney, who was passing by on his way to the loo.

'Sure,' he said, handing over his silver Zippo.

Carty pulled the Union Flag from the wall. He threw it into the hearth, and put a Zippo flame to a corner.

I said, 'Are you mad?! You'll trigger the smoke alarms and …'.

He shoved me away, and glared at the barman who'd come running from behind the counter with a fire extinguisher. Others present looked on and away, long enough to see what was happening, and longer to balance the price of action and inaction. Luckily for us, it wasn't their national flag.

'That yoke,' he said, 'won't ever fly above the tricolour again.' Glancing around, he continued, 'If any of youse want to do make anything of it, we're here …'.

We're?

By now Barney had emerged, piss spots around his fly, his eyes widening – Barney was born in England, moved to Ireland when aged 6, and was married to a Welsh woman.

'Are you trying to get us fucking killed?' he said.

Carty said, 'We'll fall like men.'

'*We'll* my hole … you will … I'm fucking starving.' He looked at me and added, 'Colin, come on and let's go eat.'

I stamped on the burning flag, killing the growing flame with my heel. My eyes on Carty all the while; I was fearful of his reaction. He shook his head slowly. Tears welled in him and began to fall. The sight of this frightened the barman into backing away. I wasn't sure if he had felt physically intimidated by Carty, but certainly the sight of the big man in emotional meltdown made an impact.

Carty put his hands to his face. When he brought them down, it was as though he had washed the colour from his complexion. Still, the tears poured. Barney stood transfixed, cigarette drooping from the corner of his mouth. I saw in Carty all the disappointment he had in himself; all he wanted to be and was not; all he wanted to change about himself and could not.

'Carty,' I said quietly, handing him a paper napkin I'd taken from the closest table.

He blew his nose into it and said he was fine. Gesturing to the barman, he continued, 'I'm fierce sorry, boy.'

I went over to the barman and told him to leave Carty alone and he'd go away. Or if he mentioned Jesus to him he could maybe make himself a friend for life. I think he left him alone. Carty went to the loo to wash off the appearance of tears. Barney and I went and joined Louis and Tommy. 'Say nothing about what just happened,' he said.

After the sun had settled it turned cold, but we liked it al fresco, watching the strangeness of this new city. We all smoked: Louis and Tommy on Czar cheroots, Barney his Major and Carty, after he joined us, brought out his pipe and stacked it with flakes of Old Clan and puffed moodily, which he probably thought looked contemplative.

'My eggs were cold,' he said.

'You were told they were there,' I said, 'and you left them waiting.'

'Will we go shake ourselves in a disco?' Barney said.

Louis shook his head, 'Ah, I think I'll go back to the hotel and have a couple before I turn in for the night.'

'Me too,' Tommy said.

'Colin?' Barney said.

'Okay,' I said, though I wasn't up for it. I couldn't let him go alone.

Carty said, like God through cloud, 'But ye're married and should be abstaining ...'.

Women were safe from us, as Tommy the Lure wasn't coming. Cruel appraisal of us, Barney said as we sat into a table in Caesar's Disco. Nightlife didn't begin till after eleven p.m.; we bled shekels hard through our pockets for beer and a couple of shots. Women danced with us, it appeared, out of politeness, and others didn't – they let us know with a withering look that they were Everest and we were merely foothill walkers. 'The thing is,' Barney said, 'they're all gorgeous … every fucking one of them. There has to be a disco someplace for ugly people … you know, a place where we'd be considered as really good-looking men.'

Tanned, slim, energetic, erotic. We knew the sun would fade their beauty and they'd look older than their years, by which time we would be in with a shout with them, but that was in the all-too-distant future.

'We may carry our horns home with us,' Barney said, 'I'm bollixed anyway … shouldn't have come out … can I ask you something personal, Colin?'

Not quite drunk, but almost. Our hotel was a block away, and we sauntered along in that direction. The skies were ripe with stars and not a cloud – a light breeze prickled our forearms and grew goosepimples, and in Barney an occasional chattering of his teeth.

'But this is strictly between me and you. Right?' he went on. 'Right?'

'Okay.'

'Seriously now … I haven't told anyone this before.'

'I said I won't open my mouth … what is it?'

'I can't come.'

'I … everyone can come.'

'Well, I can't ... I can ride for hours, no kidding, but something inside my head won't let me ... you know.'

The opposite of premature ejaculation, I thought – what do I say?

'The missus is sick of it. She used to like quickies. A quickie with me takes two hours.'

'See a doctor,' I suggested.

'I did ... he asked me if I was masturbating, and if I was, to quit it ... that's the thing I used to, right, pretty heavily but ... what? ... why are you looking at me like? Everyone wanks, even my fucking greyhounds. Even you, I bet.'

The silence between us was punctuated by a police siren.

'All I can say is this to you: don't make a big issue out of it ... the problem will just get bigger ... maybe you're chucking yourself in your sleep.'

'You think so?'

'A possibility. It could be a deep-rooted subconscious thing.'

It gave him manna to ponder.

In the hotel, Tommy and Louis were sitting to the edge of the couches, drinking beers by the neck, smoking. Louis's cigar rested in the 'u' of a glass ashtray. He was wringing his hands, his shoulders perched up the way they went when he had something to get off them.

But it was Tommy who spoke up.

'Is he with you?'

'Who?' Barney said, in spite of it being plainly obvious.

I said, 'No. He came back with youse, didn't he?'

Louis said, 'He did, and then he fecked off again, said he was going to keep an eye on youse. Did you ask him to do that, Colin?'

'I didn't. Me ask him keep an eye on us?'

Barney said, 'Maybe he's parked the bus and fecked off to bed.'

I said, half wondering if we'd walked past it, 'We didn't pass it on the way in.'

'We tried his room,' Louis said.

The situation: Tommy had signed the minibus out from the Transport NCO, and as such it was his responsibility to ensure it was returned in the same order as it'd left the yard in, while Louis was the senior NCO and in charge of us ... as things stood, both looked to be deep in the mire.

Louis's lips went thin and hard. He was thinking what to say to our commanding officer if Born Again Carty had slipped from his shiny pedestal. Barney mentioned the burning of the Union Flag, and immediately Louis said, 'And you didn't think to report his action to me or Tommy?'

'I thought you did,' Barney said, looking at me, knowing I hadn't.

'Jesus, you're well able to come now, aren't you?' I said.

'You knew about this?' Tommy said, accusingly.

'It was nothing,' I said.

'Burning a Union Flag, nothing?!' Louis said, shaking his head and then rubbing his eyes with his fingers.

He was out of tune with his normal, mild self.

Tommy said, 'It could be viewed as a major international incident.'

Barney said, 'It's only a fucking flag ... the real thing is this: where is the unholy hoor?'

'Looks like he's done a runner,' Tommy said in a low voice that pleaded to be contradicted.

I said, 'Maybe he's just gone for something to eat?'

'He's up to no good,' Louis said. 'If the bus comes back in one piece, that'll be something ... but if he's had a few drinks, he'll be liable to either crash or pawn it.'

We waited. And waited. Ate complimentary pecan nuts and took turns to read a week-old *Jerusalem Post*. Louis was asleep, his glasses low on his nose, his legs stretched, mouth open. Tommy paced the tiles up and down and sideways and across. Barney played patience with half a deck of cards.

The sun rose golden. Still, Carty hadn't shown. Louis said we weren't to leave the hotel until that stupid fucking wanker showed his face.

'I'm going to my room to have a shower,' he said.

Tommy came in from the vestibule. He'd got fed up with the tiles and had walked the pavement, hoping to see his minibus appear around the corner. I doubted if a miracle had happened here since J.C. left town.

Barney said quietly, 'Do you want to know something else?'

Tommy said distantly, 'What?'

'He hasn't got a UN driver's licence.'

Tommy threw his hands up in despair. 'You never told us that, either.'

'I thought ye knew,' Barney said.

Choices. By late afternoon, it was time to make a crucial decision.

Louis said, 'We may fucking ring the Adjutant and report this. That Carty ... I'll crucify him.'

Tommy said, 'I'll hammer the nails into his hands.'

Barney said, 'I bags the spear into his side.'

I said, 'Are we drawing lots for his clothes? His army-cum-civvies?'

The notion drew smiles. When the two senior ranks went to reception to make the call to headquarters, Barney said, 'Guess what my missus said about the me-not-coming problem.'

'Just tell me. I'm too tired to play guessing games ... we've been at that all frigging night. Yeah?'

'She fucking shouted at me that I was all hammer and no nail! In our local local! Can you imagine that?'

Louis and Tommy came toward us, a lift in their step, seemingly not laden with bollockings in their ears, but with good news.

Louis said, relief brightening his features, 'He drove back across the border.'

'The fucking tool,' Barney said, 'we're stranded …'.

My expression asked for further information.

'He's guilt-stricken over the flag burning,' Tommy said. 'He reported himself for doing it, and told the Colonel he'd have wrecked our holiday if he'd stayed with us.'

A sort of a Jesus disappearance? I thought.

'Death and Resurrection,' Tommy said.

Louis, now totally devoid of worry about looking bad in front of his superiors, laughed too loudly.

'You can only be who you are,' Barney said.

Sometimes, he could surprise us.

Doll Woman

Strawberry blond from a pack or bottle, whatever. Petite. Fifty-four, or thereabouts. You'd find more meat on a kebab. She wore make-up, but this did not stop the haunting of wrinkles coming through, like the lines of ancient trails shown up by aerial photography. I was back in town for the funeral of an old army colleague – these days I seem to have increasing reason for coming back to Kildare. To pay respects to people who I'd never imagined ever dying. And in general, death was snatching those who had always taken care of themselves, not good advertising for the advocates of the eat well and exercise brigade.

Because it was a military funeral, they brought out the band and used a gun carriage instead of a hearse. The police band had on black stylish uniforms with red piping down their trousers. In my day they wore green and greener capes. Johnny Magee wasn't top brass, or any rank close to it, but the army like to give their dead a good send-off, to herald the news with drum and trumpet.

I waited outside for the bearers to lower and slide the flag-draped coffin onto the carriage, to screw in the bolts to keep the coffin from sliding off. A lot can go wrong at a service funeral: the coffin being lowered into the wrong grave; a body falling out through the bottom of a cheap casket. None of this risk for me: when I go it'll be to the furnace, and my ashes will be spread on the mountains. I don't want my sons and daughters traipsing out to a cemetery, not that they would, mind. At least, not often. And not unless they were stuck for something, and wanted to see if I could dig deep in my pockets like I had done for them in life. Who'd want people looking down on them? Shit, I've had enough of that throughout my life.

Nancy, not her real name, we used to call her that because she bore a strong resemblance to the Drew TV character, ranged alongside me at a point along the two-kilometre walk to the cemetery. Looking back, I'm sure she'd seen me earlier on and had been thinking about what she should do: she was never one to act on impulse.

'Hi, Mick,' she said, looking up at me.

She wore a black coat with a wide collar.

'Dee,' I said, taking her hand in a brief shake, 'Jesus, good to see you … sad, huh?'

'Terrible. I only cut his hair the day before he died.'

'Still hairdressing … it's been years since … when is the last time we met?'

'Years.'

All around us, the trudging of feet, muttered conversations. Under the railway bridge, echoed voices, chestnut trees to the immediate left, behind a wall where I banged Dee's sister on our eighteenth shared birthday. Louise. We used to call her Loose.

'Oh, not as much hairdressing as I used to. And you, what are you doing with yourself these days?'

I said I worked as a private investigator down south in Waterford. Part-time. Full-time would mean I'd be working for the taxman. There was no sense in telling her too much: about the marriage break-up, about how the cops, my colleagues, had come calling to our door on the verge of dawn and turned my whole life upside down and inside fucking out. She probably knew all that, and besides, it was too detailed to push out on a graveyard walk. More than the dead listen in to conversations.

She had bad teeth. Rotten, like leaves turned brown. It was the one thing about herself she had let go, and it could only be because she was terrified of dentists – she had a dread of pain, and no kids either, which pointed in that direction. Still, in spite of the teeth, she looked well. And I had physical flaws too: overweight leaning to fat, wore glasses, looked older than I was, and had whiskey trails burning my cheeks. Devils can't be choosers.

A few in the crowd recognised me and pretended not to, not because of anything I'd done, but it was in their nature to make a snide comment to those on the fringe of their company, just to rise a snigger from a putdown.

A wind picked up, distorting the priest's words. Military Police undressed the coffin, ceremonially folding the Tricolour, and all the while Dee was linking my arm; I was certain we must have looked like a couple.

'Are you going to the Silken for the refreshments?' she'd said.

'No … you?'

'I think I'd prefer someplace quieter.'

'Me too.'

So we ended up in a little corner café on Station Road, sitting across from each other. I wondered how a silence would sit between us, but she seemed anxious to keep away a lapse in the flow of conversation. We pitched names at each other to rouse a memory we could talk about, and in this way built up a bank of deaths, people who were dying, persons gaoled, failed marriages; the latter could have been a lead-in to talk of the rock on which my marriage had perished, but we allowed it a stretch of silence and moved on to discuss Louise, who was living in Canada.

'She married a teacher,' she said.

'A teacher,' I said, trying to keep the doubt from showing – I didn't believe anyone could teach Loose anything.

'Four kids, can you imagine?'

I could. My espresso and her latté arrived, delivered by a cheerless waitress who left behind part of her mood. Dee called her back and asked her for a sachet of brown sugar.

'It must hurt her to smile,' Dee said.

'A bad day.'

'So?'

'So?'

'How are you keeping … I mean really, really keeping? I heard that you and Siobhan split up. And you were such a long time married, too.'

'I'm doing okay. You?'

'Do you ever get lonely?'

'Sometimes. How about yourself?'

'Yeah, yeah, now and then, but I have Ginger and my dolls and the TV is great, but …'.

'But …' I said. We'd once known each other well enough to talk dirty. 'You can't ride a telly.'

Her teeth killed a beautiful smile. Oral is out, I thought.

'No, you can't,' she said, her lips narrowing to closure, instead beaming her smile through beautiful green eyes.

'Did you ever marry?' I said.

'No … we won't go there.'

I thought that was a good way of warning people off sensitive issues.

St Rita's, Dee's place, is mid-terrace in an old estate populated with young Poles and Nigerians, Brazilians, unmarried mothers, and a few elderly people intent on staying put and breathing in memories. Inside, in a glass cabinet, on the mantelpiece, on corner shelving, and in every room, were dolls – even on the sill in the loo, and hanging on walls in lieu of photographs and paintings. And each owned a name. I got the feeling that the eyes of the dolls were fixed on me.

'They're my family,' she said, taking my jacket off the back of the couch to hang up.

From the hall she said, 'Beer or a whiskey? I have Powers. It used to be Daddy's, but he … you know yourself.'

I did? Then I remembered that he had stepped out in front of a train. Nobody could be sure if it had been a deliberate act.

'Beer's fine, thanks.'

Those dolls. Irises of every colour bore down on me. There were a few Sindy's, baby dolls, a lot from other cultures: Irish, Dutch, Welsh, even Amish. When she came in with the beers, I said she must be widely travelled.

'I've never left the country,' she said, sitting into an armchair by the red-brick fireplace. Ashes and spent coals in the grate, a few sweet wrappers, the shells of cashew nuts.

'I hate flying,' she said, 'and ships … dentists.'

She smiled. I smiled.

In bed, she was wild. Talked dirty, moaned, dug her heels into my buttocks. She threw the sex manual at me, but I wasn't as flexible as she would have liked

– and she wouldn't let me see her naked. By touch I knew she'd shaved there: then she let me glimpse it and I said it was nice. I don't like that sort of thing really. Lush is better. At evening's end I was wrung out, and Dee too – she wouldn't lie in against me, said she hated the feel of a sweaty body and didn't want to brush against its stickiness. All the while the eyes of her dolls were upon us, and her cat was present too, but I didn't find this out until I stepped on it by accident – it was lying at the side of the bed. Ginger hissed and lashed out a paw, drawing blood from my thumb. I went to kick the orange bastard, but he had hightailed out to the landing.

'Mick!' she said.

She'd seen me swing a foot at her moggy.

'He's after drawing blood,' I said.

'Ginger?'

'I …'.

'Show me.' She was sitting up, propped in place by her hand.

When I did, she shook her head, her beautiful mane flowing over her shoulders. She had several moles between her breasts, shaped like some constellation of stars. The cut was little more than a scratch, but it hurt more than its appearance.

'Isn't he just the little fucker?' she said.

Flecks of blood fell on to the red sheet.

'Mick …' she said, handing me her knickers to dress the wound.

Then she lay her head down on the pillow and brought my head to rest against her breasts and took back her panties.

'It's just a little prick,' she says.

'First your cat flashes a claw, now you.'

She giggled.

'Mama will make it better,' she said, before sucking on my thumb.

I thought of her bad teeth.

Neither of us had work the next day, so we took off for a drive in her aged green Nissan Micra, fluffy dice, pine freshener hanging from the rear-view mirror and pink backseat cushions in the shape of a heart.

She drove slowly, never bringing the needle above forty, on winding country roads, to a craft village she often visited because she was friendly with the guy who owned the place. Sometimes, he got in new dolls.

'Did you call down to see Siobhan, or are you going to?' she said evenly, looking straight ahead.

'What do you think?'

'No … I suppose not.'

'You don't want to talk about it, do you?'

'Same as you about marriage.'

'That's different.'

'Both are very personal,' I said, which killed conversation in the car for a few minutes.

Dee mentioned that we were nearly there, and after a short silence added, 'I was going with that fucker Paul Henry for years … he was married and I fell for the usual: he loved me, was going to leave his wife, move in with me, yeah?'

His name lingered in the air.

'I remember him … tall man, photographer … his family owned the studios on the main street,' I said.

'He's dead.'

'What happened, Dee?'

'He died about six months after we broke up; he got bad pains all over his body. He screamed all the way to the end. The doctors couldn't find a reason for his death. Sometimes that happens … you know, they can't find a medical cause.'

She said it as though it were no bad thing.

'Jesus.'

'Up his hole,' she said, then quickly, 'we're here.'

Differently coloured log cabins full of intricately crafted wares, from wool to potteries to glassware and woven garments we passed, not stopping until we reached Benny Ivor's Wood Crafts. It was dark inside, made darker by the sinister mahogany African face masks hanging on the walls. The other walls held masks from Asia, wind chimes, and the floor counters had a variety of knick-knack ornaments, like fridge magnets, pens, packs of incense and trays. The man who had called Dee about the new dolls wasn't in, but the girl said he'd left a package for her behind the counter.

'It's identical to the others you bought.'

I came alongside, and looked over Dee's shoulder as the girl surfaced the white box from the bag on the counter. Lifting the lid, she said, 'He said he hopes you'll be satisfied with it.'

A plain cloth doll, flesh-coloured, about a foot long, featureless except for two black beads for eyes, stared at us.

'Perfect,' Dee said.

She paid with her credit card, a whopping €500.

Outside, I said, 'That must be a rare doll.'

'Extremely rare, yes,' she said.

We ate in a little Italian bistro in town, themed with fishing nets, a picture of a harbour scene, a giant turtle shell. Rather than leave the new doll in the car boot, she'd brought it along in a shopping bag.

I said, 'I didn't see any other dolls like that in your house.'

'No, I move them on, what's left of them.'

'Move them on?'

'It's a voodoo doll, Mick, there's only so much life in them.'

'I see.'

'I've to think of a name for it.'

Over dessert of apple pie and custard, she started to give me cause for concern when she asked me who would be the one person in the world I'd most like to hurt.

After some moments reflecting, I said, 'No one.'

'Not even Siobhan?'

'Why would I want to harm her?'

'For your marriage failing for starters.'

'That was my fault.'

'Really?' she said, dead interested.

So I told her I'd given an alibi to the lads, the police, about a friend of mine – he'd asked me to say I had been with him on a specific night, and twenty years on, guess what? DNA evidence was used to prove he had killed a young woman.

'It's not your fault that he did that,' she said.

'Tell that to Siobhan.'

'She didn't think you had a hand in the … we're talking about Keevie Murphy, right?'

'A-ha.'

'Poor Keevie. She was a lovely woman.'

'I didn't know her.'

'You must have, she used to work at the ticket kiosk in the cinema.'

'I didn't *know* her, know her … if you follow.'

She left none of her pie, not even the crumbs, which she called 'Bystanders.'

'And I had nothing to do with her death.'

'Who said you had, Mick?'

I sighed, and asked her if she wanted to finish my dessert. Her eyes had been on it like I'd felt the eyes of her dolls on me.

'Only if you're not eating it,' she said.

I slid it across. She licked her spoon, and then said, 'Go on …'.

'Siobhan believes that I must have had a doubt about him at least once in all those years … at least one. She said the killer had a history of violence towards women.'

'Had you?' she said, chewing pie.

I'm not given to lying, in spite of the alibi that I had to retract in court, but I couldn't bring myself to admit the truth to Siobhan and now Dee. I had doubts, but I buried them, and I did so because he had something on me: a brief affair I'd had with his sister.

'No … he was a friend who I thought I knew.'

Dee simply fixed her eyes on me, and they wouldn't have looked out of place in one of her dolls.

'He raped me … and if you hadn't lied for him that wouldn't have happened. He'd have been in gaol. I don't fucking believe you. You had your doubts, for sure. Well now, you've had your last fling, Mick … I had to sleep with you … it was part of the recipe.'

'The what?'

'Recipe, duh!'

She laughed, and I thought we'd blown away the coals of burning tension.

Back at the house, she said I could stay the night, but in the spare room. She was deadly calm, polite. I couldn't wait to get away the next morning. I said we must meet up again sometime, but she just pierced me with those ice eyes, her arms folded across her breasts. She muttered 'Goodbye' and closed the front door before I was even a quarter of the way down her garden path.

Lately, I think about her in the way I used to about the circumstances surrounding Keevie's murder: I keep my thoughts to myself. About this, though: if I say anything people will think that I've flipped. Dee won't fit into the back of my mind. Her face, her eyes, those dolls, my blood on her sheet, that Voodoo doll …. The fierce, shooting pains in my legs and arms. Nightmarish health issues, rashes and coughs that perplex my doctors and leave them unable to heal.

Netanya

In Netanya that summer, Mike had met a girl called Tabitha. She was just back in town that very day after finishing a stint of annual military service in Metulla at the border with Lebanon. She was tall, though not taller than Mike, and she carried no spare weight. They had been sitting at different tables next to each other under The Scotsman's long yellow awning. They had an anxiety and impatience about them, as though they were waiting on friends to show, and had grown tired of waiting. She had on faded jeans, a short-sleeve white blouse and flip-flops she had eased from her feet. She had painted pink toenails. Her long black hair had been towel-dried, and was still wet from a swim or a shower. She sipped at her espresso and lit a cigarette. He caught her eye and gestured for a light. She smiled and handed him her plastic lighter, which had a blue eagle insignia, and they sat and smoked without saying a word; they people-watched and checked their mobile phones as though willing a message to come through. When it looked like she was getting ready to leave, he invited her to join him until her friends arrived.

'I'm not waiting for anyone in particular,' she said, with hint of a Chicago drawl.

'Just killing time,' he said.

'Yes.'

She looked at him as though posing a silent question, intended for herself, he thought, perhaps wondering what sort of guy he was beyond the crew cut, the half-starved look, the craggy face with the forehead scar. His navy T-shirt was his best clean one, his black jeans his only pair, his sandals expensive and a birthday present from his sister. Half hobo, half hippy. Free spirit. It was the image of himself he liked to portray – but Mike was someone who liked to every so often shake off the shackles that he was convinced had him bound: he was a soldier mechanic.

'Are you UN?' she said through a haze of blue-grey smoke she'd exhaled.

'No,' he lied, 'you?'

Her facial expression told him he was way off. She picked up her pink shoulder bag and sat at his table. He straightened up, and wished he'd shaved or had taken a shower with the cockroaches back in his hotel room.

'I thought you were from the Golan or Lebanon,' she said.

He shook his head, 'No, I'm not with the UN.'

'So, you're a tourist.'

'I'm working in a kibbutz just outside Qiryat Shemona. I'm free this weekend and, well, we were to meet here,' he shrugged.

He was nursing a beer, and asked if she'd like one. She said she'd like a Macabbi.

She was 28, she told him, when they were in the middle of swapping personal details. She'd asked him to guess, and he'd got close at 27. Tabitha worked in a jewellery shop specialising in diamonds. He was 32. An idea occurred to her that he had been married and the marriage had broken up. He shook his head, swigged on his beer and eyed her steadily, allowing a smile to crease his lips when he thought he saw the corners of her eyes crease with disquiet.

'You're still married,' she said.

'Are you?'

'No. I never …' she said with a deep trace of sadness in her tone, which comes from the badly let down, the betrayed, the wronged half of a love affair.

She drew the tip of her forefinger down the bottle, a line through the moisture. Then she picked at the corner of the label, glanced at him a couple of times. He could smell the coconut shampoo she'd used, and also a trace of perfume.

'My wife is dead,' he said quietly, giving her a look before averting his eyes.

She left the label alone, studied him.

'What happened?'

'What happened? Childbirth happened.'

Her features grew pensive.

'Her heart gave out,' he said evenly.

'The baby?'

'My son. He's alive. Healthy.'

'How old is he?'

'Three … he's three.'

'Shouldn't you be with him?'

'Are you hungry? I'd like something to eat that won't cost too much. What do you recommend?' he said.

After they'd eaten, they went to the beach with a few bottles of beer. He could pop the lids with his teeth, and this both enthralled and alarmed her. She said it was a feat she would never attempt; she loved her teeth too much, and wanted to keep them for as long as possible. They sat on a towel he had gone back to the hotel room for, using some minutes there to quickly wash under his arms and his genitals – he couldn't find the condoms he carried everywhere with him, and didn't want to delay any longer than he already had done. Besides, he was sure she would have one in her shoulder bag.

They were in a dune, off a narrow beach. A band played in the beach bar down the way from them, belting out a Bob Marley song about Buffalo Soldiers. They heard its faint strands, the quiet shush to shore of the waves, and then, in the middle of laughter at something witty he had said, they kissed and ignited the fuse to their passion. Afterwards, they lay side by side, her leg draped over his thigh, her fingertips light on his chest, his arm a pillow for her neck, his fingers caressing her shoulder.

Finally, they sat up, drank their last beers and smoked their last cigarettes. A half-moon and an expanse of stars beaconed in the cold ink of the skies. Sand had got in between his toes, the crevices of their behinds, under their fingernails, and irritated his athlete's foot.

Naked, she left him and walked into the sea and began to wash herself, to wash him from her. He followed her example, and later stood shivering on the beach as she used the towel to dry herself. The fabric was thin, and when it was his turn he dried himself as much as was possible in her wet.

'Do you want to come back to my apartment for coffee?' she said.

'Sure.'

It was late, almost dawn, when they reached her place. He was glad of the black sugary coffee, the bread roll she'd spread with jam for him. She said she lived there with her parents, but they had gone to visit her mum's parents in Nahariya, and wouldn't be back until Monday evening.

'So,' she said, sitting beside him, focusing on not spilling any of her coffee on the sofa.

'So,' he said, smiling.

'When are you due back at the kibbutz?'

'Tomorrow.'

'I see.'

'But you know what a kibbutz is like … I can wait till Monday.'

She sipped at her coffee and said, 'We have tomorrow, then.'

'Today,' he said.

'Oh, yes ...'.

Sunday was five hours old.

He said, 'Anything special you'd like to do?'

'Make love,' she said, putting her mug on the coffee table, 'but don't go trying to bite my neck ... I've to meet and greet people, you know?'

He nodded, 'You're okay, you know?'

'Okay?' she said, puzzled, before it came to her. 'Yeah. You?'

'Yeah.'

'I knew that ... I didn't have to ask,' she said, getting to her feet. 'I'm going to shower and get the sand out of my hair ...'.

'You want alone time or will I join you?'

'Alone time. Okay?'

'Okay.'

She smiled and left. He heard the bathroom door open and close, a bolt being drawn across. This puzzled him, but he didn't dwell on it. He watched CNN on TV, and fell asleep midway through a report about an earthquake in Pakistan.

*

He recognised the symptoms when they appeared, and tried to deny them to himself, but after a week he presented himself to the Regimental Aid Post at UN Headquarters about six kilometres across the Israeli border in south Lebanon. The doctor was Polish. He did the tests, including one for HIV, and said, 'You have contracted venereal disease, but we will not have the results of the AIDS tests for about six weeks.'

'Shit.'

'When are you to return to Ireland, Sergeant?'

'Next month.'

'Do you know this woman well?'

'I spent a weekend with her.'

'You may have given this to her, yes?'

'No. I haven't been with anyone else. Not for months. Not since I came to Lebanon five months ago,' he said, lying.

'You're married?'

'Yes.'

The doctor had a handlebar moustache. He was about 55. He peeled off his plastic gloves.

'Big problem for you,' he said.

As if I don't already know that, Mike thought, feeling panicky about what lay down the road. Moira – Jesus – we don't use condoms. She'll be mad for it when I get home – what will I say, what will I do? Fuck.

As he binned the gloves, the doctor said, 'You should see this woman, maybe, and ask her if she has AIDS … this is the big important question for you. VD is the best you hope for … let's hope it is not syphilis or AIDS … not anything so major for you or for your wife.'

Back in his billet, he lay on his bunk under camouflage mosquito netting. He'd got three days' leave, begrudgingly and reluctantly granted by his Commanding Officer, who had only relented after receiving a call from the Polish doctor to advise him that it was a necessary situation.

Christ, what the fuck was I thinking about? You risk something one time and get caught. The condoms – he had found them under his bed back at the hotel. Should have fucking known when she didn't demand that he use a rubber … should have ….

His mates asked him if he had a problem. He said he hadn't. They said he looked like a man with a problem. If he wanted to talk, you know. Talk! The army wanted their soldiers to open up to each other as they believed that talking about problems cut down on suicide. If he had talked, they'd have listened, and either slagged him off or called him a sad bastard and said he was the complete fucking idiot. At home, it'd do the rounds in the barracks and married quarters. Flaherty poked a Yid and got himself the pox, and his old doll, eh, wants him to use Viagra because she thinks he's a floppy.

In the end, Moira would find out.

If he had AIDS, he would have to tell her. If it was just the pox, he might be able to keep her at bay until he was cured. Anything else … fuck, a couple of screws had screwed up his life.

*

She was not at The Scotsman, and the apartment she had brought him to did not belong to her parents – he did not know who it belonged to, because the two middle-aged women who stood at the door hadn't got too many words of English.

'Tabitha,' he repeated.

They shook their heads and looked at each other.

'Tabitha?'

They shook their heads again, then closed the door in his face.

The next day, he met her. Earlier he had trawled through jewellery shops, hoping to see her behind the counter, knowing she would not have wanted a scene in the shop and would have had to talk to him. Had she lied to him the way he had lied to her? Probably. He was no kibbutz worker.

And he had no dead wife. What man would leave a child who had lost his mother?

It was at the beach bar. He had decided to go there for a beer, to get in under the bamboo roof and escape the midday sun. She sat at a table with a young guy, and he guessed he was the tie-in for the apartment: it was his parents who owned it. She wore the same clothes she had worn when she met him. When she saw him, the blood drained from her face. He sat in beside her on the form, and told the young guy to give them a few minutes alone. He looked hard at Mike, but he left after she'd said something to him in Hebrew. She blew cigarette smoke out of the side of her mouth.

'Thanks,' he said sarcastically.

'Don't mention it.'

'It was a shit thing to do.'

'You guys are all the same.'

'What have you got?'

'VD.'

'No AIDS?'

'No.'

'Why the fuck didn't you say?'

'Why?'

'Just fucking tell me,' he said, his voice rising an octave, drawing glances from a barman cleaning the tables. The young man stood under the eaves, kicking his heels in the sand.

'I want to give men something to remember me by.'

He resisted the urge to punch her. Instead, he said, 'I told you that I had a son … that my wife was dead.'

She looked at him sidelong and said, 'Bullshit.'

He could not contradict her, not with her eyes burning into the back of his skull.

'You know what I have. That's it … this time next month I might have worse, so count yourself lucky we didn't meet then,' she said.

He sighed, smoothed his hair, helped himself to one of her cigarettes.

'Are you going to buy me a drink?' she said. 'Do I tell my friend to go away?'

'Yeah, yeah' he said half dejectedly, half wearily, 'I'll buy you a drink.'

She said something to the young man, and he walked away.

'You've fucked me up,' he said, 'I'm deep in shit …'.

'Don't be crazy with me … be crazy at yourself. Me, you can screw later; the harm is done.'

'Are you for fucking real?'

'It's my way of saying sorry.'

'I'll stick with the beer.'

But he knew it wasn't in his nature to, and that was the real problem – it stared at him from the honey liquid in his glass.

Prairies

We heard the doctor say on the radio that if men wanted to avoid getting cancer of the prostate then they should eat tomatoes and red peppers. If they were over 50, they should have themselves medically examined. 'Prostate cancer is a silent killer,' the doctor warned.

Dad turned his head to the window, and looked through the glass at our cairn terrier crapping on the lawn he had me cut earlier that morning. He worked me for my pocket money, unlike other fathers, who gave their kids money just to keep out of their hair.

When Dad turned 50, we had a bit of a bash in a pub. Low-key. He said he wanted a low-key affair, but I think he was disappointed with that arrangement. He wanted people to read his mind, but no one could because he was never of the same mind about anything for too long. That night, he got a few beers into him and sang 'Raglan Road', the only song he knew the words to. He toasted all his dead friends and relatives with tears in his eyes. This made me want to vomit the glass of Heineken

I'd stolen to my lips when people were too busy looking at him to notice me. He was crying over people he was always giving out stink about, like Nana, who left her house to Dad's sister and a site to his brother, and a fart in the wind to Dad, because they'd a falling out over nothing much. They never made up. I never met Nana. Mam says I was born lucky.

I was about to make for my room, when something applied a brake to the idea. Dad looked so pathetic, standing at the sink with the leaky tap he'd been meaning to fix for over a year. He had on a blue short-sleeve T-shirt that he kept outside the waist of his jeans to disguise the mound of his belly. His thick, hairy forearm carried a tattoo of a red heart with an arrow piercing it. Faded. Every so often he liked to tell me that he was a hippy in his younger days, and used to tour the country in a camper van. That he had long hair and wore psychedelic clothes and sang a duet with Bob Dylan in Chicago, which I thought was pure bull. Maybe he'd sang with a Bob Dylan lookalike, or in his mind when he was stoned on hash or tripping on LSD or whatever in his psychedelic raggies.

'Remind me to buy in some tomatoes,' he said, 'and peppers, red ones.'

'Okay.'

'Lots of tomatoes,' he said.

'For the cancer,' I said.

He didn't answer. Instead, he ran the tap till the water turned cold, and then he poured himself a cup and drank it thirstily. He faced me, mopping his lips with the back of his hand, and said, 'He's coming next week.'

This was probably the most infuriating old man thing that he did: saying something out of the blue about something he had mentioned hours previously – so maddening – you know; it's like a train stopping at its final destination and then, without warning, you're back on the tracks, going only God knows where.

He explained, '*The Virginian*, are you bothered, Tony?'

He used to read cowboy books and watch western films and an old western series TG4 repeated in the afternoons. Maybe he should've quit working nights and got a daytime job. That way he wouldn't have had the time to be watching fogey old ghosts.

'The man with no name,' he said.

'Clint Eastwood, yeah?' I said.

'No, James Drury … he's the original man with no name.'

'He's coming here?'

'No, not to this town. Claremorris.'

He rubbed his lips, and I could tell he was thinking of going to see his hero. As far as I was concerned, a real hippie, even a reformed sort, would still have had enough of that in him just to go there without thinking about it.

'Why don't you bring Mam?' I said.

His expression changed. He and Mam went nowhere together. She had her mates and he had his.

He called into my bedroom an hour later, and asked me to look up *The Virginian* on the web, just to see if there was anything on it about the show. There was more trivia than anyone could possibly care to digest. Except for Dad. He played the theme tune over and over, and ran a couple of clips from the series that were available on YouTube. He said he must get himself a laptop like mine for Christmas. 'Dead handy yokes,' he said.

He talked about *The Virginian* and *Trampas* and *Judge Garth* and stuff, doing my head in. He said it was the first adult TV programme he was allowed to stay up and see. If it were not for the show, things would have been totally dark in his house. Then he said, 'We'll go see him … the two of us.' No asking. I was going, like it or not, to see an old cowboy who meant nothing to me, whose shows were nearly fifty years old, and who probably looked only a little like he used to – a ghost of himself before he'd even died.

I told Mam the next morning, and suggested that she should go with him instead. Well, you'd have thought I was after asking her to jump from the roof of the shopping mall. 'No,' she said quietly, 'no, Son … ah, no. Thanks.' I nodded. Well, what do you actually say when you're told that your parents' marriage is over in the most roundabout way imaginable? You nod, even if you don't fully understand why the hell you're nodding.

We stopped outside the church at a stop sign. He said someone was squeezing a cat, his way of telling me about the skirl of bagpipes in the church grounds. I was trying to read. I read a lot, but I had to stop reading because I sometimes got sick from a combination of shaky words and car motion. If he had to pull over and let me out to vomit he would flip, but there was no guarantee he could pull over in time, and I didn't want to risk vomiting in the car. Or on him, as I'd have had to listen to him moaning for hours, and worse, I'd be sitting in my emptyings with the window rolled down to the last, the slip breeze drying the sick into me.

'Is Claremorris a long drive?' I asked.

'It's way out west, pardner.'

Oh God, spare me, I thought.

In Moate we pulled over to eat breakfast. The café was quiet, and we sat at a table by the window. I asked him straight out if Mam and he were still living together because of me. He said that was partly the reason, and partly till I got started out on life, and partly because it had to do with finance. I said about Cosmic Jones, and if Mam was going with him, and he said they were friends. I asked him if he had a friend, and he said we should eat breakfast.

He usually took care not to speak when he was eating, so we ate in silence. When he was finished eating, he asked if I knew the cowboy philosophy. I said no, tell me.

'If it's not yours don't take it; if it's not true don't say it; if it's not right don't do it.'

'Simple commandments,' I said.

'Yeah, but still hard to keep, son, very hard.'

We moseyed on, and then all of a sudden we stopped moseying. The car broke down: the most reliable car he had ever owned, as he was so fond of saying. We got out and pushed it over to the hard shoulder. He turned the key, and swore when he got no response. He opened the bonnet and decorated the engine with foul language; I guess if he'd had a six gun he'd have pumped bullets into it.

He said, 'Give me your phone for a minute.'

'I've no credit.'

'Tony, for the love of …. You're a bleddy eejit, Jesus, Mary and Joseph … what class of a bleddy moron are you at all?'

'Where's yours?'

'The battery's down,' he mumbled.

'Yeah, Dad, so don't be getting on to me.'

He was sorry then, but didn't say so.

'And I didn't call you names,' I said.

He sighed, then apologised, and I said it was okay because I knew that saying sorry was a hard thing to do, for reasons I'm still not sure of. I used to hear him say he was sorry to Mam, and she'd ignore him and he'd get bull-thick and say he wasn't really sorry; he'd only said so for the sake of peace.

He waved down a passing car, and borrowed a phone from the driver for a few minutes to ring the AA. Then he smoked a cigarette in the drizzle and walked up and down the road, climbed a three-bar gate into a field to pee, and then got back in the car and said he was sorry for calling me names. But saying this didn't appear to be enough for him, for he kept talking, as if these new words might retract those he had said earlier. Maybe he softened their effect, but what he couldn't lessen was how he had said them: with bitterness and a desperate despair. I'd been hurt, but I knew he was hurting too. It was temper talk, he said, that's all.

It took an hour for a mechanic to arrive and work his magic. Within a few minutes he had us on our way. Thirty minutes later it broke down again, and then again, and by the time we reached the hotel where *The Virginian* was to appear, he had well and truly vamoosed.

Later he rang Mam, and said we were staying over that night as the car was acting up and it was being looked at in the morning. She didn't sound too disappointed when I was on to her to say goodnight. Dad hung around the bar for the evening while I watched TV in the bedroom. He came in late, jarred and sad, and said he'd met *The Virginian* in the lobby. I doubted him.

'What did he say?'

'Howdy.'

'Howdy?'

'Well, he was in a hurry.'

In the darkness I heard his gentle breathing in the other bed, the toss and turn of thoughts that wouldn't settle.

'Dad?'

'Yeah?'

'Did you really get to see him?'

'No.'

I had news for him. But he didn't get excited about *The Virginian* appearing at the horse show the next day.

'Well?' I said.

Nothing else was said for moments.

He sighed out loud and said, 'No. None of that; it's all gone.'

I'd already a small idea that something was wrong with Dad; yesterday he'd eaten those peppers and tomatoes, but in the hotel room I sort of grew a little more to the fact. But I didn't know it back then, and neither did I suspect that things would get much worse for him, and consequently for those who loved and thought well of him. His was a sentence on which one could have hung many meanings, and walked across many prairies without ever finding a single grain of truth in the sands.

Ritual

I spread the newspaper on the kitchen table, knowing for certain that he would be there to stare at me with his murderer's eyes, as he is on every anniversary of Alex's death. Every year the newspapers pick up on the quadruple killer, and every year for the last few there is increasing speculation in the media about his release from prison, or a transfer to accommodate those who don't want to travel too far to visit son or brother scum.

My pink Nokia did a little jig on the wooden surface, between the red-and-white salt and pepper cellars. I picked it up, and saw Nano's number in the caller display.

'Vicky,' she said.

'I know. I'm looking at the bastard.'

Silence.

Nano said, 'I'll call round later, okay?'

'Okay.'

I needed to think, to clear my head, to prepare for the annual ritual, the cleansing .... Two days after our first big row over money, Alex came home and told me that he'd volunteered for the Leb. I went crazy because I wanted him to be around when our baby was born. But then he said he'd only put his name forward to push him further up the list for the next trip. It made sense to me when he said it like that, and when I calmed down I realised that he was right: we needed the money. I said I wouldn't mind if he went after our baby was born. I often wonder if he'd pushed that news at me to break part of the storm, that he knew he was going all along ….

We hadn't got married quarters yet because I wouldn't take the one the quartermaster wanted to issue us with: it was some dive, the walls rank with damp and peeling wallpaper and an outdoor toilet with the shit backed up in it, and of course Alex wanted the kip as he didn't want to pay rent for the flat. And even though the rent for the quarters cost next to nothing, I refused to move in there. People bank on other people being desperate enough to accept anything that's thrown at them, and what's more, to be grateful for it.

'Ah Vicky,' he said.

'Ah Vicky my arse. Jesus, get me out of here. If my Ma saw the state of the gaff you wanted to move me into she'd be after yere blood, Alex …'.

'I'll get it cleaned up.'

'Why bother cleaning something that should have been knocked down a hundred years ago?'

So, we went back to the bottom of the waiting list. Then Alex started talking about buying our own place. He said they were building a rake of new houses out in Tallaght, and he kept this up for a couple of weeks, and then he said, when he'd brought home a takeaway from the Chinese, that he had some news. I'd known he was building up to something, but hadn't been too sure what it was. His oul' one was always full of mad schemes, like wanting us to buy a mobile home and park it in her backyard.

'I will in my hole,' I'd said to Alex at the time.

If he couldn't see why not, then there was no sense in telling him. I wouldn't be under an obligation to anyone, especially not his mother – there'd be payback with her. Besides, I wouldn't like to owe her the favour; it wouldn't sit right with me.

I was watching *Top of the Pops* on the telly, and he thought I was just going to fall over him. He forgot that when he was watching *Match of the Day* he pretended not to hear me asking him to get me a bar of Aero; starving for it, I was. Anyhow, I loved that song 'Fame', and even with the small rise in me I could dance as well as what's-her-name.

When I was ready, I said, saying it like I didn't really care whether he told me or not, 'What's your news, Alex?'

I was half thinking that he was going to tell me he'd been selected for a course for potential NCOs, and would be away training a lot of the time, in the Glen of Imaal and that; that I would hardly see him for six months.

'It'll wait,' he said.

I'd hoped he wasn't getting the sulks.

'Tell us how was your day,' he said.

It was a cold summer evening, the fire was on one bar to save the gas in the bottle, and I was carrying a cruel headache. I was still working in Dunnes, and would be for as long as I could manage to stick it, till the baby came. I told him my feet were sore, and I'd a massive row with a customer who said I'd overcharged her when I knew for a fact that I hadn't, because I'd triple-checked her change, seeing as it was her.

'What do you mean?' she'd said.

'Sure you're in here every week trying that oul' trick on.'

And she had been, and the supervisor knew it too, but he said afterwards that I couldn't call the customers names like that – because even though you were right in what you said, the wrong way of accusing someone can be turned and used against you. I was just being straight is all. That one would lick shite if she thought it'd fill her.

He laughed at that.

He was wearing his combat uniform. I knew he wasn't supposed to be wearing it outside of barracks, and had been stopped by the military police a couple of times and warned. He could wear his ordinary everyday uniform. I think it was to do with the combat jackets; the lads sold them, or they were stolen. A security thing, I suppose, with the stuff that was going on up north.

The combats were green, and had good and plenty of pockets, and the lads on the building sites were mad for them. The army started stamping on them to stop the loss, and the guards were given the power to confiscate them off civvies. He sat in close beside me, lounged, and touched my belly with his fingertips, then laid his hand flat on it and kissed my cheek, and didn't even take his hand away when I said I had a splitting headache, which told me he wasn't after anything.

'The CO brought me into the office today,' he said.

I smelt drink off him, but it wasn't very strong; he'd only supped enough to give himself courage.

'For what?' I said.

Alex had lovely green eyes, and they were full of life. Maybe it was the alcohol had got behind them and polished them up, for they really shone that evening.

'He said I was selected for overseas.'

I sat up straight, my spine going rigid, like lightning hitting a rod, and snapped, 'No way, Alex!'

I was on my feet, evading his reach for me, and at the table before he had even stood. That pitiful look he sometimes put on made my blood boil. I reached for the takeaway, and I was so vexed I threw it at him and spattered his combats with rice and chicken curry.

'Vicky,' he said, 'for fuck's sake!'

'You lied to me, Alex!'

'I didn't! Joey Tierney failed his medical, and I was next in line, if Iturnit down Iwon't get going for another three years!'

When Alex got excited, he joined up his words and stood on his toes a little. It was like the words would kill him if he allowed them stay inside for any length of time.

He put his hands out to beg for peace. I saw that stupid silver Claddagh ring his stupid mother had bought him last Christmas, buying it for him after I told her it was what I was getting him for a present. Such a cow, and me having to leave it in the shop where I was paying it off and instead buy him a silver chain and cross that he lost after a week. He put a foot forward.

'Fuck off … don't you come near me, Alex.'

He backed away, and began smoothing his cropped brown hair.

'Come on Eileen' came on the telly, and we liked to dance to that, and it was awkward listening to it because all I wanted to do then in that moment was dance with him. But he couldn't see this, he missed that, and if he had stepped forward I wouldn't have stopped him coming the full journey. He didn't see it because he was gone, and I was left alone with an upset baby in me and the strains of a happy pop song bouncing off the walls in a flat that smelt of curry.

He was always sending me home parcels from the Leb, full of baby clothes, pink and blue, and he'd said the stuff was really cheap out there, and he'd the neck to be sending me crotchless knickers for when I'm better; meaning for when I'd be able to do the sex again.

I missed him more than I thought I would. It's not till someone is gone that you realise the little things that he did around the place. Cleaning out the ashes, putting out the dustbin, doing the delft, listening and not talking, not saying anything, just being a pair of ears for me for whenever I had a row with Mammy or I was low in myself. I missed the warmth of him in the bed, and the heat he would leave behind him when he was just out of it, the way it was there for me to slide over onto, and I always seemed to sleep better in the ghost of his heat. Funny that.

He wrote a lot of letters, and this was hard for him because he'd left school when he'd turned 13, taken out of it by his ma to go work on a fuel lorry. 'His ma's a bollocks' were Nano's first words of friendship to me. I cracked up laughing because I'd never heard a woman being called that before.

Short letters, and usually saying the same thing over and over, and he couldn't spell – atrocious. I'd have to read him the good bits out of the porn mags we liked to read in bed. I preferred the mags to the blue films. Sometimes these were okay to watch, but more often were not. I wouldn't be prudish or anything, but that's how I am, I prefer sex and that in the mags to watching the vids that Alex sent home. I gave them to the girls to watch, and they thought they were fucking brilliant, especially the one with the man who had a huge cock.

The girls could be a scream, and I missed going out with them, but I was too big, and I wasn't in the mood for them after about an hour in their company; they'd get too loud, and when they got like that I went distant in myself, for I couldn't see the sense of what the loud laughter was all about. I did before, but maybe being with a baby changes you.

'That's fucking lovely,' Nano'd said, trying on the gold rope chain Alex had sent me for my 24th birthday.

We were in my flat the evening before the world caved in.

'Yeah, it's lovely all right.'

'He's good taste, Vicky, I'll say that for him.'

'He has, hasn't he?'

'My Gerry's taste is in his hole.'

'Ah, he's not that bad.'

'He fucking well is.'

Then I remembered that he'd surprised her with a cake and a band singing 'you're once, twice, three times a lady' in the mess, and she was mortified because this was the song that was playing when she and Mouldy Jones were having sex during one of the nights Gerry was on duty, and he got stuck in her and couldn't get out, and we had to call an ambulance. None of us knew till that night that a man could literally be trapped inside you. Gerry never found out, and if he did he couldn't very well say anything because he used to go with Maggie Doyle, and no man who had respect for his mickey would go near her. Walking she is.

'You're right about Gerry's taste,' I said.

'In his hole.'

'Tea?'

'I'll make it … you've the place looking lovely. Who painted it up for you?'

'Michael.'

'The same Michael you used to go with?'

'That was ages ago.'

'He's good, isn't he?' she'd said, looking around.

'He is.'

'Did he charge much?'

'He wouldn't take anything.'

'That was decent of him.'

'He said I was to tell no one. In case anyone else would expect it done for free.'

'You told me.'

'You're not no one.'

And she reached over and put her fat arms around me, and I thought she was going to hug me to death. When she let me be, she said, 'My Gerry didn't get his letters …'.

I'd given them to Freddie. I'd rang the barracks and asked them to send someone around to collect them. The boys going to and coming from the Leb do so on rotation: three chalks over three weeks. Alex was coming home on the last, so the new lads going out brought stuff to him and the others. I'd wanted him home on the first chalk, but he said the extra money would come in handy. I couldn't argue with him on that score, but now I often wish I had.

The army took us out there last year. By us, I mean the families of those who had been murdered.

They brought us to the actual scene during the day, but I insisted on being there in the evening, at the time it happened. So an officer brought us to the place when it was night, and he had the sense to leave me and Jamie alone with each other. It was dark, and a cool breeze stirred the fronds on the road verge. The silhouette of the crusader castle on the hill was darker than the night skies. Jamie said nothing. He smoked, holding his cigarette the same way his dad used to, sheltered by his palm, warming its lifeline perhaps.

I'd fallen asleep on the sofa, and woke sometime in the middle of the night. The TV was still on, all grey and fuzzy and singing signal. I lay there, touched my belly. The telly going and lighting the room in a sort of blue light, a Bush telly that Alex joked about. 'Are we watching the Bush tonight? What's the reception, like?' Laughing goodo then at the wit of himself, my hand sliding over to adjust his aerial.

I was thinking about lots on the sofa, wide awake, wondering why that Freddie lad hadn't given the letters to the lads. He was very quiet that lad, and had a way of looking at you when he had drink on him – not what he'd like to do with you, something more, like he would want to do that with you and much more besides. Alex didn't like him, just said there was something about him. When I thought on it, that explained it better than I had; there was something about him.

I got up and turned off the telly, then made tea and brought the cup to bed and put it on the bedside locker, where it remained, untouched.

I was up early, feeling fresh in myself, really fresh considering I hadn't slept too well. When I heard the doorbell, I thought that the rent man was early, and went to answer. I remember walking the hallway, my hand arced on my back, feeling like an elephant, opening the door to clear Dublin skies, an army officer and a chaplain. They didn't have to open their mouths; their presence said everything.

One said, 'Sorry,' and this was the last thing I heard as the roars of me silenced all else they had to say. All that stuff, the bare facts, came later, and even then they had to pierce a numbness.

Why did they let live this bastard who pulled the trigger, left my son with a photograph for a father, a few scenes in a video cassette, and a green combat jacket on a wire hanger in a wardrobe? He lives in a gaol, and whenever they write or speak of early release for him my stomach rises to my throat, for how could anyone even consider freeing a scum who murdered four young men in cold blood, and put the gun to the head of one to finish him off? How could they? Do they think that a person forgets – that because I've moved on and remarried and had more children, that it's all right? That I've got over it? I'm grand, so I am? In ways they are as bad as the scum who killed Alex, for I think they own his same lack of sensitivity and respect for the lives of others. But I will never forget. I see Alex every day, feel the goodbye kiss, the sad smile, the tears in his eyes, hear the promises on his lips, read the love you and kisses in his badly written letters.

I spit on the image in the newspaper photograph, and then I take scissors to the page, cutting around the edges, resisting the temptation to slice through him. I bring the cutting to the sink, place it in the enamel basin and set a match to a corner; I watch the flame consume his face, watch as he disintegrates into floating black motes. I run the tap, and watch the flow of water break the remnants of burned newspaper, hurrying them down the drain.

If Something Doesn't Get Better ...

Larry always used to say, 'If something doesn't get better, it gets worse; what it doesn't do is remain the same.' He was so full of regrets that, if you were to shake him hard, all his remorse would sound like some godawful alarm. He was a man used to saying sorry. But the word was worn away in him, because it meant nothing any more. He had used it too often to too many people – it was now merely an automated word from his lips. A default setting. I mean, he was one sorry fuck.

We were in a people carrier I'd popped in the parking lot outside a Dunkin' Donuts, and I was thinking about abandoning it before a cop pulled us over. A fella could drive 500 miles or longer and not be stopped in his tracks – it's the longest distance I've ever driven without a traffic cop wanting to get close to my face, and my shortest run is about 500 yards. Meantime, during my thinking, Larry was staring deep into the bag and whistling, saying, 'Fuck, fuck.'

'What?' I said, snatching the bag from his lap and putting it on mine. When I looked in, I nearly totalled us by wheel-kissing the curb and momentarily losing control.

Earlier, we'd relieved an old doll of her shoulder bag in New Haven. A morning of contrary winds, and we'd rigged things so it looked like the wind had bowled her to the ground and not a Larry shove. As soon as she was down, he was all over her like a great gentle bear, cooing in her ear after he'd slipped her bag to me. I did a runner then. The old doll was wiry and tough, and when she found her deep, husky voice she yelled blue thunder. Larry shouted and pointed in another direction, 'Thief! Stop that man!' And people actually grappled an innocent kid to the ground. Afterwards, Larry caught up with me and he had such a grin. Not a happy grin, but nervous. He was pessimistic, and always expected us to get caught – it was a huge relief and surprise to him when, after doing a job, we remained cuff-free. I hadn't checked the bag on the spot because these days cameras peer from everywhere and every goddamn angle, and a monitor-watcher wouldn't fail to notice a guy dipping his eyes and hands into a Gucci shoulder bag. So I just wanted to put a distance between us and the crime scene. Each of us had rap sheets with crimes enough to bead up several rosaries. Both of us were in our late forties, with failed everythings behind us and bad prospects ahead.

In the motel we booked into, walking a distance after abandoning the carrier in a wood, we found we'd struck it lucky: in her Gucci, the old doll had $93,098 in cash. Some loose change. Credit cards, donor card, an address book, a hairbrush with strands of old hair, spare clean knickers and some fanny fresheners.

We sat on the bed looking at that stash of greenery on the orange duvet, not believing our good fortune. We counted it three times. On TV, Captain Kirk was talking to Spock about beaming him up. Man, we were smiles. Not a sorry peeped from Larry. Larry Reddy. Larry had Irish blood in him from his mother's side. He was tall, well-built, and had a stud in his left ear. He liked to go into empty churches to pray and light votive candles. That part of him came from his mother – his father was from the Congo, and he gave Larry his huge bottom lip that people knew right off revealed a truculent nature. But before people could read the lip, they took in his large brown eyes, and these shining diamonds just took people's breath away long enough for Larry to get them over the hurdle of his father's lip. Me, I'm short and skinny, and from a poor Jewish family that Israel didn't want in the homeland, which tells it all about us. Like they'd even kidnapped Africans and settled them in the Promised Land. Mom said it was because we were the thirteenth tribe of the Israelites. When I said there were only twelve tribes, she said to cotton on to what she was saying.

'Jeez,' Larry said, gazing at the stash on the bed. He whistled long and loud.

I said that was a real backwater Negro sort of thing to do, and he said, 'Sorry.'

Before hitting up the old woman this morning, we had about $200 between us. Six previous old-timer targets hadn't yielded us a whole ton: single bills, five-dollar notes, dimes, quarters, a set of false teeth, driving licences. Seventh time lucky.

I was thinking that 96 grand split two ways was a lot of money, and couldn't help thinking that one way was a hell of a lot more. It would take me the guts of five years' slogging as a short-order cook to earn that sort of dough.

Larry said, 'What was she doing carrying so much money?'

'I dunno … how would I know?'

'We should maybe hang loose for a while.'

I'd been thinking the same. If Doris Marso – her name and address peeped out from an electricity bill – sang to the cops about how much she was cooked for, they'd see it as a wake-up call. If they could snatch us before we spent all her cash, they might get to siphon some for themselves. I know how a cop's heart works.

'There's a place close by,' I said, 'in Amish land … I used to go there with Linda and the kids. They used to love it the way people do who aren't familiar with rural.'

'Okay. Sounds fine to me.'

'For a couple of days,' I said.

'A-ha,' Larry said, somewhat distantly.

So we checked out in the morning, and took a bus to Strasburg, where I bought a camper van from a man who ran an ad in a shop window that had a Conestoga wagon parked out front. Paid cash, which had given me some bargaining leverage – I'd always wanted one of those hippie vans. It was sky-blue with a white trim, and the guy had worked it to mint condition. Larry knew about engines, and he had a good look under the bonnet and said all was in order. The owner was broke – I can smell that off a person, because more often than not the same smell lingers about my own body.

Larry had a face about the deal, and I had to almost squeeze his nuts in McDonald's to find out what was bothering him.

'Sorry, Vince … I hope you don't think I'm being mean or anything, but that van comes from your cut, yeah?'

The van cost 9,000 bucks. I was kind of hoping to sell the idea to Larry that it was sort of a company car, but I knew by the look of him that he had every dollar of his share counted and measured against his own stuff.

'For sure, Larry. I bought it out of my cut.'

Some of the strain left his face. Something else, though, lurked in the craggy lines of his forehead.

'What?' I said.

'Maybe it wasn't such a good idea to spend so much dough … the cops will be looking out for that sort of thing, yeah?'

He was right. My silence told him. But I'd really wanted the van.

He said, 'Maybe we should split the …'.

'Are you saying you don't trust me, Larry?'

'I'm not saying that, Vince. No way.'

'Cos that would hurt me here,' I said, patting my chest.

'Just that it'd be good to feel it in my hand, yeah. You know what I'm saying?'

'Sure.'

He stood and said, 'They'll be looking for two fellas.'

'I know that … don't you think I know that?'

'I got nothing to show for what we did. You have the van.'

'What do you want?'

'A new cellphone for starters. Some clothes. What I got on me is what I been wearing since we left lock-up.'

Six weeks back.

'So, Larry, we book into the Red Caboose and we split the loot, is that all right with you? I go my way and you go yours?'

'For a while, yeah … till the heat is off. Right?'

I didn't answer because I wanted him to worry about my silence.

He went on, 'And maybe we can think of doing something else. I … I'm not too happy about hitting off little old ladies all of the time.'

'You're right, we need a different plan … if we stick to the same scam, the cops will sting us for sure. But maybe we should keep our options open. In case we see a rich old dame looking for trouble. I mean it's not as if we hurt them or anything, is it?'

'We could spring a heart attack on them.'

'If so … well, it means it was waiting on them anyhow. We can't look at it like that, Larry.' He nodded, but he wasn't fully in tune with the plan.

The Red Caboose Motel is made up of maybe thirty to forty converted railway carriages from the old defunct lines – they have names on their sides like Pennsylvania West; North Line; Alaska Coy; New Jersey Express; Caledonian and the like. There's a reception room, with off it a long dining car and a museum with a model railway and gifts, some of which made me remember my kids and how they used to beg me for things – I tried to get them whatever they wanted when I had money, because I knew they were going to have do without more often than not. I forced my thoughts off the ex and the happy times we had in the North Line sleeper. Linda's half Polish. She's got little time left on her clock because of a diseased heart. I try not to let that bother me, but it isn't always possible.

That evening, we were having dinner in the dining car when Larry said, 'You sure you don't mind separate rooms?'

'No problem, Larry. We're grown men and need our own space.'

An hour ago we'd split the money in my carriage, right down to the last cent. All the time I was counting he had his eye tooth on his truculent lip. I swear he didn't goddamn blink once as I counted. He stuffed his share into a red backpack and smiled broadly. 'Happy days,' he'd said in a singsong voice.

We ordered quarter cheeseburgers and fries, and two beers apiece. The car was empty because it was pushing to closing time, and it was out of season for family visits.

After he slugged on his beer, he said, 'I think I'll clear out first thing in the morning, Vince. I can't wait around here, it's too quiet, too creepy.'

'Do you want a ride into town?'

'No, I'll be fine. I'll get a cab and a bus from there.'

'Where are you headed to?'

'I have a sister in New Jersey. She'll be glad to see me, I reckon.'

'This is egg-eating Susie, right?'

He looked at me in surprise at my having remembered. Susie had a dietary condition. She ate boiled eggs for breakfast, dinner, and tea. In the joint, Larry used to talk about how she used to talk with her mouth full of egg, making his stomach sick.

'She's off the eggs,' he said.

'Good.'

'You bet. Too many people got to steering their asses well away from her.'

We concentrated on our food as we'd run out of things to say to each other. Besides, he ate with his mouth open – it must run in the family – which wasn't a pretty sight, and I didn't want to look at the mixing process. Normally, I could keep a conversation going among a crowd of deaf and dumb, but I had begun to dislike Larry: he had a major trust issue with me. And he didn't have reason – which is a strange thing to say, given our game, our form – but I'd never turned him over, not once. Not even when tempted.

He looked to the side, out the window at the camper van. He said I should move it into the shade of the willow trees behind the purple house, so the sun wouldn't spoil the interior. Clouds were crossing its windscreen.

'Can I?' he said, 'I need to get that bag of treats out of it anyway.'

Larry had a sweet tooth.

'Sure,' I said, handing him the keys.

When I got up in the morning, he had already checked out – I hadn't been late in rising. I sat out on the veranda enjoying a smoke and a black coffee, watching two Amish men drawing a horse cart along the tobacco crops and loading it. The horse was big and strong and blinkered. The mist hadn't cleared from the rolling land, and the sky was the sort of blue you could look at for-ever. I thought that sticking with the plan to stay here for a couple of days had been a cool idea; I was in no hurry to go anywhere. And anywhere I wanted to go was going to see me eating into the stash – I knew deep down that I was going to hit the track sooner or later, and maybe the horses would run like they had cyber fuel in them, but some wouldn't have much speed in their legs and fire in their hearts – but this time if the nags failed me I wouldn't be living rough and hitting the soup kitchens. I had my camper, and in it a bed, mini-fridge, a TV ... the works. I was well set up if the four legs disappointed. In my head I had it sown that because I was so well set up for failure, there was no chance of it happening.

I didn't see it coming, but Larry caught me one all right. The fuck. He'd kept a spare key to the camper. I noticed its absence from the spot where I'd parked it the previous evening. All that was left were faint tyre prints along the earth, and a Snickers wrapper he must have eaten for an early breakfast.

He knew I couldn't go to the cops, and probably counted on my not coming after him. I wished him bad luck, and consoled myself that I could still afford to buy another van. Also, I couldn't stay at the Red Caboose for as long as I'd hoped – Larry couldn't be trusted now, and if he was picked up by the cops, he'd rat me out to them for a deal on his jail term.

When I went to check out, the woman handed me a letter, saying that my friend, Mr Coady, had left it for me. Coady was Larry's chosen alias, mine was Michaels.

Outside on the steps, while waiting for an Amish horse buggy to collect me, I read what Larry had to say for himself. He wrote sorry a few times in as many sentences.

'Vince, sorry pal. But I guess this was coming for one of us. I'm gonna flog your bus as soon as possible, so no point in you looking for me or it ... sorry, it's nothing personal. Hope you won't stay mad at me too long. Sorry and all. Larry.'

I tore the letter, binned the scraps, and wished again all the worst for that sorry fuck.

In spite of feeling low, I enjoyed the buggy ride along narrow country roads to town. It was one of those things you do that deep down you know you won't be doing again, and maybe that's why it was such a grand journey of three miles.

Any so, I lifted my spirits and bought a red camper for $6,000 from the same guy. I had wheels and money. Hopes, plans, and a feel good feeling began to wash all over me. I drove for hours, and finally pulled over to a rest area alongside the edge of a forest after the eyelids began to grow heavy. There were trucks parked, and some larger vans than mine. It was late, and after I'd emptied myself in the convenience block, I drew the curtains in the camper and turned on the TV. Watching TV and slowly sinking a beer helps me to fall asleep. I think some programmes are made specially for that very purpose – that was an old joke of Larry's.

Next thing I see Larry's face in a photo on the news, and right off I'm awake. It was like a sword had been unsheathed in my stomach and thrust upwards. He was dead, his body lying on a sidewalk with a grey blanket over it. I upped the volume, my eyes wide, mind pleading for it not to be true.

The news guy said that police suspect that the killing was in revenge for the mugging of an old woman, the mother of mafia don Gio Marso. Many officials are questioning the police role, and their lagging behind the criminal fraternity in this investigation. Damn cameras, damn everyone who ratted on us. Poor, sorry Larry.

I rushed my gear into a travel bag, locked the camper and hurled the keys into the trees. Next, I started to hitch a lift, and I've been doing that on and off since – leaving the good old States for Canada a month ago, on the first anniversary of Larry's murder. I'm working as a short-order cook in a shitty roadhouse. I don't do crime stuff any more. I'm just living in wait for the bullet. There's nothing can persuade me that it ain't coming. If something doesn't get better, it ....

That Time in Kurdistan

That time in Kurdistan, the snow came falling in relentless thick flakes for days, and blanketed everywhere so deep they couldn't go on patrol, and had to stay put in their commandeered hotel. The Iraqi guards stomped their feet on the frozen roof, and others tried to keep warm around a brazier next to a dingy-looking armoured personnel carrier in the grounds. The UN people had nothing much to do beyond sit in their rooms, drink their fill, reminisce, hatch miseries and attend the daily evening conference. Sometimes there were power outages, and Mackay's first touch with absent electricity brought him close to his mother's worst experience. He woke in the middle of the night – he always slept with the light on – and it was pitch black. He thought he was blind; he was wildly disorientated. He groped for his J-torch, not finding it quickly enough – blindness played with him. Terrorised. Wide eyes saw nothing but coffin darkness, then the weakish shine from his torch. It had taken him an age to recover, for his heartbeat to slow down, for the cold terror to leave his spine.

In the closet that the hotel became for the UN observers, Mackay noticed changes emerging among the different nationalities that made up their group. For instance, he noticed that the two Norwegians and the two Canadian officers had, since being snowed in, become friendlier towards each other, that the Senegalese, Zambian and Indonesian officers had bonded together too, as had the civilian Austrian field officer and the two Danish officers, who weren't really military men at all but dairy farmers and part-time reservists. The Irish military police stood apart. We're not part of any clique, Mackay thought, and he gathered that this was partly because they were police, but mostly because they were Irish and non-commissioned officers. The Poles, including the Commanding Officer, weren't part of any clique either, because they were communists and Poland belonged to the Warsaw Pact, while the Canadians and Norwegians were in NATO. They'd put themselves at a remove, and the others kept them there. As for the Iraqi liaison officers ... they were convinced that every westerner was a potential spy, and in addition to overseeing the ceasefire between Iraq and Iran, they were on a fact-finding mission – like a nosey person eyeing up the contents of his neighbour's house, taking inventory.

Mackay was a lone MP; his two colleagues had made it down south to Baghdad before the heavy snows arrived. He didn't miss them; they were older guys and sometimes drank too much, and the early starts and long-distance patrols to the front line and mountain posts didn't agree with them – last month, Fergus's jeep had gone over an anti-personnel mine that'd made ribbony chunks of the tyre along with his nerves, which weren't the best before the incident. Afterwards, he had gone quiet and sullen in himself. Only when sufficiently lubricated did he open up, and in this breaking of his silence he started to worry Mackay and Bull Nose, especially Bull Nose, with his fears about what might happen next, that the landmine was a premonition of sorts. Bull Nose's mother was psychic, and he spent a lot of time on the phone to her trying to persuade her to see into his future, but she said she couldn't tell him anything because the spirits wouldn't allow her to use her gift for herself and close family. So, according to Bull Nose, she knew stuff about him but refused to say. He got Fergus to ring her, and she told him to avoid heights and depths, which Mackay thought was 'pure shite', but which the lads believed made for perfect sense: heights had to do with the narrow mountain trails that had sheer drops to rivers and canyons – so far down that those looking at the jeep crash wouldn't hear the splash and splinter of impact – and the depths had to do with the trenches and hidden minefields. They said it was still okay to fly out to Cyprus on holiday – she didn't mean they were to avoid that sort of height. Mackay marvelled at the way people could work a slant.

Mackay was delighted inside and outwardly envious of the lads, as it wouldn't do to look happy to be waving them off. It was okay for them to be bubbling – they were getting out of Sulaymaniyah, away from the arduous long-range patrols, the hikes by mule to the ridge tops, the weaving between trenches where hundreds of men had been killed, the flattened villages whose occupants had been poisoned with gas, the long, lonely evenings playing cards, singing ballads, listening to the sentries suffering death by freezing on the roof above their rooms, listening to bullshit stories they had told each other for the umpteenth time, some taking on a new slant. The money was good though. God bless the Iraqi dinar, but give them USD anytime – it's the world's currency. Money can keep a man sane.

He was a sergeant, and they a pair of corporals who had no hope of attaining his rank; he was younger than them by about ten years, but his rank meant nothing here among the three of them – they were all the same. Bull Nose said so when he stated that they had to look out for each other up here – equal except when it came to taking responsibility for things. They handed him their leave requests to process, their payment queries, their reports to proofread, and often rewrite, and suchlike – for the moments of their particular need he became their sergeant. They suffered from 'Kurdistan belly' and blamed the food. As far as he was concerned they had been downing too much 'Frieda' beer, an Iraqi beverage in a brown bottle with a seabed of sediment, but he said nothing, because saying nothing probably staved off an outbreak of discord and disenchantment. The milieu was almost that of a prison, its bars made of snowflakes, in which inconsequential issues were put under a magnifying glass and developed into matters of significant importance. Men often searched for slights where none existed, but often, somehow, they managed to produce a miracle and find one, maybe several, and these infected the atmosphere, created bad blood, and for some reason, even long after things had seemingly being patched up between people, that bad blood returned every now and then to stain the air.

On his way to see Mrankowski, who had summoned him, he wondered what the Polish CO wanted. They hadn't spoken very much to each other in their time here. His room was on the second floor. Mrankowski was built like a down and out sumo wrestler. He had lips that were shaped as though he were about to kiss. He hadn't endeared himself to the other officers when he gave an order that they were not, under any circumstances, to take photographs or use a video camera, and a day after this edict he himself was out and about like Cecil DeMille, filming away to his heart's eye – it was the rumblings at the daily conference. On the last occasion Mrankowski spoke with him, it was to say that he did not want the military police to beat up his UNMOs. *Do the MPs hammer their officers in Poland?* Mackay had thought. He said, 'Yes, Sir, of course we won't.' Later on he wondered if Bull Nose had thumped the Senegalese officer, Toure, for clicking his fingers at him to bring a typewriter from one office to another. Bull Nose could turn fiery in an instant. During a power cut, one of the many they experienced, the officer had got a bang to his nose that left it bleeding and swollen. It figured, of course, but there was no proof. No *eye*witnesses. Toure didn't click his fingers any more.

He knocked on the bedroom door, and was told to enter. Inside, the CO was sitting in a black leather chair too small for him, behind a desk. There was a large Polish flag on the wall behind him, flanked by two smaller ones. He preferred to work in his spare bedroom and not in an office on the top floor, which the Austrian field officer, Thom, had furnished for him. He didn't like, Mackay supposed, to be surrounded by NATO officers.

'Sit down, Sergeant,' he said.

The officer had on his light grey uniform. There was a red flash with two white eagles on his upper arm. An inch of fat hung over his shirt collar.

'It is nearly Christmas,' he said.

Mackay nodded in agreement. It was. 'So?'

'And I want to have a party … it is good for the spirit, for this sector. I want you to organise this with Thom.'

Mackay noticed Thom for the first time. He was standing at the window, looking out at the snow falling. He had this sort of superior attitude, which kind of peeled away at Mackay's brain.

'Okay, Sir.'

'You see, Sergeant,' Thom said, moving from the window to the side of the officer's desk, 'we Middle East European countries eat Christmas dinner on the eve of Christmas, so you don't need to count in myself, or the Danes ...'.

'Denmark has moved, has it?' Mackay said.

'Karl and Harry are personal friends.'

'What about Henry? Isn't Hungary stuck in the middle of Europe?'

Thom looked at Mrankowski, who said, 'So, Thom will organise the supplies, the cook, and you will invite the Iraqi officers – especially Major Razak – and make sure they are served well, yes?'

'Of course, Sir ... will you be attending the Christmas Day dinner?'

'Yes, certainly ... it will be an official duty.' He smiled and then added, 'I will not let my hair down like with Thom.'

Thom said, 'I have a Christmas tree for you.'

'For my room?' Mackay said, being deliberately obtuse.

'The ballroom ... we have the use of this for the dinner.' He moved right next to the CO's shoulder and said, 'Now, about Devine ...'.

Bull Nose.

'Corporal Devine,' Mackay said.

'Yes. He owes sixty-seven dollars for international phone calls.'

'Why are you telling me this?'

The CO and Thom glanced at each other.

'Because,' the CO said, 'he said that we were to refer the matter to you.'

Thom said, 'I understood … understand that you are to pay for it.'

'No. That's a personal issue.'

'He is your countryman,' Thom said.

'I'm not paying his fucking bills,' Mackay said. 'Take that matter up with the Irish admin officer in Baghdad.'

'But …'.

'There are no buts … "but" isn't happening. Do I look like I came down with the last fall of snow, Thom? What the hell is your problem?'

The CO frowned, his eyebrows joined, and Mackay thought for a moment that he was going to come down hard on him, but before he could speak, Mackay stood, saluted and said, 'Is that all, Sir?'

Thom clearly thought it wasn't, and said that the bill had to be paid. The CO did a fluttery wave with his four fingers and said he would speak with Corporal Devine when he returned from leave. Meanwhile, the bill would be paid from petty cash.

The UNMO rooms were swept clean every day by a young Kurdish woman in baggy pants who, on her hunkers, brought a hard brush to the wine-coloured carpet. She also changed the bed linen daily under the watchful eye of her father, or maybe her grandfather.

Mackay wasn't sure, and couldn't ask because the pair didn't have a word of English between them.

He had thought of asking the old man in sign language, but thought maybe it was best not to go there: he could be her husband. They were in his room now, cleaning – he badly needed to use the loo, and he was glad to see they were almost finished. The loo had a portable frame toilet over the Arabic toilet, the hole in the tray, as the Canadians thought that squatting to crap was an insult to their dignity. Bull Nose said it was because their aim was bad. Mackay saw sense in that, and said that their frontier ancestors would be mortified at how sanitised their descendants had become.

After they'd gone, he showered and shaved and tried to formulate a plan for Christmas. He would delegate responsibility, of course, having learned how to do that from officers, who would do nothing for themselves if they could get away with it, much like his Auntie Mary, who used a walking stick to get around though she didn't need to; she had better legs than a Gold Cup-winning steeplechaser. The thing was this, though: he didn't want the day to go awry, to give the other nationalities reason to complain – he wanted to show that the Irish were capable of organising an event better than any German could. There was that, but something else, too: he hated Christmas. Hadn't always but did now. Paradoxically, he was hoping that the preparations for it would help him to forget certain stuff.

Henry the Hungarian had offered to prepare Hungarian goulash for starters. Mackay thought he would take up his offer, and also while in the kitchen Henry could keep an eye on Muhammad, the Egyptian cook who was about as near to being a cook as a camel was near to being a horse.

The tree arrived. It was the skinniest and most bare-leafed tree Mackay had ever seen – like the ones that people back home dipped into the skip after Little Christmas. He rigged it up in a small corner of the ballroom, facing a U of sofas and armchairs, and around these he placed three electric-radiator-style heaters, because it was unbearably cold. The ballroom had panoramic windows that looked out to the mountains and the city – when the lights were out it was as though the whole world had been plunged into darkness. There were long seconds of pure darkness, and into this came a flash of torchlight, a scrambling to light candles, to take the bluntness of the darkness away, to encourage light to grow. Mackay didn't like these sudden and unexpected plunges into sightlessness. He detested and feared these occasions; there was the blindness – his mother some years back, when he was just a boy, had gone to bed perfectly healthy and woke up blind, and her terror, her screams, had touched a nerve in his soul. It was the helplessness of that morning he hated most, the standing by, the doing nothing because there was nothing he could do. Being away from home for Christmas, he thought, doesn't mean you leave everything behind.

Henry was getting carried away with himself. He used sewing thread to tie gold-wrapped sweets to the ends of the branches, and he bubbled over with enthusiasm, moving the chairs here and there a fraction, mentioning that a rubber plant would look well, straightening a straight tree. He loved Christmas. Mackay got to thinking he might do for the angel on top of the spruce, but then reproached himself. Still, he could see why Thom had crossed him off his list – the evening dinner was his show, and Henry would take over without even meaning to – but Mackay thought it best to have someone like him on board: his energy might be infectious. Besides, he hadn't had much luck enlisting some of the others. Kachepele was in his room layered up in combat jackets and blankets, sitting on a chair surrounded by heaters, like these were some symbol to ward off the devil. His teeth chattered and he shook all over.

Other officers like the Indonesian and Malaysian were Muslims, and they smiled through their lack of interest in the whole Christmas affair. Later, Mackay pulled apart a box of crackers and removed the small plastic toys and inserted in their place small plastic crucifixes, and gave them to the pair when they were doing whatever they were at in the Malaysian's room. Mackay had his doubts about them, and considered asking Henry if he thought they were bent. Only he wouldn't use the word 'bent'; instead he would say 'lovers' in case Henry was bent and took offence. Mackay didn't try to enlist the help of the Canadians or the Norwegians, because it was these he wanted to prove himself to – the other Polish officer, the engineer, he wouldn't involve either, as they had fallen out a while back after he asked Mackay, 'How are things in Londonderry?' to which Mackay's response had been, 'The same as in Russia Poland.' That spat could have come to blows were it not for Thom, who at that precise moment got a very sharp pain in his chest, which went away in seconds.

In the kitchen on Christmas morning, Henry started preparing the goulash, Muhammad had someone peeling the potatoes, and several turkeys were steaming away inside the ovens. Mackay, meanwhile, arranged the tables alone; he put clean white sleets on the tables, glass candleholders, placemats, cutlery, glasses – later on he briefed the three waiters through an Iraqi liaison officer, whom Mackay liked because he hadn't refused the offer of a hot whiskey, and nor had he insisted on showing him photographs of his three wives and loads of kids like some of his colleagues had done. He thought it odd that they'd all married women younger than their first wife. Was that a law? He'd called home, too, speaking with his wife and his boys, his mother, which had saddened him into having another hot whiskey. And then another. There he stopped, because he knew when to – and this evening was special. A dodgy starter, a glorious meal, Irish whiskies with Christmas pudding. Flames dancing on the puddings. He didn't rate the starter, but it would be okay, and besides, it was a Hungarian dish prepared by a Hungarian – what else could you expect? Irish stew?

Almost time. Evening was in. It was dark. People had been seated, even those who didn't want to be there, wearing their Christmas cracker crucifixes around their neck, smiling, which convinced Mackay that they just had to be Buddhists. Kachepele was in his room, the heaters moved in closer to him. He had never seen snow before he arrived here – it had been a brief love affair for him, turned cold quickly, as it were. Thom, who'd said to cross him off the list, now sat beside the CO, sharing a joke. The goulash was hot, if bland. Toure was back to clicking his fingers again, doing it to the waiters, who didn't seem to take any offence. Then, neither had Bull Nose.

Mackay thought that things were going well. The starters, most of them full, hardly touched, were being cleared from the tables. People were anxious for the turkey and ham dinner. And the fiery liquid toast to health, prosperity and happiness.

The power went. Mackay's heart and eyes froze solid. A coldness stole into the darkness, a darkness that should not be present. The candles. He had forgotten to light them, and now people were bringing their lighters and matches to the wicks. He heard the striking of matches, the clicking of lighters, smelt the stink of sulphur – teardrop flames began to pulse against the darkness. There were a few muted conversations and some ripples of nervous laughter. No one was ever truly comfortable with blackness. But Mackay heard none of the chatter – he was thinking back to a Christmas morning when Santa had brought a complete and utter and lasting blindness to his mother. And how he had, even as a teenager and adult, not fully connected with nor tried to understand her trauma … all changed since his arrival in Kurdistan. He had told her this today.

House of Dara

So the old man left me the run-down hole in Connemara and a few euros in the bank. He was 69 when he died. I hadn't seen him in twenty-five years. They spread his ashes at sea. It was news that went down well with my lithium. The last time I saw him he said he never wanted to see me again. He lived by his word. Insisted I had a distorted mind, like my mother. I didn't like him. Neither did Huey, the Begging Buddha.

The cottage is in the wilderness, close to the Atlantic. It has a green corrugated roof, two bedrooms and whitewashed walls. The fields around the cottage grow rocks; no matter how many times I harvest them they keep growing back. There's an outdoor toilet and two stone sheds filled with turf. Another is home for the stinking creatures he'd also bequeathed.

Two fields beyond mine, the land begins to taper in a coat of rushes and sand dunes to the edge of the sea. On blustery days you can see the waves dance high, tips of shoes white, froth of spent energy on the wet shore – seaweed thrown there too, like scarves of the lost at sea, calling out to the souls of the land. My father calling, I sometimes think.

The broken-down racehorse shares a shed with a grey donkey, and maybe they share stories too and swap questions. Like how come we ended up with a bloke with buttons in his earlobes, a ponytail, a hash-smoking fucked up degenerate, who's 48 but looks older.

Huey Doolin and I went to school together, and we hung around a lot for a couple of years. Then we got caught up in the drift of places we had to get to, and I didn't see him until last month. By Christ, I thought. *There goes a changed man.* He'd lost a ton of weight. His skin was clear; he used to wear serious acne. It took him a while to recognise me, for my face to register, but when he did he hugged the fucking breath out of me and said things like, 'Where the hell have you been, Brother?' and 'Man, I was only praying for you last night.' The Huey I'd left behind would have taken a swim in a sewer before saying a prayer. We had a right old natter, and he said he was glad to see my head was back in order.

Anyhow, this morning I pick him up at the bus station. He brought along two friends. I knew they were coming because he called me last night to say so. I was a little late in arriving, and apologised, saying I had to stop off at Tesco to buy some groceries. One of them has a face, and that's why I thought to apologise. But it isn't that he's pissed at me for being late – his expression is natural. Born with it, maybe. I check him often enough in the rear-view mirror to know this for sure.

Huey sits up front. We eat up some miles before he says anything. Then he remembers to introduce Joey – the fed-up-looking one, and Tiger with the mid-length red hair. Feminine looking, and I wonder if perhaps he should be called 'Tigress'. It's something I would have said to Huey years ago – and for sure we would have cracked up. But Huey has changed, so I mind what I say – can we ever be soul friends again? I mean, you shouldn't have to watch your words in front of a pal; at the very least you shouldn't have to be overly cautious. He's turned spiritual, and has told me a couple of times that he worries for me. I doubt his sincerity. When I was in dock, he neither paid me a visit nor answered my letters. I think he's hoping that the medication fogs my memory.

The car radio is on an Irish language channel – I'm never really bothered what station is playing. I just like to fill the car with some noise, and it doesn't have to be loud. Once the silence is smothered, I'm happy. Huey looks over his shoulder and asks Tiger (his surname is O'Toole, and I think to say Tot, but …) for the CD. After he gets it, he asks me if it's okay to play, and I say, 'Yeah, but the player isn't working.'

I'm driving a beat-up car that failed its NCT, and all week I'd been trying to figure out ways to make some money to have the repair work done. Sure I have no rent to pay, but I've got to eat, and I have a horse and a donkey to care for too. My euros are running low. The old man left me in a situation – he'd given me things worth little, but yet worth something. Coolderry is sooooo fucking remote.

Huey says nothing about the player. He hands the CD back to Tiger and asks Joey if he's okay. Joey doesn't answer. His surname is Reagan, and he has deep-set eyes and narrow shoulders. He's the youngest in the Ford Fiesta, and he looks to be the most troubled. More than pissed off, I begin to suspect.

Just as we arrive at Teach Dara (House of Dara – my father's name), it begins to drizzle. Tiger asks if he can watch TV: *Survivor*. I've no set. I used to, but binned it one night when the reception was pretty poor and there was a soccer match on I had been dying all day to see. I get easily frustrated when things don't pan out right for me.

'Nice,' Huey says, stepping inside.

But he means basic, small. Quaint too, perhaps.

Tiger says, 'Where's the loo?'

After I tell him, he says, 'Are you serious?'

'Very fucking … you know … poor … sort of,' Joey says.

Huey says, 'Do your business, lads, we're starting after we have a cuppa.'

'Starting what, Huey?' I say.

'I'll give you a hand in with the groceries and explain it to you.'

The lads hurry in to say there's a horse and a donkey out in the field, and I say they're mine. I can be possessive about things that I don't really want. The three of them go outside, and I stare through the small window above the sink – they're fussing over the animals, feeding them handfuls of grass, petting their ears, flanks. Cracking jokes. They even delay when the rain turns hard. Joining them, I lead the animals into their shed, give them some hay and nuts. Joey asks me for their names, and I make them up on the spot, 'Valiant and Neddy.' Well, you can't very well call your pets Bastard and Fucker in front of guests.

'You're blessed to be living here,' Huey says, leading the way into the cottage.

'A beautiful smell of the sea … it's so … so invigorating,' Tiger says. He touches his cold sore with his tongue.

Joey grunts. I'm not sure if it's in agreement.

At the table, I ask if anyone wants a beer or ham sandwiches. They look at each other, and then Huey says, 'We're not here to drink alcohol, Robbie. And we're vegetarian. I gave up eating meat years ago.'

'Oh,' I say.

'Sit,' Huey says, smiling broadly like a Buddha.

I really want a beer to kill the strange feel of strangers, but Huey says, 'Come on, don't be shy.'

I've done a little of what he's doing now – but I didn't take to it back in the day, and I'm quite sure it's not for me. All that sort of shite does is to summon ghosts.

Huey blesses me, my home, and asks the spirits to increase my bounty, to protect this space, to cleanse it of negativity. Then he begins to say, 'Om …'.

This is what they … we … do. Chant. I could never imagine myself sitting in my father's home, holding hands with lads around a table, saying mantras.

In the well of silence Huey leads us into, inviting us to contemplate, to invite our spirit guides to contact us, I fall asleep. They think I deliberately snored. Huey wags his forefinger in my direction, 'You should have respect. I am trying to help you here.'

Tiger says, 'Yes, we all are, everyone has respect for Master Huey.'

Joey grunts.

Master Huey? I think.

'I think it's time we were leaving,' Huey says.

I can't read his face. It's in neutral.

'Ring for a taxi,' Huey says to Tiger.

'No, wait here … I'll drop youse in. But I genuinely fell asleep. Seriously like …'.

Huey says, 'You know, Robbie, we came here to bless your home, but also to see if it were a suitable place for a retreat. We have some money to invest in a property.'

'This is soooo ideal, Huey,' I say, coming wide awake, 'the sea is nearby. And …'.

Tiger says, 'It's the energy.'

'What's wrong with it?'

Huey says, 'It and you … there's a very grey energy here.'

'Is that bad? 'Cos I like grey. It's my favourite colour.'

Huey says, 'Now you're being flippant.'

'No. I like grey, really. Remember, Huey. I used to live in a grey tracksuits … gee, all of the time.'

Joey says, 'How much?'

'What?' I say, partly because I hadn't expected to him say anything apart from emit a grunt.

'To buy you out,' Tiger clarifies.

'I need to get it valued before …'.

'Fifty thousand,' Huey says, quick off the mark. He is a man who'd sussed his price well in advance of making an offer.

'There are five acres,' I say, 'I don't know the value of …'.

I get to thinking that fifty thousand isn't much. Not when I would have to find a new gaff. I feel a wire in my temple getting hot.

'About what it's worth,' Huey says.

It's like my car, I think; worth more to me in real physical terms than monetary. I dwell on how much it would cost me to replace my Ford. The house is worth more than Huey has offered, but I have no idea by how much.

'We'll take care of the animals, too,' Joey says.

That does entice, but only a little.

'No,' I say, flatly. It kills me to kill the offer.

Huey spreads out his hands and says, 'So be it.'

They take up the offer of a ride home. Sometimes the rain is wind-flung against the car. I try to jump-start the conversation, but none is interested in making talk. Least of all Huey – when a talker stops talking to you, you know you've lost a friend. He may look better than he did all those years ago, he may sound more confident, have more money, a belief system, but I say to him, as I pull in outside McDonald's, 'Huey, one thing about you hasn't changed: you still sulk when you don't get your own way.'

He looks long and hard at me, and says, 'Bless you my brother … and light and happiness upon your soul.'

Our meeting up is proof that old friendships, very often like old romances, fail to rekindle and aren't worth the effort. Strange things are happening in the cottage. Noises, creaks, like a bone snapping. This morning before my eyes a grey stain appeared on the walls: a handprint. I legged it out of there.

I am too afraid to go back in. I'm sitting in the Ford, biting my fingernails, not a kick in its engine. Occasionally, a shadow crosses by the kitchen window. Now and then it stops. It's as though someone is leaning forward to peer out through the glass. I feel as though the inside of my head is blazing. The same old stuff always happens when a situation gets out of hand.

Later, when strangers approach, they ask why I'm throwing rocks at the cottage and breaking the windows. They can't see my ocean-drenched Father.

'It's a donkey,' a woman says, who'd gone in to check, who I never expected to see again.

The world just won't stop playing its fucking tricks on me.

The Red Caboose Motel

I just sit, listen to the silence, watch the candle burn away in the quartz candleholder in front of my father's photograph.

There are places, situations and people that I can't wait to leave behind, and a grieving mother is one of them. An uneasiness grows within me that I cannot contain. Something else pulls at me to linger for a while longer, but my soul has already taken flight. The price for not staying is a dose of guilt. It occasionally clings. But mostly, when I break away, I feel like the root of a tree breaking surface to witness light.

And it's funny too that the black sheep of the family is now the one who does most for her; the physical things and the hardest part, the listening, the being there in the dead weight of deep silences, where no word lives or could ever survive.

The holiday had been my idea; I thought the prospect of visiting her grandchildren would give her something to look forward to, a daub of sun in her grey canvas. It does, but she also makes it sound like a pilgrimage by saying things like, 'This'll be my first time to the States without your father,' and 'We'll be over there for our wedding anniversary.' All that sort of stuff drains the energy from you.

Alan lives there, her son, my brother. More her son than my brother – there's a gap of fourteen years between us, and I suppose we didn't live under the same roof for anything longer than four to five years. He has done well for himself, especially for someone who looked like he had been going nowhere with his life. Dad sent him to the States when he was fifteen, when Alan was on the cusp of getting into all sorts of trouble. Mam had always been careful to say that it had been Dad's decision to let him go – she said this when I mentioned at the time that Alan was a little young to be leaving home. She said, 'Michael is over there.' Michael's one of our other brothers – he came back from the States a few years ago, and has been regretting it ever since.

Today, this morning, into the silence, Mam drops a bombshell: 'Monica asked me if it was okay for her to come along with us.'

Monica's is Mam's older sister. She lives in London, not far from the waxworks museum – she likes to tell people this in a quiet way, as though it is a boast of sorts. Mam didn't think it funny when I said she looked like she'd escaped from there. Monica has two bockety hips.

She is a widow; her husband killed himself. He hated the Irish, yet he married Monica. They'd hated each other for the latter part of their married lives. Last year she brought home some of his ashes and spread them on a racecourse. He hated horse racing, too. Gambling, he believed, was a disease thought up by the Irish.

'Okay,' I say, though why I said that I don't know – of course it's okay. Why not? It'll be someone else to sit in with Mam's silences.

'I know youse don't see eye to eye, but I thought if she was along you and Alan might have more time to spend together …'.

Meaning that Monica hadn't invited herself along – Mam had done the inviting.

'You don't mind?' Mam says.

'No.'

The photograph of Dad under candlelight is of him sitting in a railway carriage. He loved trains. When he got his free travel pass he travelled all over the country – I doubt if there's a track and its station that he didn't get to know. His father had loved trains too; he was a porter. Once, as a tip, he was given the keys to a Ford Cortina. This man said he and his family were emigrating to Australia, and he wanted to leave with a grand gesture. It made the newspaper – Grandad smiling. He wore his peaked porter's cap, his navy British Rail uniform, dangling the keys to a decent car. I resemble him – the hooded eyes, the chunky build, the ears and the long nose. When I look at old family albums, I sometimes come away with the feeling that I'm a living ghost.

So I book the holidays and, at Aunt Monica's insistence, two wheelchair assists. My brother meets us at Boston airport. He looks fit and healthy. He says, smiling, looking at our aunt and our mother, 'Maybe I should have brought an ambulance instead of a people carrier.'

They'd travelled light, with almost empty suitcases: they intended to return home with the spoils of shopping: tortured credit cards and fleeced bank accounts, savings husbanded by husbands no longer present to guard against the dragon mall. I'd been the one tasked with bringing a veritable tuck shop in my suitcases for Alan's kids – they love Crunchie bars and Tayto crisps.

About a week into the holiday, Alan says he's booked the midweek break for the Red Caboose Motel in P.A. in Amish country, near to where the *Witness* movie was made. As it turns out, a day before the trip Mam's stomach comes at her and she says she isn't up to the journey. By now, Monica had been wearing at her nerves, and she needed a break from her. Alan's wife puts on a brave face – she'd been looking forward to getting the two old dears out of her hair for a couple of days. Probably me too. But I'd made myself useful, and hadn't hung around the table waiting for my breakfast to be served or looking to be brought somewhere, like the consignment stores. Though the two women have money, they are war babies, and had grown up knowing how to resurrect clothes and give them life. Cheap quality is what matters to them, not lasting. No matter how often they're taught the lesson that cheap doesn't last, they never learn.

'You'll like it there,' Mam says to me, 'your Dad loved it … we were there four or five times.'

Alan looks at me, doesn't say what he's thinking – it's the spot where Dad took ill and died. This is the real reason Mam's stomach had come at her – she prefers to be at and near the places where Dad and she had been together, and not the last time and final place.

Shortly after midday, we pull in at the Red Caboose Motel. The sun is out; it has weak warmth, like a phony smile. We hadn't spoken much on the journey from New Haven. When we did have something to say, it was usually to give out about Monica in the back, who had got doddery in her old age. She had a nephew of mine parked either side. It wasn't much fun for the kids as she had taken to farting in front of people and apologising for it, but never moving away or thinking to open a window. She called it passing wind, said with a tiny smile as though to say wasn't she the bold thing.

Dad used to call her 'The Lady'. He didn't like her very much; he thought her a snob. She couldn't hear us talking about her over the noise of the air conditioning. Besides, after ten days of putting up with her, we weren't really bothered if she did happen to overhear.

She wanted to see Amish country, and Alan hadn't got it in him to turn her down, even though he thought the five-hour car journey might be too long for her to fully enjoy.

Our plan is to book her into a caboose and leave her to babysit the kids while we sip at beers and talk about Dad and how he'd loved it here. It's my first time to visit, and I could tell in an instant why he had fallen for the place. He was an open-air man, had worked on the land all his life. Because I'm much older than Alan, I can remember stuff about him that Alan couldn't have known because of the time gap, and that was why he insisted on bringing me here, to see the place where Dad had passed away, to swap memories. Because Dad was an easy sort of man to remember.

Alan goes to draw our keys from reception. About forty rail carriages, renovated sleeping cars, are laid out in four or five rows. Old railway companies show the ghosts of their former existence on their timber-framed sides, with names like Alaska, Pennsylvania, Great Northern, Delaware and Hudson, Union Pacific, Union Line. All familiar-sounding names to Alan, as he'd emigrated to the States when he was 15, and had ended up working as a city cop.

The kids are beginning to get itchy feet just as Alan returns.

'What time are we eating?' Aunt Monica says above their voices, looking at the kids, like she's calling them to order, to get in line – the old come first. She has short, iron-grey hair, reddish cheeks, and grey eyes I doubt very much had ever cried with laughter.

'You're in number thirty-four,' Alan says, then telling his kids to bring Monica's bags to her caboose.

'I don't eat hamburgers,' she says quietly.

She wears red trousers that a prostitute would think too bright, and a white blouse the sun shies away from; strings of cheap jewellery dangle from her neck. She's a baggy throat full of unsaid words.

'Am I sleeping on my own?' she says.

'In thirty-four,' Alan repeats, and then says, 'the boys are in thirty and we're in forty-one … yeah … over there.'

She says, 'I'd love a cup of tea.'

Later, Alan says she's a passive-aggressive person in the way that she goes to lift her bag, catches your eye, and holds it until you feel obliged to take it for her. He'd probably studied stuff like that in the cop academy. All I really know of her is that she has a sense of entitlement, and that her wheelchair ruse is a means for her to skip the line at the airport and at customs.

We put our bags in the caboose and go outside. Close to the front of the motel runs a railway line that a steam train passes by a few times daily, and under a veranda an Amish man with a straw hat has a black buggy for hire and two beautiful chestnut horses to pull it. Beyond the tracks there are rows of pumpkins and tobacco crops. To the other side of our wine-coloured caboose is a granary tower, a purple-painted house, and cornfields that make me think of the *Children of the Corn* movie.

'You don't remember this,' I say, 'but when I was a kid the Dad had a train set that he used to keep on a large double bed. It had green baize and bridges and tunnels with miniature trees, and a train station, and the carriages had these little figures inside sitting at tables with lamps.' I stop talking and we look at each other, and I can see the imagining going on in his blue eyes. Then I continue, 'He had to dismantle it when our brothers came along. He put the boxes in the loft, but they went missing from there. We think an uncle stole it. It was a Hornby set, expensive ... I think Dad got it from his own father.'

Jack, one of the kids, runs over to say Aunt Monica wants to know when's dinner, and why there isn't a kettle in her caboose to make tea. Plus, the boy says, she's left her pills in the car. Alan's kids are bright, typical American lookers, all blond and blue-eyed and bushy-tailed. I try to imagine how they would have looked if they'd grown up back home in less than kind financial circumstances, because there's nothing surer that's how it would have been for them if their Dad hadn't emigrated. He was so young to do that, though – far too young – but he was beginning to get into trouble, like I said, teetering on the brink of stepping outside the law. Ironic, given his present-day police role.

He tells his son we'll be eating at five, in two hours, and to tell his aunt he would bring her down a pot of tea and biscuits in a few minutes.

'She'd put years on you,' he says, watching Jack climb the steps to her caboose. Turning to me, he says, 'She's a liability. Did you hear her at dinner last night?'

'Farting?'

'Not farting, no … she said she was lucky to have diabetes or they wouldn't have operated on her foot for free.'

'She said that? I missed it.'

'Yeah, she said it.'

'She keeps repeating things, you know … and to her it's like you're hearing it all for the first time; every gory, boring detail … I think it's worrying.'

He nods, and says in a wondering whisper, 'It is.'

He speaks with an American accent. Then, Alan has lived much longer here than he had at home. His kids love their Irish heritage. In particular, they love Tayto crisps and books about Irish history: the Celts, the Vikings, anything with swords and death and black plagues.

After dinner, he shows me where Dad had dropped dead: next to the railway line, where he had been with his grandkids putting coins on the line for the trains to crush. I ease a bunch of wild blue flowers beside the track and say a silent prayer. A loud prayer from me would be a bit like hearing an ass braying 'Amazing Grace'.

That night, I drink a couple of beers. Alan admits that he doesn't do alcohol any more because it had become a problem for him; he drinks non-alcoholic beer to fool himself. He is four years into fooling himself, and I congratulate him and feel a little guilty for drinking the real stuff. He has the TV on. We can't see each other as the beds are back to back, with a dividing partition that's wallpapered with a 1950s pattern of drab vertical brown lines on magnolia.

He says, 'The dad used to get up every morning and go for a long walk. We stayed a week here at a time, and he loved it, and talked about how he wished he'd come out here years ago and hadn't listened to Mam, because, Davy, you know he had a job offer. He'd wanted to emigrate.'

We talk as night crosses into morning, mostly about Dad. He fills me in on bits of his own life too, the general shape to it, but mostly it's about the things he did with Dad when he'd visited here: bonding, father and son stuff. Alan had been back to Ireland a couple of times, and he'd worn his cop uniform at Dad's funeral, primarily to show his old teachers that he hadn't gone through life as the waster that they said he would be. But he also wore the navy uniform with pride. The uniform suited him. But I'm aware that, although we are brothers, we have been strangers thus far for nearly all of our lives – and I'm not sure if flesh and blood is the bonding connection people say it is.

In the morning, I'm first up and about. The air hits me – a beautiful aroma of pumpkins tinged with tobacco.

In the fields, two Amish men in dirty straw hats load laths of tobacco on to a cart. A haze in the distance is the last visible breath of the night. They work for about twenty minutes, until they've loaded the cart, and then rein the horses around to face into the road. The cart rolls to a large barn, where they begin to unload the tobacco. I decide to breakfast in the motel's dining car, and notice Monica walking toward the cornfields, but looking like she doesn't know where she's heading. Part of me wants to ignore what I'm seeing, but only that small part of badness in some or all of us – the bit about ourselves we don't like and spend a lifetime trying to fix.

I catch up with her just as she steps into the corn.

'Monica?'

She doesn't answer.

I take her elbow gently, and turn her from the first tall row of stalks. Her eyes are as hazy as the hills. She doesn't recognise me.

'Monica, come on.'

Alan is up within the hour. Monica is her old self by then. She says she sometimes goes for a walk in her sleep. I don't correct her. Neither does Alan. He just sighs hard upon understanding why she'd hinted at one of his boys to stay with her.

'I'd like some breakfast,' she says with surprising and demanding clarity.

The woman is hard work.

'Of course,' I say.

Alan nods. He has an idea now where all this is going for her.

At that moment, a steam train approaches, passing the spot where my father had drawn his last breath. There is the clickety-clack, the ringing of a bell, the blowing of a whistle, and yet, curiously, there is a silence deep within the noise – the sense of a soul at rest amid the clamour. When the train has lost itself in the distance, Alan says, as we turn to look at Monica returning to her caboose, 'She won't have any memory of this in a while.'

He puts his hand on my shoulder and squeezes hard.

I don't have any words in me. I get a tight feeling in my throat. So tight it hurts. But there is probably nothing to say. It is simply a frame of time in which a brother becomes a brother and an aunt begins to lose her way, and my father says goodbye in the faint whistle of a distancing train.

Mingi Street

The one-sided street meanders snake-like, fracturing in three places: at its northern tail, beyond the French Wadi-Gate – a checkpoint by a dried riverbed – where the road slims to meet a tight bend before the port; midway, when the road shoots up a long, broad and twisting way to the hilltop village; and at its southern outreaches, where the bulk of the shops squat, leaving behind the disused whorehouse, a half-built hotel, and a dump smoking its own filth.

The pock-marked asphalt yawns to Roshaniqra Border Crossing, where the Star of David flies above custom offices, pulled taut by sea winds that sweep into the caves underneath, and turning about make their way up the chalk cliffs, past bent railway tracks, through the electric fences, finding nowhere to go, and no choice but to slip out to sea, rippling the waters, before returning on the backs of the waves, newly born.

Khalil Abbas awakened to the call of the muezzin crier, and turned over on the mattress in the back room of his shop, not wanting to disturb the phlegm that slept quietly on his lungs, and yet needing to answer his throat's whisper for thick coffee and his bladder's cry for relief.

The wind howled. It moved along the tin roof, pulling at its edges, pushed against the door, came trembling through a fissure in the window, stirring curtains he never drew against the night. He landed here twenty years ago, fleeing Beirut, cleaning out his electrical shop and heading south with his family, staying first in Sidon, near the crusader sea castle. Finding they weren't safe from Israeli warplanes, or the different militias who fought like jackals over bones, he moved on, skipping Tyre, and crossing over the unofficial border the Israelis manufactured to keep their northern territories safe from guerrilla attack. Building a home-cum-shop of tin and wood to join others sprouting up to service the needs of UN troops who lived beyond the giant T-walls paralleling the length of the fledgling shanty town.

A dissonance of foreign voices: Irish, Dutch, Fijian, Polish, Nepalese, Finns, Ghanaians and Norwegians, the street alive at night, the restaurants full, and songs and arguments fading as curfew fell at eleven, and the soldiers melted away behind the walls, and the gates shut with a clanging noise that sounded Khalil's own bedtime.

He got up, went outside, and pissed against the rippled walls of his house, the stench rising to meet his nostrils a solution of medications intended to break up the phlegm and assist with his breathing.

The medications give him hope. If he had no hope, he would die. A lack of hope would kill him more quickly than the disease he knew thrived within, breaking him down, pulling his flesh inwards, giving him a cadaverous look, his complexion an unhealthy, yellowish pallor, and marking his eyes with black rings that saluted his illness for others to take in and look away.

The heart attack three years ago started it, the slide. The searing pain, the time spent in Marajoun Hospital, thinking how quickly a few days can change a man's life. An energetic, bustling trader reduced to a mass of quivering fear and a dread of getting another attack, more alive to his own mortality than ever before, rubbing his father's prayer beads between pads of thumb and forefinger till the beads had a shine that outshone his father's.

He dipped his hands in a basin with its rim broken in places, and took in the cracked mirror, the lines about his eyes like curtain pleats, and the yellow in the whites of them signifying the poison that swam through his veins. He'd hooded eyes and a beak of a nose he touched without thought.

He shaved slowly, dipping the blade in water after each swipe, removing the soap and dabs of foam flecked with grey stubble. The wind had not let up, and he knew of old that it would blow for another day at least. Early spring, and he still felt the chill of a bad winter in his bones.

He made coffee in a small pot, and poured it thick and brown, rich in coffee grits, into a miniature cup.

He nibbled at pitta bread because he felt hungry, but the hunger gave way to the nausea he expected but had prayed against happening – his appetite played tricks all the time, but he tried to eat, because he knew one needed to eat in order to live, one went with the other. If his body rejected food, it was telling him something, something he didn't want to hear and tried to shut out, but his body screamed. It screamed at him in the smell of his piss, the belly cramps, the invisible hunger, the bile it threw into his mouth, which left a sour taste to suppress the one of mouthwash.

Inshallah, he would say, to his customers and to himself. What else could he do? Nothing but wait, and enjoy as much as possible whatever time he had left. Basima would be here tomorrow, back from Beirut, from seeing a specialist about the angry veins in the back of her legs, from seeing Adiva, their only daughter, married to a pig gendarme, who whistled at traffic from under his mushroom shelter, and later returned home to beat his wife. She would also carry the results of his latest tests, tests he'd reluctantly undergone, tests by specialists in a private hospital who were so skilful they could add ten years to a man's life, or so Basima believed, and tried to have him believe, too.

Opening up his shop, he went out and stood under the awning, taking in the cancerous-looking morning, a yellow air of dust and wind. He squinted, holding a face towel to the small cyst by his right eye, and walked with a slow, emphatic landing of feet to the shop next door, where he bought bread, exchanged a small pleasantry with Fatima, the mukhtar's wife, neither of whom he liked for the way they forced their son into joining the Israeli militia, and for how they revealed no guilt over his death, the way the boy turned his own rifle on himself.

He saw them sometimes, making their way into the UN Camp, to the cemetery near the sea, burning mint leaves for their boy, who should be alive with his life in front of him, a wife and children. They have cheated themselves of so much, and their son of his life, and know but deny it. Fatima talks of bully NCOs in the militia, and of sights her boy saw in the compounds, when they came under attack from the Hizbollah; *it is true when people say someone was blown out of his boots*, and that *human flesh in a bombed car smelt like pork being roasted*. It is easy for Fatima to say these things, because surely such scenes would drive anyone mad – look what happened to her son.

Back in the shop, he pumped the heater with kerosene and set a lighter to its wick. Khalil heard the globe's wires creak as they reddened. Basima preferred to fill the small brazier with some barbecue coals and sit around it at night with him, warming pieces of pitta bread for milliseconds on the smoking coals before eating them.

Usually, she stayed in their house on the hill, and lately she was trying to persuade him to do likewise.

'You are sixty-three, Khalil, not a young man any more.'
She spoke with a dialect he loved, one from the Bekaa
Valley, and Baalbeck, the town she came from, with its
acres of Roman ruins lying under a view of the snowy
Lebanon mountains, where the scent of the last cedars
mingled with swatches of mountain flowers.

She was bending with the years, her features thickly
lined about the eyes and lips. She didn't like living on
Mingi Street, and the house he built had, at the time,
unburdened her of much. Basima hated the noise of
the Israeli half-tracks as they roared along the street,
the cars driven by young people who had little choice
of road to travel as they raced up and down the one
out front. She told him the shop wasn't doing the
business it used to, failing to realise that that wasn't
the reason he continued to keep the shop open. What
would he do with himself in the village? Sit out and
watch the dogs shade themselves from the sun, he
said, one evening, as they drank black sugary tea and
she started about him retiring.

No doubt the business had fallen away. It showed
in the boarded-up shacks that ran from his shop to the
UN gate manned by French soldiers. The soldiers spend
their money on gold, and on dining out. Mostly, they
travelled to Tyre or Beirut to shop. During the Civil War
it was different, travel was restricted, and they bought
in shops like his. The UN had cut the size of its force,
too, by as many as two thousand since its inception. It's
a lot of pockets for shopkeepers to lose.

He competed by offering credit terms and becoming extra friendly with the troops, talking at length with them, offering teas and colas with the knowledge that they would, at some point, check out his stock, and perhaps buy something. In the old days he did a lot of business with the Irish, but they bought little from him nowadays, knowing where to buy better much cheaper. Those he dealt with he could barter with, knowing at the end they would give in and buy from him, but the Ghanaians and Nepalese didn't know when to quit. They would haggle him beyond his profit margin, and he would beat his chest, shake his head and say, 'I cannot sell you this. For me no money. I buy from the man that price and I sell you this price ... you see what I make? Three dollars, no more, I swear to you the truth. You don't believe me, check my books, come check my books.' But they never did.

The Irish named the shanty town Mingi Street (Ming ee). A man called Dawson said it was a word the Irish learned in the Congo, meaning a cheap present of dubious quality, and the seller of such was known as a Mingi Man. Fake Lacoste, fake Levi's, fake just about everything. It was true, and there was no real problem with that; the problems started when the fake cost as much if not more than the genuine, and soldiers found out they'd been cheated. These days, reflected Khalil, like so much else in the world, it was hard to tell which was real and which wasn't, who lied and who didn't.

Dawson lost his smile when Khalil asked if he thought he was a poor-quality man. 'Isn't that what Mingi means? You've just told me. Believe me, my friend, I am not.' Then he smiled. He always smiled. You can lace poison with a smile to make it taste good.

He turned on the portable TV, but still his eyes wouldn't be drawn from the perspex windows, behind which he kept shelves of watches, chains, lighters, knives, small diversifications from his range of electrical goods. He considered covering them to protect them from the yellow dust, but decided not to bother, as the dust of time was on them anyway.

He felt the cold, and didn't like the wind, the way it spoke in howls, moans and whispers. An atavistic chill inched along his spine, filling the pit of his belly with an iciness, as if a freezer bag had burst in his gut. A deep cloud crossed his mind and sat there, raining on his thoughts.

In time, his house would be like the others, boarded up with thick planks, tumbleweed snagged against the door, the shelves empty, the smell of kerosene and charcoal long dissipated, the vapour of his breath no more. He would be in the cemetery by the sea, with mint leaves smoking over him, and tears moistening the scarlet anemones Basima would place in vases above his head.

He put on his jacket and a blue scarf Adiva bought him for his birthday, but he couldn't shake off the chill. Netanyahu was on TV, saying Israel would respond in due course to the Katyusha rocket attacks on Qiryat Shemona last night. He sighed, rubbed his eyes, drank some cola to moisten a dry tongue. Outside, the wind played up and down the street.

He knew them all on the street, their petty jealousies, the ones who had come, and gone, the ones who had died, and like him were dying. Ata the gay hairstylist ordered out of Sidon by the Hizbollah, who didn't take to his pink string vests and claret short shorts, Jesse the commando who sold booze to the messes and turned dollars into shekels and back again, Sammy the coffee man, Porno Joe, Willie Whitevan, Tom Cruise, one-armed Monsour the tailor, Chicken George, Pablo's Bar, Ali Strawballs, he knew them all, not by their true names but the ones accorded them by the UN troops. He had alliances with them all at the beginning, when each helped the other, at a time before they realised they were eating from the same cake, and small and large rivalries didn't exist. It all changed. One watched what the other got, and did. The more successful you became, the less popular you were among the other traders. He was always middle-of-the-road popular.

He closed shop early, and drew the drapes so no one passing would espy him through the shop windows. The yellow dust storm had lasted all day, and as night fell, and it fell quickly, he heard the distant rumble of thunder, and knew it was on the march, heading this way, from the sea, where once he'd seen Israeli patrol boats battered about by a mini tornado. There would be little sleep tonight.

Opening the back door, he spat outside into the night, on to a muddy patch lit up by flash lightning. He emptied his lungs of phlegm, knowing that before he lay on the bed his lungs would refill, and the spittoon by his side would not remain idle. He felt cold. He moved in the heater, and filled Basima's hot-water bottle. After taking his medication, he slipped under the duvets and lay on his back, looking at the red globe, the lightning when it flashed silvery on the concrete floor, listening to the tip tap of rain falling hard on the tin roof, the soft drip of water coming from a spot where it always leaked, landing in the basin, in which he put a towel to deaden the noise.

The storm lasted most of the night, and sleep didn't come till after the call to prayer spread from the minaret in the village, and the thunder had rolled across to distant hills and wadis. He slept then, and didn't waken until he heard the loud knock on the back door. He opened his eyes, bleary for moments in the morning light.

'Khalil?'

Basima. Her tone contained fear and a heightened premonition that something had happened.

'I'm coming,' he said, the words growling over the phlegm in his throat.

Opening the door, he stood aside to let her pass. He took in the scent of her perfume, the red-painted lips, the rouge on her cheeks – things she only wore on her visits to Beirut, or on some major shopping expedition.

'Such a time of it,' she said. 'The traffic in Beirut is terrible.'

He nodded, felt his stubble, wishing he had woken early and cleaned himself up. She spoke of the weather in Beirut, the cold, the wet and muddy streets, the buildings coming down, the ones going up, and of Adiva, who was at home in the village.

After she said this, she waited for his response.

'For a visit?' he said, the seeds of her words taking root.

'For longer, yes, much longer than a visit.'

He said nothing. He supposed that Adiva could help in the shop. He lit the stove, and put on a pot of water to make coffee. Basima warmed herself in front of the heater.

'Your legs?' he asked.

'I need an operation on the veins.'

'Adiva … that pig of hers?'

'Oh, he doesn't mind her staying. I told him she was needed to run the shop. He put a face on him, you know his face,' she lifted her nostrils with her thumb, 'but smiled when I said Adiva would be paid for her troubles.'

'Run the shop,' he said quietly.

Two birds with one stone. Her daughter away from a man who beat her, and a husband home to die. Basima was a clever woman. He nodded, turned his back to her, and stepped onto the shop floor. He killed the tears in his eyes with a blink.

Basima put her hand on his shoulder and he rested his on top, his palm pressing down on her ring. Her voice cooed in his ear, her words gentle, but telling, 'It's time.'

The Stand House

His cleaner, Iris, visits three times a week. She washes and irons his clothes. She is Nigerian, and seems a good soul. He hired her through an agency, and likes her for her hearty laugh. He pays her a little over the going rate, and is decent with a bonus at Christmas. Something is never spoken of between them, for it needs no mentioning: she is also his 'check-in' lady – he has a fear of dying and not being found for days. A bit like a man fearful of wakening up blind, who keeps a torch on his bedside locker. Neither matter, he supposes: being dead to the dead; a blind man having a torch within hand's reach.

He is less than a week out of hospital.

Next of kin … he had erupted in tears when a nurse had asked him that simple question for her admission form. The tear storm caught them both by surprise. He has no next of kin. No one for someone to tell someone else that he is in hospital or at the morgue. The chilling reply to her question formed in his head and spilled as tears. If himself, or close to it, he would have dredged a smile and said, 'No, no one, love.' Then he thought to mention his solicitor, and surrendered her name quietly, almost embarrassingly. Chirpily, the nurse said, 'See, everyone's got a next of kin.'

He no longer eats at home, preferring to dine at a little Greek restaurant down a back street that prepares a variety of vegetarian meals. He hasn't eaten red meat since the beef crisis back in the eighties. Doesn't believe in the so-called experts who are wheeled on and off TV to say that beef is safe to eat. Trust is another issue similar to truth. Not everyone can be trusted to be trustworthy all of the time.

This June Saturday morning he stares off into the dissipating London fog. High in the sky, not long there, there's half an orange sun on display, a shy sort of glow, wreathed with silvery strips of cloud.

He finds his thoughts alternating between drifting and focusing, and while he does not mind the drifting so much, the focusing bothers him – he wonders if he is staring as his father used to stare in the weeks before he died: into a remote distance?

The future is honest – it holds the date and precise time of his death. That is fact, a truth. The past he can't change, and he would oh so dearly love to alter some of its aspects. Mostly small things, some major: to speak less coldly to her; to smother a habit before it had set up home within him; to have spent time … more time with Eleanor … he would love to own these as truths.

Honest truths. The future is easier to shy away from, because it holds little for him by way of charm. At least it is so for the elderly. Youth owns the future. They grow into it, very often pass it by.

He wonders if a truth originally shaped as one is viewed forever by people as such? *There's a thought. Truth change?* Or is it how we perceive truth? Constantly on the search for ways and means to make a truth palatable for our conscience to digest? Dilute?

'Questions, questions,' he whispers. *Stop tormenting yourself. Live in the present.* It is the only truth left to him: that he is breathing London air – he can neither take a breath back nor plan for two ahead. Advice imparted to him by a man fifty years his junior at a talk presented by one of the circle's invited guest speakers.

Distort the truth. Historians do it all the time ....
Stop!
He takes a deep breath, holds, exhales.

He is an old man with time on his hands, but little of it left to him. He is not dying, but is at an age where death has forfeited its sting of surprise. At least he thinks so, but he is occasionally uncertain of this: he suspects it is possible for an old person expecting death, on the lookout for it, to be taken completely unawares when it eventually arrives.

Traffic noise is beginning to grow. London – he has always loved the city, its people, its essence – Dublin is his birth city, but it has no place in his heart: he would afford it none. He is Irish, born of English parents who spent their working lives in Ireland. Considers himself Irish because you can't lie away an accent.

By nature, he is not morbid. By nature, he is even-tempered, and quiet-spoken. A week past his seventy-eighth birthday, a day he spent alone in his Russell Square apartment, he counts his blessings: he is well, apart from the occasional turn – his mind is clear; no muddied memories, no bouts of confusion. *At my age, what else should I expect?* It is very much a case of a worn-out body in need of running repairs.

He had a wife and a daughter, one of whom he knows for certain he has outlived. He has a tiny circle of friends that are engaged in a slow diminishing. Usually, three or four of them die within a couple of weeks of each other, and this generally happens in November, which his circle calls 'The Month of Sorrows'. He does not miss them when they are gone; he is not cold, but he has learned how to distance himself from sorrow, to look at it from a remove of himself, something he tried to explain to a friend, since deceased, but wasn't sure if he quite understood his point.

'I don't follow,' Ed Harty said.

'It's like I'm outside my body, and looking at myself looking at what's going on … does that make sense?'

'No.'

He was 53 when he sold the Stand House. A broken man, alcoholic, smoker, gambler – the latter three addictions he eventually managed to see off, the former … well, he doubts if broken people can ever be fully mended. There are days on which they can feel they are on the mend; he has learned that these are watering holes of respite, no more. 'Being a broken man can become an addiction, too,' he told Harty. 'One can get to like wallowing in self-pity.'

'I doubt that. Something remains not right, you know. But what is it that remains broken?' Harty had asked.

Albert said, 'I … I don't know. I suppose soul, spirit, heart, mind … all four?'

Over a mug of tea, he tallies the spend of his years: twenty-five in Dublin, twenty-eight at the Stand House, a pub opposite the Curragh Racecourse. He had lived above the pub and lounge, rented out a couple of rooms too, because outside of the flat racing season business was less than brisk, and the money earned from letting came in handy. And it was a comfort not to think he was alone in those spacious upstairs living quarters. Especially after ….

His customers were mostly men from surrounding horse racing stables, of which there were many: jockeys and grooms, professional punters, losers, winners, drinkers and non-drinkers, passers-by, historians, hard-bitten ladies, murderers, rapists … they all walked through the doors of the pub he had bought with his parents' legacy and a slender bank loan. Summer race meetings at the Curragh, Derby and Guineas' day, but no jump meets: the racecourse and its stand and paddocks a trio of winter ghosts.

Harty, the week before he died, mooted the Curragh trip at the circle's weekly meeting in their local. Every year, Harty said, it was either the beaches at Normandy, the war cemeteries, or someplace else that reminded them of the dead. 'Why not a bleedin' change for a change?'

Albert finds nothing at all wrong with the annual outings to France. He believes it's important to remember the fallen; it would be a sin not to. Harty proposed the Derby at the Curragh as an alternative event and destination, having remembered speaking with Albert about the pub he had once owned there. But Harty didn't genuinely want a new destination; he was getting a dig at Vize Hickory, who had dropped him from the pub's snooker team. To Harty's disgust, Vize said it sounded like a fucking jolly good idea. In any regard, Harty won't be coming along to the Curragh. Vize, a decorated war hero, a former high-ranking military police officer, is organising the three-day visit.

It's a little chilly on the balcony. He is three storeys up. He loves his apartment, its warm colours, his paintings of racehorses, places he has visited down the years. His retirement is long, having quit on a working life after selling up the pub in Ireland for a handsome profit. Not a man for risk investment, he bought six properties, and these he rents through a property agency. Who will inherit them when he dies is a matter that now and then causes him a degree of bother, though he is aware that it should not, as he will be beyond caring.

In the kitchen, he boils up the kettle and puts a teabag into a green mug. He drinks copious amounts of tea. Everyone encourages him to drink water for his health, to aid his pipeworks, but he can't bring himself to unless it is flavoured, though of late he has begun to sip at sparkling clear water.

It is mid-June, and in three weeks he'll be back in a country he hasn't set foot in for decades, or thought much about either. There have been times when he resolved to visit, but the resolve melted for one reason or another: usually trepidation. At least with a group of people, as with the Normandy tours, there is a sharing of sorrows and a little banter, a sense of togetherness; Ireland though, if he'd went alone, would be another matter entirely. Resurrections of all sorts might occur.

The Circle is called 'The Red Lion's Inn Circle'. Harty used to say, 'The in circle,' on a chuckle. A pity he's dead. He was good for a laugh and getting a rise out of people. His family buried him with his snooker cue and a cube of blue chalk. Vize didn't mention the fact that he had dropped Harty from the snooker team, skirting around the issue by saying, 'Ed was a valued member of our circle and a fine snooker player, turning out to represent the Red Lion even when he didn't feel the Mae West …'.

'Eight members will be travelling to the Derby,' Vize says when he rings in the afternoon, disturbing Albert during his nap, 'in total. I tried to book the Stand House Hotel, but bloody hell … they've gone out of business, though their site is still on the web, old boy.'

It is the first he has heard of his pub being a hotel. The new owners must have extended.

'A fine hotel too, good-looking leisure centre, the width of the road from the racecourse. Bloody recession is what I say, Albert. Goddamn awful tripe.'

He does not know whether he likes or dislikes Vize. He is 70, or has been for the three years Albert has known him. He wears a tweed jacket, and a handlebar moustache he keeps waxed. Uses snuff. Drinks whiskey, always Jack Daniels. Twice divorced. Two grown-up daughters who shun him – things Albert learned from Harty, who was good at finding out things about people. Whether his information is true or not is a different matter.

Albert is the most senior member travelling to Ireland, and as such, like their president, he won't be expected to share a room. It used be a circle policy for all members to share hotel rooms, but members had voted to add rules to the circle's charter after Michael Harty, Harty's older brother, went walkabout in the middle of the night, stole into Vize's bed and groped his genitalia before proceeding to drown him in vomit. A lurid business, which saw the elder Harty banned from the circle for twenty-four months; in effect a lifetime

banishment, as Michael has about six months to live.
Another likely victim to the Month of Sorrows. Neither
is it lost on Albert that Vize may have also punished Ed
for his brother's night-time violation. Murky people do
murky things – another Harty observation.

He does not feel well, in a general sense – there is
no specific pain, nothing for which he can dispatch
a painkiller to conquer. He is not sure if he is up to
attending the meeting at the Red Lion this evening. It's
only round the corner from the apartment block, but
it may as well be in Siberia when he feels like this. He
has learned to listen to his body, and from experience
understands that the times he did not were the times he
ended up in dock, strapped to a heart monitor.

Wandering into his bedroom, he takes out the small
leather suitcase he had bought for a song some years
back at a January sale in Harrods. Packs what he thinks
will be enough, and a little over enough in the case of
underwear. Iris had said she would help, but he has a
thing about doing as much as possible for himself.

His computer confirms what Vize had told him
earlier about the Stand House Hotel, Conference and
Leisure Centre. What he hadn't said is that the whole
lot had been demolished and turned into a car park.
No. Surely they mean that the hotel has been levelled,
not the pub?

Back … when? He'd once submitted a planning
application to remove the porthole windows and Ionic-
design archway at the entrance, but later withdrew it,

such had been the ructions created by the authorities and locals – later, the Council placed a preservation order on some of the property's features. How can something deigned as having historical significance and subsequently afforded cultural protection come to lose its status? *Cui bono?* As Vize would say.

It bothers him, even at the Red Lion that evening, when he is distracted enough not to have heard several questions posed to him by members, to the extent that they grew worried for him.

Vize intrudes quietly into the silence.

'You're not with us this evening, Albert. Is everything all right?'

'My apologies … they knocked down my pub. I can't believe it.'

'Nothing's permanent,' Vize says, consolingly.

So very true, Albert thinks. It is a fact he always loses sight of.

'Deposits in by the end of the week, gentlemen,' Vize says, glancing at his watch. Albert thinks that Harty might have been right about Vize having a woman in his life.

'She's 'bout fifty … he's giving her socks I'm told.'

His voice alive in his ear as ever. As with other ghosts long dead, he knows that Harty's voice will fade and eventually disappear.

They congregate outside the Red Lion on a misty morning, waiting for the minibus to arrive and bring them to the airport. He knows they are there waiting solely for the bus, and not for him to join them. He has decided to listen to his body and to his mind. Yesterday evening he had broken the news to Vize, who promptly called around to the apartment. He sat there, legs crossed. A reach of sunlight in through the window failed to touch his canvas desert shoes. Concern etched wavy lines across his forehead.

'Albert,' he had said, with a shrug, after listening, 'I completely understand.'

'You do?'

'Yes.'

Understood that he had googled and viewed the flattened site where his pub once stood, where his daughter had died, where his wife had walked out and never returned – he doesn't know to this day where she got to or if she's alive, because her letter had begged him to leave her alone, not to come looking. Of course he did go searching for her, a year later, but she had not changed her mind. He and his drinking, the distance at which he had put himself from her when Lynn died, had chased Eleanor away.

'I'm puzzled though about something …', Vize said. 'You say the hotel was gifted to this racing authority, and they proceeded some time later to level it?'

'Yes, it appears so.'

'And you had a preservation order lodged against you?'

'Yes.'

'So, these the new owners must have managed to get around that obstacle in some way.'

'Obviously, Vize, they did.'

'Hmm …'.

'What?'

'It smells.'

'Yes, it does. Frankly.'

Vize had served in Intelligence in Northern Ireland.

He said, 'Do you know what, old boy? I often say this about the Irish … they do apathy very well, except for your northern brothers.'

'Your thoughts?'

'For what they're worth … vested interests. It had to be in someone or some party's interests to knock a spanking new hotel to the ground … one that had a profitable leisure centre, too. But …'.

'But?'

'It may well be all above board. I know quite a few hotels that have fallen shut and silent. If you can knock a white elephant, why wouldn't you?'

It is Albert's turn to say, 'Hmm …'.

'Best to let it go, Albert. Nothing lasts, isn't that so? And things come to light when they're ready to and not before.'

It is not in him to dance with the devils that are some of his memories, to explore what dirty truths lie behind the demolishment of his former pub, if any. There is a not a lot of time left for him to do or care about much – a truth that greatly pains him.